"Ms. Shal... immediate... love story... She knows how to deliver."
—*Rendezvous*

* * *

"Rachel, I can't talk to you when you're wearing that stupid hat." Before she could react, Ben whisked it off her head.

And froze.

Her soft, flowing hair was...gone, leaving a short, choppy cut of maybe an inch or so. The extent of everything she'd been through—the accident, the pain, the slow, ongoing recovery—suddenly hit him. He hated himself for reminding her, for reducing her to tears.

But he'd forgotten—Rachel would never allow anyone to see such a thing. Crying in public would be unacceptable. Crying in front of *him* would be tantamount to disaster.

Instead, as regal as ever, she remained calm, her head high. "Ben, go away."

Gently he put the cap back on her head, his fingers brushing over her warm, smooth skin. "I'm sorry."

"Don't even look at me."

He realized they were not on the same plane, that she apparently thought the sight of her had sickened him. "No, wait. Rachel—" He dragged in a deep, ragged breath. "You look...alive. Isn't that all that matters?"

## JILL SHALVIS

has been making up stories since she could hold a pencil. Now, thankfully, she gets to do it for a living, and doesn't plan to ever stop. She is the bestselling, award-winning author of over two dozen novels, including series romance for both Harlequin and Silhouette. She's hit the Waldenbooks bestsellers list, is a 2000 RITA® Award nominee and is a two-time National Reader's Choice Award winner. She has been nominated for a *Romantic Times* Career Achievement Award in Romantic Comedy, Best Duets and Best Temptation. Jill lives in California with her family.

# Jill *Shalvis*

## The Street Where *She* Lives

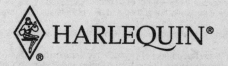

# HARLEQUIN®

TORONTO • NEW YORK • LONDON
AMSTERDAM • PARIS • SYDNEY • HAMBURG
STOCKHOLM • ATHENS • TOKYO • MILAN • MADRID
PRAGUE • WARSAW • BUDAPEST • AUCKLAND

If you purchased this book without a cover you should be aware that this book is stolen property. It was reported as "unsold and destroyed" to the publisher, and neither the author nor the publisher has received any payment for this "stripped book."

ISBN 0-373-83578-7

THE STREET WHERE SHE LIVES

Copyright © 2003 by Jill Shalvis.

All rights reserved. Except for use in any review, the reproduction or utilization of this work in whole or in part in any form by any electronic, mechanical or other means, now known or hereafter invented, including xerography, photocopying and recording, or in any information storage or retrieval system, is forbidden without the written permission of the publisher, Harlequin Enterprises Limited, 225 Duncan Mill Road, Don Mills, Ontario, Canada M3B 3K9.

All characters in this book have no existence outside the imagination of the author and have no relation whatsoever to anyone bearing the same name or names. They are not even distantly inspired by any individual known or unknown to the author, and all incidents are pure invention.

This edition published by arrangement with Harlequin Books S.A.

® and TM are trademarks of the publisher. Trademarks indicated with ® are registered in the United States Patent and Trademark Office, the Canadian Trade Marks Office and in other countries.

Visit us at www.eHarlequin.com

**Printed in U.S.A.**

# CHAPTER ONE

HE'D ONCE BEEN CALLED a selfish bastard, and Ben Asher figured that to be a fairly accurate assessment. He lived his life on his own terms and kept his emotional entanglements pared down to, well, him. Thanks to his freelancing job as a photojournalist for *National Geographic* and *Outside,* among others, he could pack up and leave at the drop of a hat, without looking back. Even now, after only a few months of being in the Amazon, he'd be moving on to his next assignment soon.

Good old Africa, here he came.

He moved through the strangling, thick, wet, green growth so unique to the Brazilian jungle, finally breaking free into a small clearing containing a couple of temporary structures. He crossed the clearing and stepped over the threshold of the reserve's office, which, due to the proverbial lack of funds, was the size of a postage stamp. They'd been without electricity and phones for nearly a month, only just today getting the phones turned on. Warily, he met Maria's glare. Apparently the calls were coming in too fast and furious for her liking.

Maria, his temp, had been forced to walk approximately twenty-five big, whopping yards from the office to the radio hut to radio him about this call. Noting it was hotter than hell outside, he figured he understood. *"Gracias."*

She didn't respond, but then again, she rarely did.

She'd come to him from his previous assignment near Rio, where Ben had uncovered a so-called American ministry. The "minister," Manuel Asada, had run an international charity scam, which through the years had earned him untold wealth. Targeting churchgoing, generous souls in the name of humanity, Asada had solicited funds and promised to build villages and feed the poor.

Instead, he'd pocketed everything, killing anyone who defied him or got in his way. He also had a nasty habit of abusing the local women. Maria had been one of them. Together with her testimony and Ben's photographs evidencing some of the crimes, Asada was now languishing in a Brazilian prison, but would soon be extradited to the States. There he'd face some of his swindled victims in court, not to mention murder charges on no less than three counts.

Secretly, Ben hoped Asada remained in Brazil, where he had a better chance of actually staying in a jail cell. He'd sworn vengeance on everyone who'd taken him and his profitable business down, including family members and loved ones. Luckily, in Ben's case, that meant fewer people than the fingers on one hand.

He picked up the phone. "Asher."

"D-daddy?"

At the sound of his daughter's quavering, frightened voice, his heart stopped. "Emmie? What's the matter?"

Loud, crackling static filled the line, reminding him that thousands of miles separated him and his twelve-going-on-thirty-year-old daughter. "Emily?"

Nothing, just more static, and Ben damned the poor phone lines, the pathetic equipment, the shack he'd called home for two months. "Emily!" Panic had a bitter taste, he discovered. Sweat trickled down his back as he sank to a rickety chair. The humid air made his shirt cling to him like a second skin. "Come on, come on," he muttered, and banged the phone on the scratched, beat-up desk, swearing uselessly before whipping the phone back up to his ear.

"Daddy?"

Sagging in relief, Ben relaxed his folded-up, taut legs, and promptly smashed his knees into the wood. He took in a breath of the closed-in air around him. "I'm here! Are you all right?"

"Yes."

*Thank God.* "Where are you?"

Not a good father question, he noted with disgust. Any father, any *good* father, would know where his daughter was at all times. Not that *his* father had ever taught him such things, but he knew how parenthood was supposed to work.

"I'm home," she said.

She meant her home, of course, which she made with her mother in South Village, California.

"You've got to come." Across the too many miles and years, her voice broke, killing him. "Please, don't say you can't."

Ben spoke to his precious, only child far too seldom. And she *was* precious. She was also brilliant, which never failed to both amaze and terrify him. In any case, it would be easy to blame his heavy travel schedule as a photojournalist or even the fact that his cell phone rarely worked for the lack of time they'd spent together. But the truth was, it was his own need to roam at will, to never set down roots that caused the problem. The story of his life. He was nearly thirty-one years old, and had yet to figure out the cure for insatiable wanderlust.

He didn't need a shrink to know that came from his

upbringing. *Work harder, Benny boy, or we'll send you back.*

That bit of wisdom had come directly from Rosemary, his foster mother. *Don't say the wrong thing, Benny, we'll send you back. Don't rock the boat, Benny, we'll send you back.*

He'd gotten the message loud and clear. Don't say a word, because no one wanted to hear it.

Well, he'd cut out his own tongue before giving his own daughter a similar message. "Em? Talk to me." The static was bad, but he thought he heard a sad, little sniff, and his stomach hit his toes.

"It's about Mom."

As it had for thirteen long years, just the thought of Rachel caused conflicting emotions to race through Ben—pain and regret. Regret and pain.

Mostly pain.

Whoever had said time heals all wounds was full of shit.

"It's really bad this time," she said with another little sniff.

Okay, he got it now. Ben relaxed marginally, because for spending so little time together, he and Emily were well versed in this play. The last time it'd been "really bad" Emily had wanted to day trade on the Internet with Rachel's investment account. The time before that she'd been campaigning to be homeschooled so she could travel with *him,* which besides being a really bad idea— what did he know about kids?—had nearly caused Rachel to blow a gasket.

Ben leaned back, scraping his too wide shoulders on the narrow, splintery chair back. "What is it this time, she won't let you take an extra math class?" His daughter was famous for overloading on school in order to avoid socializing—which Ben blamed on Rachel since he'd never asked for more schoolwork in his life. The irony of the whole thing amazed him. It'd taken one hundred percent of his energies just to survive his childhood, and yet Emily, free to enjoy her youth in a way he couldn't have even dreamed of, chose to work herself into the ground. "You don't take enough time to be a kid—"

"No, you don't understand!" A sound crossed the airwaves, one that sounded suspiciously like a sob. "She's had an accident…. We tried to call you, but we couldn't get through, and then Aunt Melanie said I should try again…"

Black spots filled his vision. Probably the steamy, muggy weather. But that was a lie, a damn lie. After all these years and all the heartache, he still didn't want Rachel hurt.

"An accident?" The black spots blossomed, showing him remembered visions from all those years ago. His first sight of her, in English class at school; tall, willowy, hauntingly beautiful. She'd been so far out of his league, him being nothing more than a foster kid from The Tracks, a sleazy area of South Village no one wanted to lay claim to. But she'd looked at him that day, from eyes that held a mirroring loneliness, a mirroring pain, and he'd fallen a little bit in love on the spot.

He hadn't expected her to feel the same way, and had figured he'd hit the lottery when she'd smiled back. As he'd gotten to know her, and her demons, he hadn't had a chance in hell at keeping his distance. Their time together, every single minute of those six months, the intensity of it, the passion, had been heaven on earth. Until she'd taken it all away, nearly destroying him in the process.

"She got hit by a car and almost died."

My God. That lovely, giving, warm, unforgettable body broken and bleeding and hurt? Vaguely, he caught a horrifying list of injuries.

"…and a cracked pelvis, too. Broken arm, ribs, leg and ankle, all down her left side where, um, the car slammed into her."

Ben couldn't process it, couldn't begin to imagine.

"And there was some brain injury, but the surgery went really, really good."

The hope in Emily's voice sliced through him like a razor blade. "Brain injury?"

"Yeah, it made her talk funny at first, but she's better now. Sometimes it takes her a minute to, like, coordinate herself, but the doctor says that's temporary."

"Okay." Ben realized he'd been holding his breath and he let it slowly out. Guilt sliced through him for every not so charitable thought he'd ever spared about Rachel over the years, and there'd been many.

"The doctors say she's going to be fine," Emily said in his ear, her voice still wavering even as she became the comforter. "But, Daddy, she needs help."

She couldn't need money, Ben thought. Rachel had inherited gobs of it from her workaholic father who'd probably entered hell pissed off that he couldn't bring his fortune with him. Not to mention, Rachel was hugely successful in her own right as a popular cartoonist. Her famous comic strip, *Gracie,* earned her so much dough it made him dizzy to think about. But maybe she'd lost it all in the stocks or something. "I don't have much at the moment," he admitted having just last week made his regular substantial charitable donation.

What was the point in saving, when he didn't have a place to keep it or someone who needed it? He had no family besides Emily, at least none that wanted to claim him. Being the eighth of nine wards in a foster home that gathered kids in the name of "Christian" duty— and for the monthly stipend—he'd gone all his life without material things. When he'd finally had the money to buy stuff, aside from his cameras, he got no satisfaction from it. If anything, material goods just tied him down. And after his first seventeen years of being held to one spot, being untethered was his greatest joy.

In fact, he'd been untethered for just about his entire adult life, cohabiting with some of the most rural and isolated people on earth. If it weren't for Emily, he might never have reemerged into "society" at all.

"It's not money she needs." Emily hesitated, and Ben waited anxiously. His daughter was not only sharp as hell, but capable of reasoning far beyond her years. And she was reasoning now, silently, which always scared him.

What could Rachel, a woman who needed no one, possibly need from him?

"She wants to go home to recuperate. But she can't really manage by herself. So she's going to have to go somewhere else to get better, like a convalescent home. And then I'd have to go to Aunt Melanie's and change schools. She's really freaking out worrying about me."

Damn it. *Damn it.* He didn't want his daughter separated from her mother, and with Rachel's sister one hundred and twenty miles north of them in Santa Barbara, that's exactly what would happen. "We can hire a nurse," he said.

"She's trying, but it's hard to find someone."

Once upon a time, he'd known Rachel better than anyone. She'd had it tough, in a way even tougher than he had. As a result, she trusted no one. She'd rather lie down and die than accept help from a stranger.

Actually, unless she'd changed in thirteen years, she'd rather lie down and die than accept help from *him*. That feeling was mutual and had been since the day she'd decided he was no longer welcome in her life. It still bugged the hell out of him how easily she'd moved on, while he'd mourned and grieved her loss for years.

But he was over her now, *very* over her.

"Daddy, she's determined to do it all, for me, but she's going to hurt herself. Please? Please won't you come?"

His daughter had rarely asked him for anything. And yet all he could do was panic at the thought of being caged, tied down to one place—*that* place—for God knows how long.

"Please," she whispered again, her voice barely audible. "Please come home."

The hustling, bustling, urban South Village, just outside Los Angeles, had never been his "home"—he'd had no real home. But since he hadn't told his daughter about his past—about being found nearly dead in a trash bin when he was only two days old—he couldn't very well explain it to her now.

And just because the word *home* was foreign to him didn't mean it was that way for Emily. He'd give anything, *everything*, to ensure she never knew what it was like not to have a home.

"We need you, Daddy."

A new coat of perspiration beaded his forehead. "She'll refuse."

"She knows she has no choice. It's you, or hiring a stranger."

"You know how she feels about me."

"Yes." She cleared her throat and spoke in a perfect imitation of Rachel. "You're 'wild, rough and un-molded.'"

Oh, yeah, that was a direct quote. He could hear the faint smile in his daughter's voice, the daughter far too understanding and old for her years.

His fault.

"And *danger* is your middle name," she intoned, still quoting.

Hmm.

"Oh! And you're a selfish…" She lowered her voice. "Well. You-know-what."

"Yeah."

"You're also—"

"Okay, okay." Nothing like being humbled by your own child. Maria shoved an envelope in his hand. It was grimy, but then, everything here was. Addressed to him, it looked as if it'd been to hell and back before arriving here. The postmark date was five weeks ago, which didn't surprise him. It was amazing it had gotten to him at all.

Inside was a perfectly spotless, perfectly folded piece of white paper. The chilling words read "I'm not done with you yet."

Ben lifted his head and covered the mouthpiece with one hand. "Did you just get this?" he asked Maria in Spanish.

She nodded her head and looked at him from guarded black eyes.

Fear clawed Ben's belly. "Asada."

Maria paled at the name.

"Radio the authorities," he said, still speaking Spanish. "Make sure he was extradited to the States as planned."

She nodded and turned away.

As helplessness coursed through him, Emily continued to chatter in his ear. "You won't be sorry, Dad! We can all be together. You know, like a family."

Oh, boy. He'd have to deal with that later. For now, he had bigger issues. Asada had once sworn revenge, and now somehow appeared to be free to carry out his threats.

Five weeks free, if the postmark meant anything.

For the first time he could remember, he only half listened to his daughter's monologue about all the things they could do if he was there. Under other circumstances he'd be amused and a little intimidated by Emily's plans to make them a cozy nuclear family.

Maria came back, speaking in rapid-fire Spanish, shocking Ben, both because she was actually speaking unprompted, and by the words coming out of her mouth.

Five weeks ago, Asada had escaped in the middle of extradition to the States, adding the murder of two guards to his rap sheet in the process, and was thought to be somewhere between North and South America.

Christ. "Emily," he said hoarsely, gripping the phone. "Tell me about your mom's accident."

"She was hit by a car."

"When?"

"A month or so ago, you've been unreachable until now—"

"I know. Who hit her?"

"I don't know. The police haven't caught anyone."

Ben dragged in a steady breath. "Okay, listen to me. I don't want you to open the door or talk to any strangers, do you understand?"

"Daddy." She laughed. "I'm twelve, not four."

"Yes, but—"

"You gave me this talk years ago, remember? Don't worry."

"Emily—"

"Just say you'll come back here to be with us while Mom gets better." She hesitated, then went for the kill. "I love you, you know."

Ah, hell. He was such a goner.

And he was going to South Village, California.

"I love you, too, baby. With all my heart. Now stay safe." *Please, God.* "I'll be there fast as I can catch a plane."

## CHAPTER TWO

*Even at the tender age of five, Rachel knew what moving day meant. A new room, a new nanny, all of her toys in new places. She didn't want to go, not again, neither did her sissie, but what they wanted didn't matter.*

*"Goddamn it girl, suck it up." This from her father. "Go find your mother if you're going to snivel."*

*Her mother waved her nearly empty glass of that stuff that looked like water but smelled bad—it would be years before Rachel came to know vodka was her mother's drink of choice—and said, "Don't look at me, there's nothing I can do."*

*A common refrain, one Rachel had learned to live by. With no more control over this move than the last one, or the one before that, she sat on the step, hugged her doll close and waited for the movers.*

"Rachel."

She tried to blink the porch into focus, but suddenly she wasn't five years old anymore, it'd all been just another dream. She'd had a lot of those lately. As it had for the past month, the creeping, insidious pain joined by a nauseous claustrophobia jerked her fully awake. Logically, she knew the claustrophobia was from being trussed up like a mummy. But even worse was the sweat-inducing panic she felt from her complete lack of control over anything, including her own body.

"Oh, good, you're awake."

She grimaced at the deceptively kind voice of the nurse who carried needles, and used them often. "You couldn't possibly need more blood."

"Oh, just a little."

"No way."

Unperturbed, the nurse sat by Rachel and took out her blood kit.

"I mean it. Don't even think about it." But even Rachel had to let out a laugh, though it shot a bullet of sharp pain right through her. Most of her was still covered in either soft bandages or plaster casting. She hadn't been able to move on her own since she'd crossed the street a month ago, heading toward Café Delight to have lunch with her agent, Gwen Ariani, and instead had been mistaken for a roadblock by a speeding car.

Among other physical problems she had, her brain seemed to have the hiccups, making coordinating movement a circus event. Her doctor told her that would probably be temporary. Probably. Good God. Forget the fact she needed fine motor skills to maintain her comic strip *Gracie;* things weren't looking real good for the rest of her nice, cozy life. "I am not a pincushion."

"Spunk." The short, dark-haired nurse named Sandy nodded approvingly. "Give 'em hell, girl." She swabbed Rachel's arm, but had the good grace to look apologetic as she wielded the needle. When she was done, she patted Rachel's hand—bandaged to the tips of her still healing fingers. "Oh, and hey, good news. Most of the bandages come off today. Dr. Thompson will be here this morning."

"And how about the casts?" Rachel found herself coming to life for the first time that day. That *month.*

"You're going to go from plaster to air casts."

"What's the difference?"

"You'll be more mobile and lightweight. It's a good thing." Sandy headed for the door. "Now, don't you worry your pretty little head over any of the details. I'll be back with the doctor in a few."

Rachel studied the ceiling, her new hobby. There were eighty-four ceiling tiles in the room. She'd worry her pretty little head all right—the "pretty" part no longer applying, of course. She'd worry because she *knew*. They would release her, maybe as early as the end of the week, but it didn't mean freedom.

For at least a couple of months she needed help, a fate worse than death as far as she was concerned. She'd learned her love of control from her overly controlled, overly authoritative, overly guarded childhood. That she would need someone to help dress her, help her move around, help her in every way, was extremely... frightening.

What she really needed right now was a powerful, virile husband.

Ha!

To get a husband, she'd have to seriously date someone. To do that she'd actually have to let that someone into her life. And to let someone into her life, especially a *male* someone, she'd have to... Well, she'd have to do a whole hell of a lot, including honing up on the social skills she'd let get so rusty.

Since that wasn't about to happen, Rachel had no choice, no choice at all. A nurse. A *temporary* nurse. Either a huge, beefy woman or a male, it didn't really matter at this point. She had so little pride left.

Just as long as she and Emily got to be at home, together, nothing else truly mattered.

Which brought to the surface her greatest worry. How

was she going to manage without being a burden on her teenage alien—er, daughter?

Her hospital room door opened again, and she heard the voice of Sandy, coming back with Dr. Thompson.

Closing her eyes, she feigned sleep. It was unlike her to pretend anything, but in this case, where everyone persisted in talking to her as if she'd suffered permanent brain damage, eavesdropping had become a necessity.

She wanted to know their plans for her, because no way was she accepting anything but release papers. No convalescent care, no way. Forcing her taut muscles to relax wasn't easy. Over a month after the accident she couldn't yet quite remember, and every inch of her still ached.

Even her hair.

And she *itched*. Beneath the cast on her arm and lower leg. Beneath the multitude of healing lacerations. Beneath the stubbly hair growing back after the buzz cut she'd required for surgery to ease the swelling of her brain.

If it didn't hurt to smile, she might have let out a wry one. All her life she'd cultivated her long, blond tresses—only to lose them in one twist of fate.

At least she still had her...what? She didn't have her health, she didn't have her life as she knew it, she couldn't draw, couldn't even hug Emily—as if her daughter even wanted to be hugged.

"If she doesn't hire help, Sandy, she's not going to heal properly." This from her doctor.

"Well...her daughter was talking to Outpatient Services earlier," Sandy told him. "She signed up for home care, I believe."

Rachel stopped breathing. Emily had already arranged for an at-home nurse? Melanie had obviously helped, but that seemed completely out of character, because though Rachel's sister had come through for her after the accident, it wasn't Mel's usual habit to think ahead for herself, much less someone else.

For years Mel had complained that Rachel didn't need her enough, but the truth was, when Rachel *did* need Mel, when she tried to confide something that was really bothering her, Mel often shrugged it off as not important. That, or she went overboard in her response.

A perfect example had been when Rachel and Ben had split. Feeling like a basket case, she had attempted to talk to Mel about him. But in her exuberant need to protect her baby sister, Mel had taken it as an opening to talk bad about Ben every single time the subject came up. Thirteen years later she was still doing it.

Rachel had learned to keep her problems to herself.

Besides, Mel had already gone above the call of duty, using vacation time from her job in order to take care of Emily while Rachel had been in the hospital, handling the house and all the responsibilities that went with that. Handling everything.

Rachel knew how much Melanie needed to get back to her own life, especially her independence. She and Emily would manage. With—oh, joy—a hired nurse. Having someone in their home, living with them, would make her terribly uncomfortable, but—and this was the good part—she *was* going home.

After a distressingly nomadic childhood, and after being woken at all hours of the day and night to be poked and prodded at for a month, her own bed would be heaven. Quiet, calm, tranquil heaven.

EMILY BOUNCED into Rachel's hospital room, a barely contained bundle of energy. She wore a tank top, baggy jeans too loose on her hips and clunky sandals. Her face was completely void of makeup, as she hadn't yet found that particular vice, but she had two silver hoops in each ear. Her bright-green eyes were shining through her too-long blond bangs.

Her ever present laptop was tucked beneath her arm.

In spite of her exhaustion from a brutal physical therapy session, Rachel's heart swelled at the sight of her greatest joy. In having a child, Rachel had learned to share herself, to receive love as well as give it. It was because of Emily that she felt whole.

Whole being relative at the moment.

Given the shift of the shadows on the walls from the gently dancing pines outside, hours had passed since Dr. Thompson had removed some of the bandages. She was now a new person. Granted, a new person with little to no hair, fresh new air casts on one arm and leg, and a healing broken pelvis. A new person who still hurt...but she felt marginally better nevertheless.

Or at least lighter. The bandages on her multitude of abrasions—which had covered part of her face, her torso and good arm—were gone. Because she could, she bent her right arm, watching with relief when the still-scabbed limb did what it should. And if she ignored the wild trembling that indicated it was weak as a baby's—something her physical therapist promised to fix "in no time"—things were good. "Emily...look at me go."

Emily looked suitably impressed. "Nice. Before you know it, you'll be drawing again."

At the moment, she couldn't even lift a pencil, much less think with the wit required for *Gracie,*—a character who was brave, brassy and bold, everything Rachel wasn't—but she'd get there.

*God, please, let me get there.*

To hide the fear from the girl who saw everything, she forced a smile. "Did you come with Aunt Mel?"

"Yeah." Emily plopped into the bedside chair, her pixie-blond hair once again swinging into her expressive eyes. She set down her laptop. "She's busy flirting with your doctor again, but as my supposedly mature aunt, she didn't want me to know, so she sent me in here."

Melanie had a long history with men. Very long.

"She thinks I don't know about the birds and the bees." A quick cheeky grin flashed, reminding Rachel that before the accident, she and Emily had been on shaky ground due to Emily's certainty she knew everything, which naturally meant Rachel knew nothing.

"I bet I know more than she does," Emily added.

A sexually aware preteen—every parent's nightmare. "Emily—"

"Oh, Mom, I'm just kidding."

Uh-huh. But no way was she going to start a grudge match today. "You really doing okay?" She wished she could reach up and touch Emily's face, her hair. She missed their closeness, missed everything. "Tell me the truth."

"Well, I'm better than you. The nurse told me they took out all your stitches. And most of the bandages, too." Leaning in, Emily scrutinized every inch of her face until Rachel wanted to squirm. She could only imagine how she must look. The bruises had to be fading along with the swelling, but they were probably still putrid yellow and puke green. And her hair, her glorious hair… "They haven't brought me a mirror, so…" She managed a weak laugh, but Emily leaned even closer, still serious, still inspecting.

Rachel turned away and fought the burning behind her

eyes. "I probably look fit for Halloween, even though that's months off yet."

"Oh, Mom." At the soft, choked-up voice, Rachel turned back, shocked to find love on Emily's face. *Love.*

"Don't you know?" she whispered. "You look beautiful." Her eyes were shining like two brilliant stars. "So beautiful, Mom."

Rachel managed a smile past the huge lump in her throat. "Which means you're beautiful, too."

"Yeah." But it was Emily's turn to look away now. "But I know who I really look like...."

When she trailed off with no clear intent to finish, Rachel sighed. *Not a coward,* she reminded herself. *Never a coward.* "Like your dad."

They stared at each other awkwardly while Rachel's heart sank. No, she wasn't a coward, and hadn't been in a long time, but bringing up the subject of Ben Asher with Emily was usually trouble.

He was the one person Rachel and Emily never agreed on.

How could they? Her daughter saw him as a hero, larger than life. A man who put others' needs before his own. A man who brought justice to people who couldn't get it for themselves.

He *was* that, Rachel admitted to herself, and more. So much more.

SHE'D CHANGED SCHOOLS *again, halfway through senior year this time. On her first day, a boy sauntered into her English Lit class late. With a slow, lazy smile and even lazier gait, he strode down the center aisle with a devil-may-care attitude that had wild whispers falling in his path.*

*"Did you know he's from The Tracks?" one cheer-*

*leader hissed to another, just behind Rachel. "Lives in a foster home with eight other kids."*

*"He's still hot," came a hushed reply.*

*"Hot, yeah. But dirt poor."*

*"Such a waste."*

*Rachel couldn't help but notice no one else in the classroom gave him the time of day. Given his laid-back air and languid stroll, he could care less. He wore Levi's with a hole over one knee, a dark T-shirt with a frayed hem and ripped sleeve and had an ancient Canon camera slung over his shoulder. His hair was wavy and long, past his collar at the back, the front tumbling over his forehead. He tossed it back with a lift of his head.*

*His gaze focused in on Rachel.*

*She wasn't used to that. She was invisible. It's what happened when you were always the new kid, and she was good at it. But he saw her, with eyes that were sparkling and full of trouble. He took the one empty seat in the classroom.*

*Right next to her.*

*"Hey," he said with a slow, devastating smile.*

*She looked behind her to see who he was talking to, and he laughed.*

*She felt like she'd been hit with an electrical current.*

*"Got an extra pencil?" he asked.*

*A little overwhelmed by his sheer presence, by the fact he was even looking at her, she handed him her pencil. Boys didn't look at her often, mostly because she never made eye contact and never bothered making friends. Why should she when she'd only be moving again soon enough?*

*"Got some paper?"*

*She'd given him a few sheets, and an eraser, too. And by the end of that first hour he'd convinced her to share*

*her notes, and help him study for the next test. She'd
tried to explain she wasn't the girl to get to know if he
wanted to be popular, but he laughed.*

*"Popular?" He scratched his jaw and shrugged his
bony shoulders. "Not my thing." His eyes roamed her
face, seeming to see more than anyone else ever saw.
"But you...you, I'd like to get to know."*

*And he'd done just that, gotten to know her, in a way
no one else ever had.*

*Not then, and not since.*

"MOM?" Em's worried gaze ran over Rachel's face.
"Stick with me now, you're freaking me out."

Right. Stick to the present, much better than the past.
They were talking about Ben. Ben, who took the most
amazing photographs of the underprivileged and dis-
played them boldly in print for the more privileged pop-
ulation to squirm over. His thought-provoking articles
that accompanied those pictures usually won him
awards, and instigated a surge of charitable donations to
better circumstances all over the world—and appease
their guilty consciences. She knew this because she'd
followed his career over the years for no reason other
than morbid curiosity.

But he was just a man. A man who'd shown her more
passion and emotion and life than anyone before or after.
And though it had been thirteen long years, she still
resented it with her entire being. Resented *him*.

"Look, forget it, okay? Forget Dad for now." Emily
chewed on her fingernail and strove for casual. "So...
what was for lunch? Puke-colored Jell-O again?"

Rachel took a deep breath, heart aching. "Emily,
honey...you *are* like him. Just like him. In so many
ways."

Emily blinked twice, slow as an owl, and Rachel couldn't blame her. Rachel often hadn't been willing to talk about Ben. Not a great parental decision, she could admit now. "Yes, you look just like him. You know that. And since he's drop-dead beautiful, you are, too. So beautiful, Emily."

Emily looked stunned at the turn of the conversation, which made Rachel doubly glad she'd had it. "So..." She cleared her throat. "You and Mel hired someone for us? You going to be okay with that?"

Emily's glow faded and she stared at Rachel's hand, which she gently clasped in her own smaller one, nails polished with chipped purple glitter and chewed to the quick. "I wish you wouldn't worry about me so much."

"It's a mom thing. Am I going to like her?"

"Oh, man, would you look at the time?" Emily pulled her hand free and bounced up. "Gotta go. Homework."

"Nice avoidance technique. Who is she, Em, Attila the Hun?"

"You're funny, Mom. You should write a comic strip."

"Emily Anne, what are you up to?"

Innocent eyes glanced back, solemn and full of intelligence. "What makes you think I'm up to something?"

"Intuition," Rachel said dryly.

"Hey, I'm just getting you where you want to be, Mom. *Home.*"

## CHAPTER THREE

DESPITE HIS desperate need to get to South Village immediately, it still took Ben nearly a week. Two days to get out of the jungle. Another two waiting for a seat on a small plane to get to an international airport. And then nearly two days more of connections and travel.

Finally, Ben landed in Los Angeles and nearly choked on the smog. It wasn't even noon and the temperature had already hit ninety-five degrees, a sweltering, shimmering heat that made the air so thick that breathing was optional, and unadvised.

Granted, he'd suffered far worse, with much more humidity, for long months at a time. But somehow, spring in Southern California seemed more hell-like than anything he could remember.

Okay, so it was more than the weather. It was the fact he'd come back to his inauspicious beginnings after all these years, a place he tried not to think about, much less visit. He'd left here at seventeen, scrawny, too poor to even pay attention, and sporting a broken heart. He'd done his damnedest to stay far, far away.

For the most part, he'd managed, convincing Rachel's sister Melanie to bring his daughter to wherever he happened to be. To further her education, he'd said in his defense of dragging a young girl to all four corners of the earth. Dirty corners at that.

Melanie had bought the excuse. So apparently had

Rachel, and Emily had been delighted with her annual travels with her father.

As a bonus, he hadn't had to face this place in a good long time. But he was here now, courtesy of his own terror over a madman who may or may not know about his daughter, about Rachel.

Ben had contacted the local authorities here in the States, and had been passed over to the Feds. They'd been polite, helpful and dishearteningly doubtful that Asada would be stupid enough to show his face here in Southern California. After all, just the week before, he'd been featured on the television show *America's Most Wanted*. Unless Asada had a death wish, he was deep in hiding. Still, they'd promised to do drive-bys to surveil at Rachel and Emily's place. And they'd promised to take a look into Rachel's accident, to see if maybe it hadn't been an accident at all.

A thought that made his blood run cold.

He had a meeting tonight with one of the FBI agents he'd spoken to, Agent Brewer, and hopefully would learn something more. Something like they'd caught Asada.

Riding the airport escalator to the ground floor, Ben took a long, critical look at his own reflection in the mirrors that lined the walls. A grim stranger stared back. He'd have thought he'd had enough grimness in his life, that he didn't need to borrow more, but just being back "home" seemed to have uncovered some vast store of it deep within him.

He hadn't told Emily about Asada. No way was he going to be the one to introduce her to the truth about the cold, cruel, dangerous world he lived in.

And Rachel…well, he'd wait and see on that one. For all she knew, he was coming to help her. Though why on earth she'd agreed to such a thing was beyond him. He figured desperation must have played a huge role, but for the life of him he couldn't imagine the only woman who'd ever brought him to equal heights of ecstasy and depths of misery being that desperate.

Of course, he no longer knew her every thought and whim as he once had. Right now, she was injured, hurting…he wouldn't put more stress on her shoulders by bringing up Asada.

No, Asada was his cross alone to bear.

He stepped outside, and the heat sapped his energy. Or maybe it was the reality of being here.

*Your own fault.*

With a sigh, Ben slung his backpack over his shoulder and headed toward the rental cars, resigned to his fate.

To RACHEL, South Village was home sweet home. Beyond being the busiest and most energetic pedestrian neighborhood in California, South Village was her life. The casual elegance of the charming town was no faux city walk like Universal City, but authentic, steeped with the blend of history and early California legend that came from being one of the original mining towns in the late 1800s. Since then, the place had been subjected to face-lifts, decline, then more face-lifts, and was now enjoying an upswing.

In a few square miles one could eat at a restaurant owned by a famous celebrity, check out the best and latest in live theater, grab a drink from a sidewalk café, buy a present from a funky bookstore or an original boutique, or simply wander the streets drinking fancy iced coffees, taking in the sights.

But that's not why she loved it so much. Here she

could surround herself with people. Here she could lose herself in the crowd. Here she could just be.

Here she'd granted herself the luxury of learning a place inside out for the first time.

She lived on North Union Street, right in the heart of downtown. On her left sat One North Union, an old hotel remodeled into an array of art galleries. On her right stood what had once been the sheriff's office in the great Old West, and was now her neighbor's house. On the other side of that was Tanner Market, nearly hidden from view on the street by a brick courtyard filled with flowers, fountains and wrought iron.

In her opinion, what made the block of beautiful buildings was *her* house. Thanks to the syndicated success of *Gracie,* she'd purchased the old firehouse five years ago. The three-story brick structure had already been shined up, gutted and restored for modern use, but Rachel and Emily had customized it further, turning it into the home of their hearts. Every wall, every floor, every piece of furniture, had been lovingly agonized over and decided upon based on comfort.

This was her first real home—already she'd lived here longer than anywhere else—and if she had her way, her last. She sat in the wheelchair she was determined not to need by the end of the day and looked around. It'd been nearly a week since she'd been promised release from the hospital, and finally, finally, after more physical therapy, after long discussions with her doctor, here she was.

Already, amazingly, she could feel the improvement in her bones. Just being home did that, she mused sitting in the big, open living room that had once housed fire-fighters. A month and a half ago, she'd *stood* in this very spot every single day, staring down at the street below, watching people stroll by, smiling, laughing, living. She loved it here, right smack in the middle of organized chaos. Here she was home. Safe. Just her and Emily.

Now, fresh from the hospital, with her head still spinning from her doctor's orders to take it easy, she was waiting for the new nurse, telling herself she'd be out from under the nurse's care as soon as possible.

"Here, Mom." Emily came up behind her and wrapped a shawl around her shoulders.

She hadn't even realized she was cold, but now she could feel her limbs shiver. Her brain still fooled her like that sometimes, and it disturbed her, this horrifying lack of control. But the bone-melting exhaustion frustrated her most of all. Her good hand trembled where it rested on her thigh. Her shoulders slumped, making her bad arm ache all the more, and she'd only been sitting five minutes.

For a woman used to running five miles before breakfast, then working a full day, then chasing Emily around on a racquetball court, the lack of energy was demoralizing.

She felt used and abused. Washed up. And so discouraged she could hardly stand it. She wanted to jump up, wanted to run through her house, wanted to see each and every room she'd made theirs. She wanted to go into her lovely studio upstairs and touch her easel, her colored pencils, fresh clean paper. She wanted to draw, paint, *scream*...anything other than sit here helpless. Helpless made her feel like a child again.

As that child, she'd had money, privilege, material things...everything but stability, security and safety; the three *S*s which meant so much to her. Her father had spent his entire adult life taking over troubled corporations and turning them around, gathering millions as he did. He gathered the money to himself in a way he never had his own family. There'd been no laughter, no shared family dinners, no affection and certainly no love in their household.

Melanie, the oldest by two years, had usually commanded the fleeting attention of their parents. Given Mel's penchant for trouble, most of that attention had been negative. Still, she'd thrived on their nomadic existence, making friends with ease—especially male friends.

Not Rachel. As the years passed, she'd promised herself that someday, she was going to find her own home and never leave it. In her senior year, her father moved them to South Village, and by the time Rachel had graduated, it was time for her parents to move on.

Mesmerized by the place, Rachel stayed. She utilized family contacts to get her sketchings purchased by the local paper, she'd gone to college at night studying art and the rest was history.

Home sweet home.

"Mom?" Emily moved in front of her and kneeled. "It's only natural to be this tired, right? Didn't the doctor say so? I mean, coming home took a lot out of you."

"Yeah." Rachel felt the burning need to throw something or have a good cry. Even her daughter had changed, as now suddenly Emily didn't want to do anything to upset her. Rachel wondered how long that would last, how long before they went back to being two circling, snarling tigresses. "Lying in that hospital bed for five weeks was hard work all right."

"The way *you* stress it was. Do you want to lie down?"

"I'd like to never lie down again."

Emily laughed. "Don't worry, in no time you'll be yelling at me to go out and play instead of doing homework."

Rachel sighed, it was all she could do. "I'm proud of your grades, Emily. So proud. But you're too young to work so hard."

"I like working hard."

"But…" Rachel frowned as the thought flew from her head. Frustrated, she closed her eyes and concentrated so hard it hurt, but it was no use. She couldn't remember what she'd wanted to say. "I really hate that. How can I yell at you if I can't keep a thought in my head?"

"Practice," Emily assured her, looking cocky. Probably because she was in charge here and knew it. Role reversal was a powerful tool in the hands of a preteen. Terrifying.

The doorbell rang, and suddenly Emily's grin dissolved. Her healthy glow faded as she stared at the door.

"It's the nurse." Rachel looked at the door with what she imagined was a twin expression to her daughter's.

"Early." Emily chewed on an already gnawed fingernail. "Go figure."

Definitely that good cry would have to wait, because Emily looked more nervous than she did. "Oh, honey. It'll be okay." It had to be. "Besides, it's temporary, remember?"

"Yeah. Um…you might want to remember that."

It was instinctive, wanting to hug her daughter. So was the move to do just that, which had her body shooting sharp little bites of pain as a reminder that she couldn't do anything on the spur of the moment. As she sagged back in her chair, she took a deep, careful breath.

"Mom?"

"I'm okay." Okay being relative of course. Careful to not move a muscle, all of which were quivering, she said, "Let's get this over with. I'm sure you and Mel did a great job picking her out."

"Uh...now's probably a good time to mention Aunt Mel had nothing to do with this." Emily continued to chew on her fingernail, staring at the door with a curious mixture of dread and joy. "She doesn't know, no one has any idea...."

The bell rang again, following by three raps on the wooden door.

An impatient nurse. Great. She really *was* getting Attila the Hun.

Emily tossed her chin high and headed for the door. Then, ruining the confident stance, she hesitated. Quick as a bullet, she shot back to Rachel and dropped a sweet kiss on her cheek, and gave her a very wobbly smile. "I'm really sorry, okay? You know, like, in advance." Then she strode to the door and opened it.

Standing there, one shoulder braced, his other hand flat on the opposite jamb, head bowed as he waited with a barely contained edginess, was the one man Rachel had thought to never see again.

Ben Asher lifted his head, and his dark, melting brown eyes unerringly found her across the foyer. "Hello, Rachel."

He'd come. He'd come back. And unbelievably, all she could think about was her hair, or lack of. Though it screamed in protest, she lifted her weak, shaking arm, checking the position of the soft cap she'd used to cover her bald head. "You."

"Yeah. Me." He straightened to his full height, which was considerably over six feet. Without being asked, he moved inside, dropping a duffel bag and backpack to the ground with a heavy thunk. Then he hauled Emily close for a big hug. "Hey, sweetness."

"Hi, Daddy." She squeezed him back, then untangled herself and grinned at him.

Bigger than life, he stood in the foyer, set his hands on his hips, and with frank curiosity, looked around him, taking in the large open airy room with the bricked wall, the hardwood floors, the fire pole in the center.

"Mom." Emily licked her lips, dividing a look between her parents. "I sort of asked Dad to come."

Ben shot his daughter a wry glance, complete with arched brow, and Rachel had to wonder…had Emily really asked…or begged?

Did it matter? He hadn't come for her, he'd come for Emily. Of course he'd come for Emily, to take her on one of their trips. How she'd ever thought otherwise, even for that brief, humiliating flash, was beyond her. She closed her eyes against the sight of him, but it didn't matter; his image was indelibly printed on her brain. He was so much the same yet so different, her breath was gone, simply gone.

He'd always done that to her, way back when they'd been seventeen and he'd been her entire world. God, had she really ever been that young? She'd thought her pain couldn't possibly get any worse, but just looking at him made her want to double over with the agony from the inside out, making her feel like she was nothing but an emotional powder keg ready to blow. "I don't want you here," she said with remarkable calm. Not even for a few minutes. She wanted him gone so she could concentrate on her Attila-the-Hun nurse still to arrive.

Ben's lips curved, forcibly reminding her of Emily. Oh yes, her daughter was indeed a true gorgeous chip off the old gorgeous block. She'd just forgotten how much.

"I understand the sentiment, believe me." Gaze still on Rachel, he extended an arm, bringing Emily back into the crook of it, hugging her again. "How are you holding up, Emmie?"

The voice. The face, the same rugged, tanned, open face, framed by the same sun-kissed, light-brown hair Rachel had loved to run her fingers through. It was still long to his collar, with the same tousled look that assured her he used his fingers far more often than his comb. His clothes were clean but nondescript, allowing him to be the chameleon he was, fitting in wherever he felt the need. Even so, an aura of strength and confidence exuded from him, and Rachel could only return his stare.

It'd been thirteen years since she'd last seen him. Why did it suddenly feel like yesterday?

His movements, as he held his daughter and came farther into the room, were fluid and lithe…everything hers weren't. Muscles rippled beneath his T-shirt and faded jeans, reminding her of her own weaknesses. But his eyes, still holding hers, reflected her same discomfort.

Finally, Ben broke the unsettling eye contact to look at Emily. "Tell me you asked your mom before you called me."

"Asked me what?" Rachel's heart started to beat heavy in her chest, threatening to burst not yet healed ribs right open.

Ben shook his head at Emily, love and irritation swimming in his gaze. "Chicken," he chided softly.

Emily lifted a shoulder and gave him her saddest, most pathetic look.

With a soft sound of annoyance and love all mixed

in, Ben let go of Emily and came toward Rachel in long, easy strides, hunkering down before her wheelchair with such casual strength she wanted to kick him.

If only she could have lifted her casted leg.

He sported a day's worth of dark stubble, but it didn't hide the fact he had beautiful cheekbones and a strong, wide jaw. His mouth was full and, she had to admit, still sexy as hell. How in God's name she could look at him and notice such a thing, after all this time, was beyond her.

But those eyes, those dark, haunting eyes. Such a deceptively soft color, and yet there was nothing soft about him. Try sharp. Probing. *Blunt.*

"You look like hell," he said, proving the point.

"Yes, well, I've been in hell."

Nodding slowly, he reached out and touched her pale fingers with his sun-kissed, callused ones. She felt the jolt all the way to her toes. So did he if his quick inhale meant anything, which proved one thing—as much as it shocked her, for she was *not* a sensual, sexual creature by nature—they were still explosive in each other's presence.

"I'm sorry you're hurting," he said.

He spoke the truth; it was his nature. Stifling an emotion wasn't in his genetic makeup. Which made his pity more than she could take. "Don't feel sorry for me."

Amusement flickered briefly across his face. "I wouldn't dare."

Trussed up as she was, her senses were on overload, especially her sense of smell. His scent came to her— warm, clean, earthy male—and it was so achingly familiar, her traitorous nose flared, trying to catch more of it. He always had been a disturbing combination of untamed outdoors and infectious sensuality, full of passion, of fire, zest for life.

No, he hadn't changed a bit.

But she had. He might have once walked away from her, but she was tougher now. Impenetrable. She just wished he hadn't come for Emily now, when she was shaking with the effort not to fall over with exhaustion.

"You're in pain now?" he asked, perceptive as ever.

*Hell, yes, because just looking at you brings me pain, stabs into my carefully hoarded memories. Reminds me of my failures.* "I don't want you h-here." Stuttering on the last word as her brain once again failed her was the ultimate insult, and as if it was his fault, she glared at him.

Ben pursed his lips as he studied her, rubbing his jaw. The growth there made a raspy noise that seemed to cause a mirroring tug in her belly. God, she remembered him, just like this. Looking at her, through her, *in* her. She'd always been positive he could see far more than she'd wanted him to.

Which was all tied up into why she'd asked him to go. Once upon a time he'd been everything that had been missing in her life, and everything that could destroy her. When he'd done just that, she remembered thinking how naive she'd been to think she could handle a man like him.

She wasn't so naive now. She *knew* she couldn't handle him.

"I can't go away this time, Rachel." His voice was full of apology and a pent-up frustration to match her own. "I promised Emily I'd stay."

She jerked her gaze to her daughter, who was hovering behind Ben, wringing her hands, biting her lip.

"That's why I said I'm sorry, Mom," Emily said

quickly. "I know, I know, I'm probably grounded for a month."

"For *life*."

"Yeah, well…" Emily laughed nervously. "I deserve that."

"No, she doesn't." Ben shook his head, watching Rachel. "She was frightened. Alone and worried about you. And she wanted me to be here."

"For one of her trips with you while I recoup. Fine. *Great,*" Rachel added. "Thank you for that."

"Don't thank me for caring about my own daughter. Emily is everything to me."

"I thought that was your camera."

That caused a shocked silence.

"Is that what you really think?" he asked softly.

The present and the past commingled, and for a moment she couldn't tell where she was or when. He'd always had his Canon around his neck. He'd had an amazing talent for reaching past his subject, capturing the heart and soul in a way that had never failed to steal her breath. At seventeen, he'd been determined to use that talent as his ticket out, knowing the odds but not giving up.

Ben never gave up.

Compared to his outspoken and obvious ways, Rachel fought her battles differently, internally, but she didn't want to be so cruel as to hurt him with words simply because she was in pain. "I'm sorry. I know you care about Emily."

"Damn right I do. She needs both of us. How else will she ever learn to do certain things? *Feeling,* for instance."

Once again, she considered kicking him. "You don't know me anymore." Every word was a trial to get out past the sheer exhaustion creeping through her body, but she wouldn't collapse, not until she was alone. "It's immaterial anyway. You can't take off with her right now, she's in school and summer break isn't for another month."

Emily didn't look relieved, which was her first hint. Her second was Ben's direct, unwavering stare.

She stared back, the truth sinking in. "No. *No.*"

"Afraid so," Ben said evenly, even lightly, though his eyes alone expressed his own unsettled emotions. "I'm staying. Until you can care for yourself."

"*You're* my help?"

"Yep."

Being so tired made remaining even moderately social difficult. Being in pain and betrayed on top of it—by her own daughter no less—made it impossible. "I'd rather go to a convalescent hospital."

Emily shifted closer. *"Mom."*

She'd deal with Emily and her betrayal later. "I mean it."

"Fine." Ben rose in one smooth, swift motion, making her dizzy when he looked down at her from his full height, his gaze inscrutable for once. "I'll just take you there myself."

*"Now?"* she croaked.

"As opposed to never? Yes, now." He put his tense, lived-in face uncomfortably close to hers. His eyes flashed. "You don't want me here, then you can't stay either. You didn't expect Emily to handle the burden—"

"No, of course not." *Burden.* Lovely.

"Well, then…" He moved behind her. Strong, tanned hands reached for her chair. Tough forearms with long blue veins over ropy muscles flexed as her chair shifted.

*He'd do it,* she decided. Yes, he would, because if

there was one thing she remembered quite clearly about him, it was that he never bluffed. Hadn't she learned that one night so many years ago, when she'd let her fear of intimacy overrule her, when she'd rashly told him to get out of her life, and he'd done exactly that without a backward glance? "No."

Before she could draw in another ragged breath, her chair stopped. Once again, Ben's face filled her vision. Expecting pity, she braced herself.

Instead, she got anger.

"Are you done being a child about this? Because if you are, great. We'll stay right here. We, as in you and me. Together."

"I'd have been better off with Attila the Hun," she muttered.

"You probably would have," he agreed grimly. "But I promised Emily."

And though he would do many things, one thing he wouldn't ever do is go back on his word. "You're crazy to do this. You can't do this, we can't stay together, it would be..."

"Like old times?" he mocked.

His direct gaze was unflinching, reminding her just exactly how they had been together and how good it had been. "You have no idea what it's like," she whispered.

"You mean being forced by circumstance to give up on everything?" He laughed harshly. "Yes, I do. I grew up that way."

"Ben—"

"Forget it. It doesn't change anything." He squatted in front of her chair, setting his big hands on her armrests, his leanly muscled body crowding into her space. "But I'm a fair man. I'll make you a deal."

Her traitorous body actually wanted to lean closer.

Her nose wanted to wriggle and catch a better scent. Her body wanted…his. "You'll go after all?"

"Nope."

His fingers touched hers again, making her wonder if his body was reacting in the same way as hers. "Something not quite as good, but it'll have to do."

She eyed him suspiciously. "What?"

"Soon as you can physically kick me out, I'm gone. What do you say to that?"

They both knew that even at her physical peak, she couldn't have budged his long, powerful frame, not if he didn't want to go.

He might appear lackadaisical to some, even easygoing. But that slow, lazy way he had of moving was deceptive, like a sleeping leopard. She knew exactly how tough, how resilient he was. Or at least how he'd been.

"Deal?"

Again, her past and present mingled together, leaving her blinking fiercely to keep the sudden tears of frustration to herself. She would *not* cry, not in front of this irrational, infuriating man. "Deal. But only because I'll be better very soon," she vowed.

Damn his far too good-looking hide, he let out a sardonic laugh that seemed directed at himself. "Believe me," he assured her, surging to his feet in one graceful movement. "I'm counting on it."

# CHAPTER FOUR

BEN PRETENDED that he could actually breathe in this too big, too terrifyingly normal house that he wasn't welcome in, and managed a smile as Emily showed him around.

He couldn't quite wrap his mind around the fact that he was here. That he'd stepped foot inside South Village and hadn't imploded on impact. That he'd seen Rachel, and had felt...*something*. She'd felt it, too, but given the attitude and daggers she'd shot him, she hadn't liked it any more than he had.

The refurbished firehouse was interesting, if one was into huge, open, elegant spaces. The rooms had high ceilings and windows everywhere that showed off the interesting view of the city that never seemed to sleep. There was a firefighter pole right down the center of the place, and a spiral staircase of wrought iron. Braided rugs adorned the shiny hardwood floors, and artwork from around the world decorated the brick walls. So did photographs.

None of his, Ben couldn't help but notice. No skin off his nose. He'd come into this house with a mental wall twelve feet thick just to keep Rachel out of his head, and no doubt, she'd done the same for him. She was good at building walls. Hell, she was the *master* at building walls.

The furniture was new, tasteful and very Rachel. In

other words, expensive. And yet, he could see Emily racing through these rooms, sliding down the pole from one floor to another, perfectly at home.

"You're really going to stay home for a while?" she asked him.

Ben's insides knotted at the small, hopeful tone, even more so than at the word *home*. He'd spent most of his childhood here in South Village trying to get out and all of his adulthood trying to forget.

Now he was back, indefinitely.

Dropping his things on the bed in the room that was to be his for the duration, he turned to her. "Yep." Because she was looking unsure, he opened his arms, relieved when she leaped into them, hugging him tight.

"I know you said you would." Her head didn't come up to his shoulder. Against his chest, she smiled. "And you haven't ever broken a promise, I just wanted to hear you say it again."

God, she was young. She was so smart that sometimes he forgot how young she was. Honest relief flooded him that he was able to give her something, *anything,* other than his usual phone call. "I'll stay as long as it takes," he promised, thinking of Asada. He'd gone to see Agent Brewer on the way here, but there'd been no news.

So he concentrated on the here and now, how Rachel had looked downstairs, how she'd stopped his heart with just her eyes and how incredible it felt holding his kid— God, *his kid.* He wondered at the sharp ache in his heart. Why did it hurt so much to love her? "How does that sound, my staying as long as it takes?"

A grin split her face, a glorious answer, and his strange hurt faded.

Face flushed with happiness, she wriggled away. She danced and whirled to the door, all gangly arms and legs, and for a moment, Ben was lost in time, seeing Rachel as she'd looked thirteen years prior.

She'd been all arms and legs, too, he remembered. And the pang came back, sharper than before. What a miserable time in his life that had been, struggling to survive when he'd been little more than a kid. And Rachel had been his bright spot.

His hope.

Just as Emily was now.

"I'm gonna cook tonight," she announced proudly. "A celebration dinner. Mac and cheese."

"Celebration?" He doubted Rachel would be up for that. Her once creamy skin had seemed nearly transparent and bruised with exhaustion. She'd barely been able to hold her head up as she'd flashed those huge, angry, hurting eyes on him. If he hadn't still been so unnerved at being here, so tensed and battle-ready, it might have broken his heart. "I don't think tonight is a good night—"

"It's a *perfect* night," Emily assured him. "Mom's where she wants to be and I have both my parents in the same place."

*Uh-oh.* Ben might claim not to know a lot about the intricate workings of a female mind, but he knew warning signals when they blared in his brain.

And man, were they ever blaring now. "You know my being here is because you managed, God knows how, to pull a fast one on your mom." And because a madman wants to destroy me. "Not because she and I are back together."

Emily sobered. "Are you mad at me?"

With Asada on the loose he'd have had to come regardless. "No," he said honestly.

"Mom's mad."

"Good guess. Em…tell me you know this is just temporary."

"You just wait." She twirled again and executed some sort of ballet movement that had his eyes crossing as he tried to follow her. "You're going to love being here so much," she said, breathless now, "that you won't want to ever leave us."

Damn. "Emmie—"

"Gotta get the dinner started. Catch ya in a few!"

And she was gone, leaving Ben blinking in her dust.

*He was doing the right thing,* he assured himself as he sank to the bed. Though he felt like he was suffocating here, he *was* doing the right thing.

He would not do as he'd been doing for years. He would not run and lose himself in some jungle. Or in some guerilla skirmish. Or in some forsaken desert somewhere. His camera and his need to capture the good photo, the story would have to wait this time.

He slipped his hand into his pocket, bringing out a copy of the second letter he'd received from Asada, which had been farther down in his stack of mail back in the South American jungle.

The authorities had the original, another fastidiously clean piece of stationary with precise folds and meticulous handwriting. In contrast to the pristine paper, the text was enough to make him feel sick: "Dear Ben, Just as you have ruined my life, I will ruin yours. Your most faithful enemy, Manuel Asada."

The South American authorities were on Ben's side completely. Asada had escaped, and this wasn't only an embarrassment, but a huge threat. If they didn't find him, it was only a matter of time before he'd set up another charity scam or kill without conscience to protect his business.

Or come here to exact revenge…if he hadn't already. Ben felt a terrible, agonizing certainty Asada had somehow caused Rachel's accident.

It wouldn't happen again. Yes, eventually, Ben would have to explain the regular police drive-bys to Rachel and Emily, but now that he'd seen Rachel and the extent of her injuries, he was more convinced than ever she shouldn't know until she was stronger.

Besides, how did one explain to his daughter and the woman who hated him that he'd inadvertently put their lives on the line? That there was a madman out to get them? It would make Rachel all the more dependent on him, something she'd hate with every fiber of her being.

Right or wrong, he had to wait. And if in the meantime, it put more pressure on him to protect them, to be something he'd never been able to be in Rachel's eyes, then so be it. It was nothing less than he deserved for bringing them this danger in the first place.

BEN FOUND RACHEL right where he'd left her, sitting in her chair in the spacious living room, facing the huge set of windows. That damn ugly cap was still in place, hiding her hair from him. Her right arm and leg were in air casts. He knew that her ribs were cracked and that sitting there for so long must be torture. But he knew also that it had to be painful to shift positions.

She should have looked ridiculous. Miserable. At the very least, pathetic.

Instead, she looked as beautiful as ever. Maybe more so. Despite the fading bruises, her face was aristocratic, her skin smooth. Her body, what little he could see of it, was still long and sleek, and still made him yearn.

He could vividly remember a long-ago night when they'd sat in a hidden-away spot in the botanical gardens behind city hall. Rachel's long blond hair rippling over his arm, that lithe, soft body spread beneath his in the grass, her huge, melting eyes filled with heat and fear and hope as she gave herself for the first time, to him. His first time, too, and in spite of the fact their birth control had failed them—the condom broke—that night still stood unrivaled to anything he'd experienced since.

She didn't acknowledge him as he moved into the living room, and he wanted her to. "What happened to the person who hit you?" he asked.

"They never found him."

He sucked in a breath. Oh yeah, Asada had done it. Emily could be next.

Ben's stomach quivered as he mentally added this to the long list of things he'd screwed up. *Are you good for anything, Benny boy?* No. No, he wasn't.

Unaware of his personal hell, Rachel stared down at her hands, her words coming out slowly. "I'd almost rather it be a hit-and-run than someone who'd just made a terrible mistake. This…this torture of mine wouldn't be erased by destroying someone else's life as well."

That Rachel had once nearly destroyed *his* life didn't escape him. By the time she'd finished with him, Ben had felt every bit as battered and bruised as she looked now, except his injuries had been invisible.

Did she really look at him and feel nothing? And why did he care? Did *he* feel something when he looked at her?

Yes, he could admit, he did. Mostly anger and humiliation. She'd been taught to not express herself, but somehow he'd gotten Rachel to open up to him. It'd been like watching a flower bloom, beautiful and arousing. They'd been two lost souls made into one, yet she'd thrown it away with an ease that chilled him even now.

Good, *there* was more of that anger he needed in order to keep his distance. He'd just see her comfortable, then go make some calls regarding her accident and then stay away from her until he could leave. But when he stepped closer, took in her grim expression, her pale face, the way her good hand clasped her casted one, he was filled with alarm to see her trembling with the effort to remain upright. "Hey, let's get you get into bed."

She didn't respond, which made him feel like an unwelcome slug. Not a new feeling for him, but it bugged him nevertheless. He put himself in her line of vision and reached out for the cap that shaded her eyes from him.

"Don't." Coming to life, she struggled to lift her arm, holding the ugly thing in place.

"I want to see your eyes." *Liar. You wanted to see if her hair was as glorious and thick and curly as it used to be.*

"Why?" She flashed those eyes up at him now, wide and furious and full of pride as she stubbornly held on to the cap.

At least the temper was a hell of an improvement over the sadness and vulnerability. Not that he really cared. She'd fixed that for him a long time ago. He was simply here to make sure he didn't bring his personal hell down on her.

"L-leave the cap."

"I want to see the real you, what you're thinking."

"I'm thinking I wish you could leave."

He couldn't help it; he laughed. It was that, or lose it entirely. *Go away, Benny. Go away, Ben. Go away...* "I just remembered one of the things I used to admire most about you," he muttered. "Stubborn as a bull." He rose, moved behind her and grabbed her chair. "Nothing's changed. Let's go."

When he would have shifted her chair forward, she set her good hand on the wheel. "No."

Afraid to hurt her fingers, Ben stilled. "I'm taking you to your room where you'll lie down and rest, damn it. You're so tired you're shaking. You have black circles under your eyes, you haven't been eating near enough and—"

"You're my nurse, not my mother."

He looked down at the top of her head. "Well, since we both know what a peachy job your mother did, let's leave her out of this."

"How dare you throw my past in my face! You, of all people."

Oh, he dared, and she'd riled him good now. *Their past* was exactly what had brought them here together. *Their past* often kept him up at night with flashes of remembered heat and passion.

*Their past* was one of the emotional highlights in his life, pathetic as that was to admit.

Torn between being infuriated and turned on at the same time, he let loose. "And as your nurse, I say take off the stupid hat." Before she could react, he whisked it off her head.

And froze.

Her soft, flowing hair was…gone, leaving a short, choppy cut of maybe an inch or so. Then there was the three-inch long jagged surgery scar behind her left ear that made him want to throw up. "Rachel. My God," he whispered, horrified at the extent of what she'd been through. Clasping the ridiculous hat to his chest, he turned the chair so he could look into her face, prepared to hate himself for reducing her to tears.

But he'd forgotten, Rachel would never allow him to do such thing to her. Crying in public would be unacceptable. Crying in front of *him* would be tantamount to a disaster.

Instead, regal as ever, she remained utterly calm, her head high. Eyes bright, she sent him a fiery look. "I h-hate you."

Oh, yeah, he believed it. He even deserved it, more than she knew. Gently, he put the cap back on her head, his fingers brushing over the warm, smooth skin of her neck. "I'm sorry."

"Go away."

"Rachel—"

"No! Don't even look at me."

Her fair skin had reddened furiously, and he realized they absolutely were not on the same plane, that she apparently thought the sight of her had sickened him. "No, wait. God. Rachel—" He dragged in a deep, ragged breath. "Look, my horror is for what you've been through, not for what you look like. You look…"

*Stunning* was all he could think, staring into her wide, lovely eyes. Brave and lovely and desirable. But she'd never believe that. "Alive. Rachel, you look alive. Isn't that all that matters?"

She didn't say a word, but her chest rose and fell with her agitated breathing, and being nothing less than a very weak man, his eyes caught there, mesmerized by the surprisingly lush twin mounds of her breasts.

"You mean ugly," she whispered.

A sound escaped his throat before he could control it. "No. That's most definitely not what I mean." He drew another deep breath and shook his head to clear it. "You're wrong, very wrong."

"Just go away."

As those were hauntingly familiar words, he swore softly beneath his breath, fought with the demons that urged him to do just that, then placed his hands on her chair. ''We're out of here.''

''To where?'' she asked, panic laced in her voice.

''To where I should have taken you when I first got here. Bed.''

FROM EMILY'S PERCH on the open loft, lying flat on her belly next to the top of the spiral staircase, with only her eyes peering over the side, she watched her parents and bit her lip. This was not quite the joyful reunion she'd imagined. But she was no longer a child. She knew life sometimes sucked. And yet…she could fix this. She could. If her mom and dad weren't happy to see each other, she'd just make them happy. How hard could it be?

All her life she'd been told how brilliant she was, how extraordinary. She loved that word, *extraordinary*. Mostly because when she looked in the mirror she saw nothing but frizzy hair that gel didn't fix, too many freckles and a geeky smile. Where was her extraordinariness? Maybe it would come when she got boobs, but what if she never got any and, just like her Aunt Mel, had to buy them?

Her mom had said her extraordinariness came from her brain, which worked like a well-honed machine. Well, she'd made good use of it then, regardless of the tangled web she'd woven by gathering them both here. She wouldn't waste the effort.

All she had to do was get them to fall in love. Unfortunately, she knew little about that particular emotion. Desperate, she'd just gotten off the phone with Mel, figuring since her aunt had a new boyfriend every other day, she'd have lots of ideas. Emily had explained she was asking for a friend, but Mel had laughed and said she and her friends were too young for love.

*Thanks, Aunt Mel.*

Far below her in the living room, her father pushed her mother's wheelchair. His face, now that he thought no one was looking at him, had lost some of that easygoing, laid-back attitude that was so innately him, replaced by a tenseness that shook her.

What was the matter? Well, besides everything?

Her mother's expression, tight and angry, didn't surprise her in the least. Emily had some serious kissing up to do. Probably dishes for a month, maybe more. She'd probably lost TV privileges too. Losing her beloved reality shows and MTV seemed like a small price to pay if they fell in love again.

When they were gone from view, she slid down the fireman's pole and dropped to the middle of the living room, trying to ignore that tingling of guilt in the pit of her belly. Because, darn it, if she was as special as everyone said, then she knew what was best for her parents. And what was best for them was to be together, on the same continent for a change. That's why she'd done it, blabbed about her mother's situation to her father. Told Aunt Mel that they'd hired a nurse. Let her mother think Mel had gotten them that nurse.

Because now that everyone had done what she'd wanted, things could fall into place. All she had to do was make it happen.

MANUEL ASADA crawled through the Brazilian jungle for days upon days, and finally came out at his compound. Exhaustion and unaccustomed lack of even the most basic luxury had him weaving with weakness. He'd been on the move for too long, and could barely think, but the sight of his old fortress gave him a surge of energy.

It'd been searched and pillaged, of course, because thanks to Ben Asher, the authorities were hunting him down like an animal. Damn them all, his home was now barely a shell of what it had once been. Windows gone, inside gutted, dirtied…trashed. Disgusting. They'd pay for that, too.

That he'd gotten here at all was a miracle. He'd made it by the skin of his teeth, bribing when he'd had to, pulling from his dwindling stash of cash as it had been necessary. And it had been, several times. The entire experience—jail, the escape, being on the run—had sent him reeling with memories of his penniless, loveless, thankless childhood.

He could kill for that alone, that he'd relived being a professional beggar by the time he was four…but first things first.

His compound, once hopping with activity, mocked him with silence in the growing night, making him shudder. God, he really hated silent and dark.

Most of his minions had fled or been taken to jail, which left slim pickings. Two were still in the States, quaking in their boots, awaiting his further instructions after screwing up the murder of Rachel Wellers. He'd had some time to think about that now. By all accounts via his laptop, which he'd plugged in at various villages when he could, the woman had suffered greatly and continued to do so. Asada liked that; he liked that a lot. He intended for them all to suffer even more. Soon as he got himself reorganized. "Carlos, the place is filthy."

"Yes, but you've been gone a long time." The man's voice wobbled with fear.

As it should. Everyone knew how Asada felt about dirt, how crazy it made him. Being treated like a parasite in a filthy jail cell hadn't helped. Nor had being on the run ever since.

They couldn't go inside; there'd be men around, looking for him to do that very thing. But beneath the compound lay a secret underground bunker. They'd once used it as a supply container but now it would become his home.

Carlos raced ahead of him as they made their way toward the hidden door that would lead to a set of stairs. Manuel waited while the trembling Carlos used his own shirt on the dusty door handle. They stepped inside but didn't turn on the light—they couldn't, not while he was still being hunted like a dog, and besides, there was no electricity. It was unthinkable that after all these years of building his empire, amassing fortune upon fortune, that this could happen. But it had.

He had been brought back to zero. Back to the old days, when he'd begged for money, sold himself, whatever it took. With a deep breath, he strode inside the dark, damp cellar and lit a single small oil lantern. Then he very carefully pulled out his small laptop from his pack, blew a speck of dust off the top. He didn't turn it on, not yet. He wanted to conserve the gas in the generator. But he'd go online later, to check on the progress of what was happening in the States.

Once upon a time, just above him had been the center of his universe. Now, on top of this Brazilian mountain, hunkered beneath his multimillion dollar compound that gave him his multimillion dollar view, and he didn't even dare go up there to survey his domain.

The fact that he couldn't so much as show his face anywhere without possible retribution filled him with an unholy fury for which he had no outlet. He stalked over to a box of office supplies and pulled out a sheet of stationery. "You're going to hike back into the city—preferably without getting yourself killed—and get this mailed," he told Carlos.

"Sir, the others and I, we were wondering when we were going to get paid—"

The others were a handful of equally pathetic, worthless minions who deserved to be hung for letting this happen to him, their savior. "Go away until I'm ready for you."

"Yes, but—"

"Go away and don't come back until the entire cellar is spotless, not one speck of dust left."

"*Sí.*"

Alone again, Manuel begun to write. "Dear Ben..."

# CHAPTER FIVE

BEN PUSHED Rachel's chair forward, then hesitated at the base of the spiral staircase in her living room. "Where's your bedroom?"

Rachel hesitated, too. It just seemed too surreal, having him right here, behind her, his hands so close to touching her where they rested on the wheelchair grips by her shoulders. Plus, he'd leaned down to hear her answer, which meant she could smell him, feel his heat, his strength…

"Rachel? Your bedroom?"

How had this happened? How was he standing here, in control, in her house?

Because she'd been outsmarted by her own child, that's how! All those years of successfully avoiding him, and here he was. Unbelievable. "This is so not necessary."

"Your bedroom, Rach. Or, if you'd rather, I can take you to mine." He shifted her chair around to look at her, so that she couldn't avoid his dark eyes that had already managed to see past her carefully erected defenses.

She stared at the silver stud in his ear and did her best to ignore the blatant sexuality that rolled off him in waves. "Mine will do," she said primly.

His sigh brushed over the cap she'd shoved back on her head. Then he straightened, his hands on his hips.

His shirt pulled taut over his chest that she remembered being lean, almost too lean.

But he'd filled out. He was still rangy, still tough, but his young body had grown into a man's.

Not that she was noticing.

"Someone else could help me," she said desperately. "Anyone else. It doesn't have to be you."

"*Where* is your bedroom?"

She sighed. "Upstairs."

He eyed the firefighter's pole, then the spiral staircase. "I don't think the stairs are going to work."

"The elevator."

"You have an elevator." He let out a low whistle. "Why am I not surprised?"

Since he'd walked in her front door, she'd been holding herself tense, and it hurt. She wanted to be alone, to let go. The only way to do that was to appease him for now. "The place is a renovated firehouse. It came with the elevator. I didn't add it."

"You sound a little defensive."

She ground her back teeth into powder. Hell, yes, she was defensive. She was always defensive. She'd learned young to shut herself down, happily existing in an emotional vacuum. Until Ben had come along, that is. Without a dime to his name, he'd done what no one else ever had—showed her all the things so missing from her own world…passion, emotion. *Life.* He'd wanted her, not just physically, and had never failed to show her so.

The force of what he'd felt back then, crashing into her cold, impersonal world, had terrified her. With good reason. Their fundamental differences had turned out to be a bridge impossible to cross.

*Yet, you'd crossed it,* came the unwelcome thought. *For six months you crossed it and thrived on it.*

Ben pushed her into the elevator. They waited in agitated silence for the doors to slide shut, and once they did, Rachel wished they hadn't.

The space was small and lined with mirrors, which meant she could see herself, reduced and weak and defenseless in the damn chair. Worse, she could see him standing tall and strong behind her. "This is ridiculous."

"My being here?" Ben locked his eyes on hers in the reflection of the mirrors. "Get used to it."

That got a rough laugh from her, and a sharp pain shot through her ribs for the effort. It robbed her of breath, of all thought, and she squeezed her eyes shut, tensing up with a small cry.

Big hands settled on her thighs, surprisingly gentle for their size, as was his low, urgent voice. "Relax. Let it go. Breathe, Rachel."

No, she wasn't going to breathe, that would hurt worse. She was never going to breathe or move again. "Go…away."

*"Breathe,"* he repeated, running his fingers lightly over her thighs. "Come on, slow and easy. In and out."

She did and, shockingly enough, it helped. So did his voice, talking to her softly, over and over, reminding her to relax, breathe. Slowly, she opened her eyes to see him kneeling in front of her. "That…was your fault."

"Undoubtedly. Everything is my fault. Keep breathing now. Slow and easy."

"I know how to breathe."

He surged to his feet as the elevator door opened and turned away from her. "What I'm surprised at," he noted casually, pushing her off the elevator, "is that you still know how to laugh."

She sucked in a gulp of air and tried to pretend that comment didn't hurt worse than her ribs. Oh, yes, she knew how to laugh—*he'd* taught her. Had he forgotten? Forgotten everything they'd once meant to each other?

She was silent as he wheeled her down the hallway lined with collages of photos from the years past, starting with Emily's birth. One shot of Emmie—small and red, wrinkled and furious, howling as she told the world how she felt about being born. Another of Rachel holding her bundle of joy, smiling with wet eyes at the now quiet baby, who stared right back at her. The two of them. Even then, it had been just the two of them against the world.

Later photos of Emily learning to walk, sitting on Rachel's lap while Rachel drew a *Gracie* comic strip on her easel, another of Emily putting candles in a homemade cake for her mother's birthday.

There was a shot of Melanie on one of her visits from Santa Barbara, puckering up for Emily's four-foot teddy bear. A picture of the firehouse when they'd first purchased it, before renovations. And then subsequent pictures of Rachel and Emily and Melanie, covered in paint as they worked on the place. There was a picture of her neighbor Garrett with Emily riding on his shoulders. A picture of Gwen, Rachel's agent, her arms around both Rachel and Emily, who held Rachel's first impressive royalty check.

Behind her, Ben said nothing, and she wondered if he was even looking at the pictures, looking and feeling odd for not being in a single one. Did he feel left out?

Strange, but she didn't want him to. Despite everything, she didn't want that. She had Emily, her greatest gift, her greatest joy, because of him. She owed him for that, which was why, whenever he'd asked, she'd sent Emily to him via Melanie.

Bottom line was, she had this house and Emily. This

was her world—stable, safe and secure. It meant everything.

In comparison, Ben had a duffel bag and a few cameras to his name. That was it as far as she knew. He liked it that way, or he had.

That they'd made it together for even six months so long ago seemed amazing now.

"Rach?" As if she were the finest, most fragile piece of china, Ben set a light, careful hand on her shoulder. "You okay? You've gone quiet and pale on me."

His fingers brushed her collarbone like a feather, and a shiver raced down her spine. Not signifying cold, but something far more devastating. "I'm...fine."

Another brush of those fingers, a testing one this time, while his eyes held hers. "Rachel," he murmured. "It's still there. Can you feel it?"

"I—" *No,* she wanted to say, but lying was ridiculous when surely he could feel the blood pounding through her body at just a single touch. Again, he squatted in front of her.

"You still have those eyes," he murmured. "The ones that make me melt."

She let out a nervous smile.

He smiled back.

"I have no idea why I'm smiling at you."

His fingers traveled up, up, cupped her face. "I don't care. Just keep doing it."

She stopped breathing. His gaze was locked on hers as he slowly let his thumbs stroke her jaw. Her body responded, giving her a jolt of pleasure instead of pain for once, as if it recognized that this man, and only this man, had given her such incredible pleasure.

Ben let out a rough, disbelieving sound, then cupped

the back of her head, gently holding her still as he shifted his mouth toward hers.

*Move,* Rachel told herself, and she did—closer, matching up their lips. It was unfathomable, unthinkable. He had no business touching her, and she had no business wanting him to, but she did. Oh, how she did.

The first light touch of lip to lip dissolved her bones, and all the pain with it. Needing the balance, she put out her right hand, gripping his chest. Beneath his shirt, his heart thumped steadily. A bit dazed now, she simply stared up at him.

With a soft murmur of her name, he changed the angle of her head and connected again. His mouth was warm, firm, giving, so beautifully giving that her eyes drifted shut and she lost her ability to put words together, to do anything but feel.

His tongue lightly stroked her lips. Struck by a familiarity and strangeness all at once, she moaned, then again when a slow, deep thrust of his tongue liquefied her. She fisted her fingers in his shirt, holding him close, making him groan deep in his throat.

The sound was raw, staggeringly sensual, but then he was pulling back, letting out a slow breath.

She did the same, but it didn't change the fact she could still taste him and wanted, *needed,* more.

But that had never been their problem, the wanting.

"Your bedroom," he said a little roughly.

"The next room down."

He moved behind her, gripped her chair. Once inside, he stopped. There was a picture hanging on the wall, an eight-by-ten from two years before, of Emily wearing a sundress, beaming from ear to ear, holding up her elementary school diploma. Her eyes sparkled with such joy, such life, it hurt to even look at her, but Rachel looked anyway, just as she sensed Ben looking.

Did he see it? The resemblance, not so much physical, though that was there, too, but the very essence? The soul? It must have been like looking in a mirror.

God knows their daughter hadn't gotten her sense of adventure and spirit from Rachel. Before Ben, she'd had nothing like that until he'd come along and had shared his. He'd done more than share: he'd somehow gotten so close, he'd breathed his very being into her, bringing her to life during the time they'd had together.

But Emily...she'd been full of life from day one.

"She's beautiful," Ben said quietly. "Like you."

"Ben—"

"Let's get you into bed."

For a moment she thought he'd said "let's get into bed," and her heart jerked. Yes.

*No.*

But when he came to stand in front of her, his face was grim, so obviously her brain was messing with her again.

"Don't try to move," he said. "I'll lift you."

She stopped breathing, realizing just that very second what his being here really meant. He was going to have to help her, look at her.

Touch her.

Before the panic fully gripped her, he moved, not toward her, but to her dresser, where he randomly opened one of her drawers. Shaking his head at the rows of socks, he closed it and opened another.

"What are you looking for?"

He lifted a loose, flowing silky camisole and matching bottoms, and his eyebrows at the same time. "Wow."

The two pieces were the palest of blue, softer than

baby's breath, and her favorite thing to sleep in. And yet dangling from his long fingers, the innocent pj's suddenly seemed like the sexiest things she'd ever seen.

She was not putting them on.

"You used to wear buttoned-up-to-the-chin flannel to bed, remember?"

"I was a kid."

Something flickered in his eyes. "Not so much."

Before she could come up with something to say to that, he'd tossed the pj's on his shoulder and started toward her.

In spite of the exhaustion, the pain, she managed to shake her head. "I am not putting that on for you."

He turned down her bed and laughed, a low, husky sound that grated at every hormone in her entire body. "You're right about that. You're putting it on for you."

"Ben."

"Rachel," he mimicked, then in opposition to his easygoing toughness, he slid his arms around her, making her breath back up in her throat, making every single thought dance right out of her head.

"Easy now," he murmured. "It's loose and stretchy, so it should go on easily." And gently, so gently she felt like she was being lifted by air, he rose with her in his arms. "Okay?" His eyes roamed her features, his mouth tight in concern.

A concern she didn't want. "Put me down."

He did, on the bed, and a myriad of things hit her at once. Pain from the jarring, no matter how careful he'd been. Comfort from the feel of her own bed after so many weeks. And sheer overwhelming devastation from the feel of his hands on her.

Then he reached for the buttons on her short-sleeved

blouse. She let out a sound that make his gaze jerk up to hers.

"You can't undress yourself," he said reasonably.

"I'll— I'll sleep in my clothes."

"Oh, that'll be comfortable." He looked into her stubborn face and sighed, stroking a light finger over her cheekbone. "You're wearing your exhaustion like a coat. Just let me help you."

She opened her mouth and he put his finger to it. "There was a time you let me help you with anything. Remember?"

She didn't want to remember, but somehow his touch, like his kiss, insinuated itself past her bone deep weariness and pain, and struck her like a bolt of awareness lightning. "Get Emily. She'll help me."

Slowly Ben shook his head and removed the bunny slippers Emily had put on her feet at the hospital. "She's making you dinner. Mac and cheese. She's under the impression you're going to bounce right back now that you're home. Bringing her up here now, when you look half a breath away from death, would only scare her."

She closed her eyes when his fingers brushed over her buttons again, squeezed them tighter as he pulled the blouse open and gently off her shoulders, past the cast on her arm, taking such slow, aching, tender care with her broken body she felt her eyes burn.

*No. No falling apart until you're alone.*

He unhooked her bra and slid it off before pulling the stretchy, laced pj's top over her head, very tenderly guiding her casted arm through the wide armhole. The material tugged at her nipples, and a shocking bolt of desire streaked through her.

Her eyes flew open, met his. Once upon a time he'd caused that reaction, in quite different circumstances.

Did he remember? Judging from the strain in his face, the slight tremble to his hands as he dragged her loose pants down her legs, hardly shifting her casted leg at all, he did remember.

Determined to feel nothing as he pulled on her pj's bottoms, then covered her up with the comforter on her bed, she concentrated on breathing, concentrated on *not* going down memory lane every single time she so much as glanced at him.

He moved off the bed and opened her bedroom window, letting in some of the early evening breeze. And unbidden, another memory hit her. Him crossing her bedroom just like he was now, his tall, lanky form turning to shoot her a crooked grin as he eased open her window and swung a leg over the sill at the crack of dawn, preparing to leave after a long, forbidden night of touching, kissing, talking, loving.

Now, Ben's mouth curved wryly with the same memory. "I guess this time I can use the door instead of nearly killing myself climbing down the trellis. Remember?"

Her body shuddered. It was damn hard to feel nothing, to refuse to go down memory lane with him saying "Remember?" in that sexy voice every two minutes. "Tell me again why you have to do this, Ben. Why you have to stay."

He turned away. "Do you really think that little of me, that you believe I wouldn't?"

"I think you're crazy if you expect me to fall for the reasoning that you want to be here, in South Village, tied to one house, one spot, when everything within you yearns to be on the move."

He moved to the door. "Well, then, call me crazy."

"But *why?* You can't want to be here."

"This has nothing to do with what I want." He glanced at her over his shoulder. "Just get better. Get better and it'll be over before you know it. Then you can go back to your safe, sterile life and forget I bothered you for one moment of it."

The door shut behind him, and before she could obsess, sleep took over her battered body, releasing her from thinking, aching, wondering.

But not from dreaming.

*TWO MONTHS BEFORE high school graduation,* National *Geographic contacted Ben. They wanted him to intern with one of their photographers for the summer in Venezuela. If that worked out, he'd have an assignment waiting for him in the fall in South Africa.*

*"Come with me," he said to Rachel.*

*They sat in their hidden-away spot in the botanical gardens behind city hall, their common meeting place, halfway between their respective houses.*

*Rachel lifted her gaze off the letter in his hands and stared at him. He was more animated than she'd ever seen him, even in the throes of passion, and she knew why. He'd been waiting his entire life to leave this town, and now he had a chance.*

*But she'd been waiting her entire life to stay in one place longer than it took to order and cancel cable service. She'd moved once a year for as long as she could remember, and she was weary, so damn weary.*

*She loved South Village; loved the joyous crowds, the urban streets, the sights, the smells, everything. This town was her life, her heart. She loved it here and didn't want to leave, not even for Ben. If she left, her life with him would be no different than it was now—just a blur*

*of moving, moving, moving, when all she wanted was
a home.*

*"Rach?"*

*"I want to stay."*

*"No, we have to go. There's nothing for me here, you
know that."*

*Actually, she'd only guessed, as he never told her
about his family. It was the one thing he'd always refused to discuss.*

*"It's my future," he said hoarsely, telling her only
how much this meant to him, but not why.*

*Oh, God, letting him go, watching him walk away,
would be like ripping out a part of her, the best part. "I
can't." Her heart got stuck in her throat because she
knew. He was destined to go.*

*And she was destined to stay.*

*"You'll come," he said confidently. But they didn't
speak of it again because shortly after that Rachel
caught the flu—a nasty bug that dragged on and on,
weakening her, tiring her.*

*After watching her throwing up every afternoon at
four o'clock on the dot for a week running, Ben took her
to a clinic. "Does she need antibiotics?" he demanded
of the doctor, squeezing her hand as they waited for an
answer.*

*"Nope." The doctor shook his head. "What you're
cooking isn't contagious. It's a baby."*

# CHAPTER SIX

THE PHONE WOKE Melanie Wellers at what felt like the crack of dawn. Opening her eyes, she stretched lazily...and came in contact with a warm, hard, undeniably male body.

Oh, yeah, nice way to wake up.

Those male arms tightened on her, and a low growl sounded in her ear. "Mmm, you feel good."

Yes, yes she did. She always felt good with a nice warm body to strain against.

Jason, no, Justin...yes, *Justin,* she remembered with a fond sigh, had so gallantly offered her a ride home from the bar last night where she'd gone after work in need of a stiff drink.

Her boss had been a son of a bitch all day, she had bills coming out the wazoo and she hadn't gotten the raise she'd counted on. And yet Jason—damn it, *Justin*—had promised to make it all go away for a night.

Lord almighty, he'd kept his word.

The phone kept ringing, and it started to grate on her nerves. "Gotta get that, sugar," she said, slapping his bare ass playfully as she stretched across him for the cordless on the nightstand.

Then she caught sight of the time. Ah, shit! Late for work, again.

*Can you see me now, Dad?* With a sardonic twist of her mouth, she glanced heavenward. Or maybe she should be looking down toward hell, as that was a far more likely place for her father to have ended up. *Late for work, Dad, and proud of it. Roll in your grave over that one.*

Hoping it wasn't her boss, she grabbed the phone.

"Aunt Mel?"

A smile broke out onto her face, and only part of it was relief. "Hiya, Emmie, baby."

"Are you busy?"

Mel glanced at the extremely gorgeous, extremely naked man in her bed. He rolled over and shot her a come-get-me smile, making her laugh. "A little. What's up? How's your mom?"

"That's what I wanted to tell you, she's good. She's great. So great you don't need to take any time off this weekend to come down here, we'll be fine."

Mel's relief became tinged with something a little sour. She was the older sister and, stupid as it was, she had this bone deep need to be needed by Rachel.

Rarely happened.

Still, for weeks she hadn't taken a spare breath, going back and forth from Santa Barbara to South Village, and not only had it crimped her social life, she really needed to rack up some extra hours at work. "Are you sure?"

"Positive. Mom says do what you have to do, we're fine."

"You got a nurse, right?"

"Things are really, really fine. So, uh, we'll just see you *next* weekend. Or the weekend after."

"Next weekend for sure…" Melanie narrowed her eyes and paused. As the Queen of Liars, Cheaters and Manipulators, she could smell a con a thousand miles away. "You didn't say, Em. Did you hire a nurse?"

"Yeah, it's, um, working out just great. Really great."

Apparently tired of waiting, Justin ran two hands up Mel's legs, slow and lazylike, toying with what he found between them.

Melanie's eyes crossed with lust. Did she really want to grill her niece when she had this gorgeous man ready and willing to worship her body?

Then that gorgeous man slid a finger into her. "Okay, then," she managed to say. "I'll call you in a few days to check up on you. Bye, sweetie—"

Justin disconnected for her and tackled her flat to her back, holding her still while he smiled wickedly into her face.

"What are you going to do with me now?" she asked a little breathlessly.

"This." Then he put his mouth where his fingers had been, scattering her thoughts like the wind.

BEN HAD GOTTEN *her pregnant. Seventeen years old, the world finally, finally, at his fingertips, and he'd really screwed up this time. He reached for Rachel's hand and found her fingers icy. "It's going to be okay."*

*Choking out a laugh, she pulled her hand free. "Really? How is that Ben? I'm having a baby, for God's sake."*

*Yeah. A baby. His stomach rolled, but that could have been hunger given he hadn't eaten since breakfast. Nothing new in that. He'd planned never to be hungry again on the other side of the planet.*

*With Rachel at his side.*

*Looking at her in the moonlight, with her long hair and haunting eyes, his heart constricted. God, he loved her. Ridiculously so. Who'd have thought the no-good, black-hearted nobody had it in him to feel this way, as though he couldn't breathe, couldn't do anything if she wasn't in his world?*

*And they'd made a baby. By accident not design, they'd come together and created a life, a perfect little life, and suddenly his panic turned to something much lighter, something much closer to...joy. "Marry me."*

*"Ben—"*

*"Look, I love you, that'll never change. And we'd have gotten married eventually, we'll just move the plans up a bit."*

*"But...where will we live?"*

*"Well, we'll start out in South America, but—"*

*"Ben."*

*"We'll have to hit Africa in the fall, and then—"*

*"Ben."*

*He was losing her, he could hear it in her voice, so he kept talking, fast as he could. "And then we'll go to Ireland, because—"*

*She grabbed his hands, brought them to her heart. Her eyes were huge and wet, her voice so low he had to lean close to hear her. "Ben, listen to me. You love me, and that's my own miracle, believe me, but I can't. I can't become Mrs. Asher."*

*"So don't change your name," he said deliberately misunderstanding her. "I don't care, Rach, I just want you."*

*She let out another choked sound, this one a sob. "I can't...I can't give you what you want. We're too different."*

*"Different doesn't matter." He was going to have to talk her into wanting him. His stomach rolled and pitched again. No one had ever just wanted him, no questions asked. "Look, I'm going. You're coming with me. We love each other—"*

*"No! God, you don't get it!"* Her face twisted. *"I...don't love you. Okay? I don't love you."*

*He couldn't move. Couldn't breathe.*

*"I'm sorry."* Drawing in a deep breath, she stood. *Her eyes were still wet but inscrutable now, hiding herself from him. She was good at that. "I won't see you again before you go."*

*With the words* I don't love you *echoing in his head like a bad refrain, he could just stare at her.*

*"Goodbye, Ben."*

*"Rach—"*

*"Go. Please,"* she whispered brokenly. *"Just go."*

*It was a hauntingly familiar request for him. She didn't love him and she wanted him to go. Fine. He wouldn't beg. "Goodbye, Rachel," he said, but she'd already walked away, vanishing into the night.*

In hell with the memories, Ben woke up with a gasp. He lay in a white bed with white fluffy pillows, sweat streaking his body, air chopping in and out of his lungs as if he'd been running a marathon.

Nope, not hell, but close enough. The walls seemed to close in on him, strangle him.

How fast could he get out of town? Out of the country? Asia should be far enough for today. Surely he could get to Asia. With a vicious oath, he scrubbed his hands over his face, just as someone leaped onto the mattress at his side. Battle-ready, he whipped around.

Emily sat at his hip, with a wide cheeky grin. "Morning, Daddy."

And just like that, his heart sighed. Sagging back against the mountain of fluffy pillows, he let out a shaky breath. Asada. Rachel.

Emily.

Revise. He *was* in hell. "Morning, sweetness."

She wore cargo pants low on her hips, a tank top in neon yellow that made his eyes vibrate with the brightness, and held her laptop in her arms. She bounced a few times for good measure.

"Didn't you sleep well?" she wanted to know.

"Fine." Not fine, not really. Late last night he'd gotten a call on his cell phone from one of his editors. They'd received a letter at the magazine's head office, forwarded from his last job. It'd been handwritten on fancy, stiff, olive-colored paper. "I'm still going to make you pay," it had said.

Obviously Asada, but that it'd come to Ben in South America gave him hope—Asada still didn't know where he was.

Or whom he was guarding.

When Ben had finally gotten into bed there'd been the nightmares of Asada finding this precious woman-child right in front of him, of losing Rachel and Emily now, in the present, as he'd lost Rachel so long ago.

Bounce, bounce. "You looked tired, Dad." Bounce, bounce. "Maybe you should sleep some more."

Bounce, bounce.

"Em, you're scrambling my brain."

"Sorry." She stilled—a momentary miracle, he was certain. "Mom's still sleeping. Wanna go out to breakfast and get artery chokers before I have to go to jail?"

"School isn't jail, Em."

"*This* school is."

"No luck getting your mom to home school you yet, huh?"

"None," she said on a dramatic sigh.

"What are artery chokers?"

"Scrambled eggs, a mountain of bacon and the best hash browns you've ever tasted. It's at Joe's, a sidewalk café right around the corner. Mom hates the place, but she doesn't know how to enjoy herself.'' Hopeful smile. Bounce, bounce. ''Oops.'' She stopped bouncing. Again. ''Sorry.''

Cracking a glance at the clock, he managed to contain his groan when he saw three fives all lined up. ''It's not even six.'' In his body's time zone—God knows which one that was exactly—it felt like the middle of the night.

''Duh. That's why Mom's still sleeping. Come on, she'll never know.'' Leaping off the bed, she grabbed his arm and tugged. ''We can get a milk shake to go with it, double chocolate. They're huge.''

Ben rarely ate before noon unless it was a hunk of bread or cheese on the run. And it'd been so long since he'd been in the States, much less in a civilized country with sidewalk cafés that served huge chocolate milk shakes and ''artery chokers,'' he supposed he couldn't blame his stomach for quivering hopefully. ''Give me five minutes to shower—''

''Shower later.'' She pulled him out of bed, making him grateful he'd pulled on a pair of knit boxer shorts before tumbling into bed the night before. The jeans she tossed him hit him in the chest, his shirt in the face.

''Hurry.'' She bounced again, from foot to foot this time. ''I'm starved.''

''Okay, forget the shower, but I still need two minutes.''

''Da-a-ad!''

''Two minutes,'' he repeated, putting his hand over her face and gently pushing her out of the bedroom, shutting the door on her.

Her sigh came through the wood. ''I'll wait on the porch. Two minutes. One hundred twenty seconds, okay? Not like Mom's two minutes, which are really twenty.''

"Em, no. Not the porch.'' He didn't want her outside, unsupervised, ripe for a kidnapping. "Wait inside.''

"Yeah, yeah. Two minutes, right?''

*"Inside.''*

"Gotcha.''

He used half his two minutes to call for his messages, hoping Agent Brewer had checked in. After this latest letter, they'd promised to double their efforts, but there was nothing new this morning.

Ben brushed his teeth and ran his fingers through his hair. One glance in the mirror assured him he wasn't quite ready for a public appearance stateside. His hair was long and he needed a shave. His face seemed leaner than he remembered, and he had new lines fanning out from his eyes. Not laugh lines, given his life and what he'd done, but hard-living lines. Artery cloggers...yeah, he supposed he could use a few weeks of high-fat, over-processed food. Scrambled eggs, bacon and hash browns with his daughter seemed like a good start.

Risking his last few seconds before Emily came looking for him, he left the bedroom and because he was an idiot, a glutton for punishment, his hand touched the handle of Rachel's door, twisted it. Pushed. The huge bed was still, covered in pillows and comforters, with an unmoving lump beneath them.

He moved closer. Nothing of Rachel showed, so he gently pulled the covers away from her face.

Her head was covered by a handkerchief, her face creased in a frown, but after a beat, she relaxed back into the deep sleep of the exhausted, flat on her back.

Maybe she wasn't quite on her deathbed as Emily had led him to believe, but she was hurting, he could see it in the tight lines of her mouth, the delicate purple bruises beneath her eyes. All the painful injuries made her seem so vulnerable, which was hard to take because Ben remembered her well, and one thing she'd never been was fragile. A pillar of strength, most definitely. Full of immense courage and pride, yes. Stunningly intelligent and mouthwateringly gorgeous, yes. Fragile, no.

It made him feel fragile in return, just looking at her.

Letting out a soft exhale, she turned to her good side, winced, then went still again. Her creamy shoulders were in view, as were the straps of that amazingly sexy pj's set he'd put her in yesterday.

He let out a slow, slow breath. He hadn't allowed himself to think while he'd had his hands all over her body, but he was thinking now. She'd been hauntingly beautiful at seventeen, but at thirty, her beauty had only ripened, deepened. She had the little birthmark on her right inner thigh. He'd noticed that yesterday. He'd loved that birthmark, had loved to put his mouth to it and—

And those thoughts were going to lead to nothing but trouble. As if he didn't have enough. He took one more long look, feeling like he was dying of thirst and she was a long, tall drink of water.

Once upon a time he'd been ashamed of how much he'd needed her, a woman who'd prided herself on never needing another soul.

And yet she needed him now. She needed him now and didn't even know it.

She let out a little murmur, a half whimper, and broke his heart. "You're okay," he whispered, and lightly stroked a hand over her shoulder. She'd always had the softest, sweetest-smelling skin, and that hadn't changed, either. He let his fingers linger, as suddenly and rather desperately, he wanted his mouth there. Everywhere. "Just sleep."

Beneath his touch, her response was instant and shockingly gratifying. She relaxed. Just because he'd spoken.

The curve of her breast pushed at the top of the camisole, and he had to take his hand off her and stuff it into his pocket. Feeling like a pervert for wanting to touch her, he covered her back up, and reminded himself why he was in South Village.

Why he couldn't hop on the next plane out of it.

Turning away, he caught sight of a stack of mail on her dresser. At the mac and cheese celebratory dinner last night, right in this room, Ben had met Garrett, Rachel's neighbor. Apparently he always brought in the mail for them. Ben had wondered darkly what else he brought Rachel, but decided he was a fool for caring.

He started to walk out of the room, but jerked to a stop when he caught a glimpse of an envelope sticking out of the stack of mail. The sight of the fancy, stiff olive-colored paper backed the air into his throat. With a quick glance back at the still sleeping Rachel, he slid the envelope out from the stack.

It was addressed to him, in the carefully scripted handwriting he was beginning to recognize all too well. The return address said simply Asada, South America, postmarked a few days prior.

A new letter. Recent contact. With the envelope burning his fingers, he moved into the hallway and ripped it open, his hand shaking as he skimmed the words: "Ben, Worried yet? Frightened yet? Good, because we're still not even…"

"TOOK YOU *FIVE* minutes," Emily muttered when Ben finally came down the spiral steps. She sat cross-legged in the foyer, a long phone cord trailing across the floor to her laptop, which according to Rachel, she used to chat with her only friends—and cyber friends at that. She unplugged it and stood up. "Next time take the pole down, it's faster."

He'd taken the extra minute to call this latest letter in to his FBI contact. "Right. The pole."

"Ready?"

He forced a smile. "Yep."

They stepped outside. Ben checked and rechecked the front door lock as they stepped outside, then looked around with an eagle's eye. There was a male jogger, a newspaper delivery guy on a bike weighted down by bags of newspapers and a woman in a sports bra and tiny shorts on in-line skates.

Nothing out of the ordinary for South Village, but the urge to wrap Emily up and tuck her away someplace safe for the rest of her life was strong.

Then there was Rachel. How he felt about protecting her was far more complicated. She'd once turned her back on him with ease.

And yet he found himself utterly incapable of doing the same.

Garrett sat on his front step reading a newspaper and drinking coffee, looking big and muscled and capable of taking down anyone he chose.

Ben sighed with resignation. "You going to be there for a little while?"

Garrett eyed him over the top of the paper. "Yep."

Ben hitched a shoulder toward Rachel's front door. "You'll keep an eye out for a few?"

Garrett looked at the house, then back at Ben. "You expecting trouble?"

"I always expect trouble."

Garrett nodded. "I'll keep an eye out."

Since neither Asada nor the bogeyman jumped out and announced themselves, he and Emily left the small front gate for the street.

Though it was still spring, this was Southern California, where there were two seasons—hot and hotter. Even at the crack of dawn Ben could tell the day would be on the fiery side of hell by noon.

"Phat day, huh?" his daughter said, and led him down the sidewalk.

"Phat," he repeated, and made her laugh.

They passed a dinner theater and a do-it-yourself ceramic studio. And a shocking amount of people for just after 6:00 a.m.

"Early commuters," Emily announced cheerfully. "Did you know on the weekends we're up to twenty thousand people walking through here?"

That was 19,999 too many if you asked him.

They passed an ice-cream shop, which was also open. And also packed. "Don't you love it here?" Emily asked. "You can buy ice cream 24/7."

Love it? The crowds, the noise, the hustle and bustle, sucked the soul right out of him. What he'd love would be to leave right now, put ten thousand miles between him and this place. He didn't belong here, on the very streets that had made him miserable. Hollow.

He should be used to that hollow feeling—he'd been raised on it. Then he looked into Emily's happy, expectant eyes, and pushed away that feeling.

At least for now, he was going nowhere but crazy any time soon.

"This is it." Around the corner, Emily gestured to a small outdoor café that had heavenly scents making his nose and stomach come to life. The tables were wrought iron and close enough that Ben could catch snippets of everyone's conversation around them. Already seated were an eclectic mixture of urbanites, construction workers and shoppers. Ben sat and opened the menu that had more choices for coffee than for food.

"When summer comes," Emily told him, carefully setting down the laptop she never seemed to be without, "I'm going to ask the owner if I can work here."

"When you're twelve, summer isn't for working."

She frowned. "What is it for?"

He'd never been a normal twelve-year-old, so hell if he knew. "For hanging out with friends?"

Some of the sunshine went out of her eyes. "I'd rather work."

Ben remembered his preteen years pretty much sucking, too, but Emily came from a different universe. "What's the matter with friends?"

"Nothing."

"Em."

"The other kids are all weird."

"Weird, how?"

"The girls are into boys and the boys are into skateboarding."

"Well, then things haven't changed much."

She lifted her menu in front of her face, blocking him off. "I'm hungry."

Okaaay. Leaning forward, he hooked a finger in her menu and lowered it. "Just let me say one thing."

"Do you have to?"

"As your dad, yes."

With a dramatic sigh, she set aside her menu, looking more than a little wary.

"Worrying about you sorta comes with the territory of being your dad. I can't help myself."

"Do you *want* to help yourself?"

"Huh?"

Her eyes were shuttered now. "Would you rather you didn't have the territory at all?"

How was it he forgot how smart she was? "No, I want the territory. Emmie." He touched her hand when she looked away. "I want to be a dad. *Your dad.* I love that."

She bit her lower lip. "Sure?"

"I'm very sure, sweetness, but thanks for checking."

She grinned.

He grinned back. "So..."

"So, I'm fine."

"Promise?"

"Promise."

Short of alienating her by pressing, he had no choice but to drop it. They ordered enough food to keep their arteries clogged for the year, and Ben spent the entire meal trying to spot Asada, or someone sent by him, in every face.

He hated that. He hated the helplessness, the vulnerability. With Asada in hiding, the cat-and-mouse game was on, with everyone Ben cared about as the mouse.

After breakfast, they started walking back. "Turn here," Emily said, pointing to an alley between a lingerie shop and a gallery. "Shortcut."

In his world, an alley was a death trap. "Let's walk around the building and—"

"Hear that? Oh my God, look!"

Before he could stop her, she'd run into the alley, set

her laptop on the ground and scooped something up into her arms.

By the time he reached her, Emily was jumping up and down with the bundle still in her arms. "Can we keep it, can we, can we?"

The "it" in question was the smallest, ugliest puppy on the face of the earth. Drab brown, flat face, hanging ears...the thing couldn't have weighed more than three pounds soaking wet. In Emily's arms, it seemed to sink in upon itself, ribs sticking out, eyes huge and pathetic and right on them. When Ben came close, it shrunk back with a whimper, then licked Emily's hand.

"He's a stray." Emily hugged it tighter. "No collar. Oh, look...he's half-starved." Emily blinked up at him. "He's an orphan, Daddy."

Ah, hell. "No."

"But we can't just leave him here."

"Yes, you can. You just put him down and walk away."

Her face creased into a disapproving frown. "Mom said you're a hero. That you save people. How can you say such a thing?"

Rachel had called him a hero? He couldn't fathom *that* conversation. "Em...we can't just bring a dog home."

"But I've always wanted one...always." Her lower lip began a slow thrust outward. "Especially because I'm so lonely..."

Ah, *man*... "Em..."

"Oh, Daddy, isn't he adorable? We *have* to take him home and feed him."

The puppy, sensing victory, seemed to perk up.

Ben closed his eyes but it didn't matter. He could still see that grungy, mangy, pathetic face.

"Please, Daddy? *Please?*"

He strained for a valid reason that would get him off easy. "Your mother—"

"We've been meaning to get a dog, I swear! Just before Mom's accident we'd decided to rescue one from the pound, but I can rescue this one instead."

The puppy licked Emily's cheek now. Blinked chocolate-brown eyes at Ben. Then whined softly, as if too hungry to put any real energy into it.

Damn it, he couldn't stand when someone—or something—was hungry.

"And look, his ears are darker than the rest of him, they're so cute."

And dirty.

Emily rubbed her face against the dog, looking so happy it was almost painful to look at her. "We can call him Patches," she said.

Patches sighed in bliss, and exposed a sunken-in belly for rubbing.

Ben sighed too, and found himself rubbing that soft belly. "Only one problem, Em."

"No. No problem."

"Yep." Besides his zillion others. He stroked the soft belly again and gave Em a wry smile. "Patches isn't a him."

# CHAPTER SEVEN

SEVENTEEN AND PREGNANT. *Her father would kill her. Her mother would hiccup, spill her vodka, then burst into tears...or maybe just pass out.*

*Melanie would care. She'd wrap Rachel in a hug, then offer to drive her to the clinic that Rachel had driven her to twice now.*

*But Rachel wouldn't consider that route, not for herself. Yet the alternative...keeping the baby... How could she? Everything she was going to be, everything she wanted for herself, depended on the next few years. Years in which she'd have to work hard to make it all happen. She wanted a career, she wanted security and stability. But most of all, she wanted a home, a permanent home, right here in South Village.*

*And she wanted to never, ever, be dependent on anyone for anything.*

*But now she had someone depending on her, a defenseless little someone. What did she know about babies, she wondered half-hysterically. Babies needed warmth, caring, unconditional love, but she didn't even really know what those words meant.*

*Ben would have given her all of those things, and his name along with them. But he also wanted to drag her to the four corners of the earth and never settle down.*

*Tonight, she'd looked into his incredible eyes, had seen the love he had for her, and had nearly, very nearly, caved. And yet, ironically, it had been the enormity of what he felt for her that had held her back.*

*So, she'd given in to the fear and told him to go.*

*And with shocking ease, he had, leaving her here, alone, just as she'd wanted.*

*While a little part of her couldn't help but wonder…how deep could his love really have been if he'd shaken it off so easily? With a choked sob, she put her head to her knees.*

And awoke to the sun piercing in her window. Just a dream, a horrible, wrenching dream. She started to sigh in relief, but the pain kicked in, and she remembered.

Not just a dream. It'd all really happened.

But she was no longer a young woman all alone. She had Emily now and they were a family, so anything was bearable. To prove it, she struggled to sit up. Her vision wavered for a second and her ribs sent pain jabbing to her brain. Tightening up, she braced for more. But shockingly enough, despite the aches, bumps, bruises and casts, it was nothing she couldn't bear.

Standing up, however, was a different story entirely. She tried until she was gasping for breath and sweating, but she couldn't do it.

Okay, not quite ready, she finally decided, sitting panting on the edge of her bed, swiping at her brow. What now? The pj's were a problem. They were sheer and completely inappropriate for ignoring ex-lovers who were suddenly back in one's life.

Yes, he'd already seen her in it, several times as a matter of fact since he'd checked on her during the night, helping her to the bathroom, bringing her water, and my God, the heat in his eyes had given her sunburn. She'd felt his unbelievable wanting, and had actually felt the same. How did one go thirteen years without setting eyes on someone and then see him again and want so badly? How did that happen? Well, however it worked, she didn't care to repeat it.

*Clothes*. Number one order of business. Getting the pj's top off wasn't so difficult, her new air casts were surprisingly lightweight and easy to maneuver. She simply nudged the straps off her shoulders with her good arm, refusing to give in to the pain that was beginning to make itself known in her bad arm, and let the thing fall to her waist. With a good amount of wriggling, she managed to kick off both the pants and the camisole in one fell swoop.

Getting something else on...not quite so easy. Realizing she had no clothes within reach, her scramble out of her pj's suddenly didn't seem such a wise move. And...yep, that was the doorbell. Naturally. Because she sat there in nothing but panties.

Her robe lay across the foot of her bed. Using her good leg, she grabbed it with her toes and pulled it toward her. So far so good. But the terry cloth was thick and heavy, and one sleeve was inside out and—

The doorbell rang again.

Damn it! Where was Emily? School already? Without saying goodbye? Did she have lunch money and her homework? And where was Ben? She was almost afraid to wonder, because with her luck, she'd conjure him up here while she sat there looking like a black-and-blue poster child for abuse, huffing and puffing like a junkie to boot.

By the time she got herself covered—forget tying the sash, she was cooked. She was a complete shaky mess, never mind the hair, or the fact she hadn't brushed her teeth. Grateful for the wheelchair Ben had left right by her bed, she sort of half fell, half dropped herself into it. Okay, good. Panting for breath, out of shape and not happy about it, she set her hands on the wheels and paid the price for forgetting how bad her arm and shoulder still hurt. "Right arm only, right arm only," she whimpered to herself, hugging her left arm to her chest.

But right arm only meant she could only wheel herself in circles. Frustrated, she tried one more time, and let out a huffing scream when she got nowhere.

"Rachel." Garrett strode quickly into her bedroom, set of mug of delicious coffee down on her nightstand, and reached for her wheelchair. "Let me help you."

Her next-door neighbor was tall, dark-haired and studiously handsome. He wore wire-rimmed glasses and yep, there was his palm digital organizer sticking out his breast pocket as always. Good old dependable Garrett. He mowed her small lawn every Saturday, played Frisbee with her daughter whenever they were both around, and minded his own business. Usually.

"I was on my porch," he said. "And heard a thump. I thought maybe you'd fallen."

"And couldn't get up?" she quipped.

"Well, I knew Emily and Ben had gone to breakfast... I rang the doorbell and called out your name to warn you I was coming in." He lifted the key Emily had given him after the accident, then unhooked the brake Rachel had hooked on the left side of the wheelchair. "Try that."

Of course that worked. Feeling stupid, she sighed, making sure to keep her fingers clenched over the lapels of the robe and praying a sudden wind didn't whip through the house. "I don't suppose you'd feed me your coffee intravenously?"

He brought her the mug. "Try drinking it the old-fashioned way."

She eyed him over the top of it, trying, as she occasionally had, to feel some sort of attraction to him. Why didn't looking at him rock her world, the way looking at Ben did? It made no sense. Garrett was a dentist, which meant he rarely traveled and made a decent living. He gave to charity. He was kind to old ladies. He also played tennis fanatically and had a sailboat. It all added up to him having his own life. He wouldn't depend on her for anything including entertainment. Bottom line, he was handsome, intelligent and funny.

And yet...not a single spark.

As she sipped the coffee, another voice called out her name, and then shortly appeared in the doorway. Adam Johnson this time, her accountant, her financial advisor, her friend and Garrett's physical opposite. Height challenged, blond, and not athletically inclined, he was, however, extremely intelligent, funny and one of the sweetest men she'd ever met.

In three separate momentary bouts of loneliness, Rachel had dated him. Each time he'd made her smile, laugh, think. She'd enjoyed herself immensely and might have made it an even four dates—a record for her—if not for the accident.

And, of course, the fact she didn't feel any more attracted to him than she did Garrett.

Adam had one hand wrapped around a dozen pink roses, the other around a thick file—hers, if she were to guess. He could undoubtedly tell her to the penny how much money she had at that very second.

"The front door was ajar," he said, moving into the room. "I hope it's okay I just came on in. No one answered my knock and I got worried..."

"I'm sorry." She managed a smile, though in truth all that rush to get dressed and in her chair had done her in. She felt like a drooping flower. A hurting, drooping flower. "I'm fine, really."

"Mom!" Emily stopped short in the doorway.

"Welcome to Grand Central Station," Rachel said, but then her breath backed up in her throat because Ben appeared behind Emily, wearing cargo pants and a black T-shirt, looking wild and edgy and dangerously sexy. He was taller than Adam, darker than Garrett and, given that there wasn't an ounce on him that wasn't hard, lean muscle, he was far more solidly built than either of them.

In his slow, purposeful way he looked around the room, missing nothing with his dark, deep, direct eyes— not the two strange men in it, not the fact that she wore only a robe or that she was holding it shut, *nothing*.

Her pulse picked up speed as his gaze took a leisurely tour over her body. Clenching the robe even tighter, she drew a careful breath. She'd expected to feel a reaction when she looked at him—she always had. But this morning it came with an unexpected twist watching him against the backdrop of the other two men.

Ben Asher wasn't the most handsome, polished or cultured man in the room, but he was simply and by far the most potent, lethal, one-hundred-percent male she'd ever met.

And she couldn't take her eyes off him.

"Dad and I went out to breakfast," Emily announced, an unmistakable glow about her.

Rachel looked at Ben.

He looked right back.

"And, um, I'm going to school now." With her heart in her eyes, Emily looked at Ben. "Thanks for breakfast."

"Don't you need to go over something with your mom?" he asked.

Uh-oh, Rachel thought. "What?"

"Um…" Emily bit her lower lip, a sure sign that she was thinking. And when Emily started thinking, God only knows what trouble she'd come up with. "After school, okay? I'm late."

"Em—" Ben said warningly, but before he could press, Garrett stood. "I've got to get to the office," he said.

"He dates really pretty models after he makes their teeth white," Emily said.

Garrett grimaced. "I'm a dentist," he offered a little sheepishly.

"A dentist to the stars," Emily bragged.

Ben nodded without judgment, even though Rachel knew this life had to be as completely foreign to him as his world was to her.

Not having been previously introduced, Adam thrust out his hand toward Ben. "Adam Johnson. Financial advisor and friend to the pretty patient." He hoisted the flowers, then held them out to Rachel.

She tried to take them with one hand while holding her robe closed with her injured arm, but as had happened so often since the accident, her brain didn't quite get the message to her fingertips, and as she reached out, they fell and scattered at her feet. "Oh, Adam." Frustrated, she sighed. "I'm so sorry."

"No problem, there's always more." Adam went down on his knees, offering her a sweet smile as he scooped them up.

"I, um, gotta go," Emily said, and gave her father a long look that apparently spoke volumes between them.

"After school then," he said firmly.

Emily nodded, turned to high-five Garrett, then threw herself at Ben and kissed him. "Bye, Daddy."

"Bye, sweetness."

Rachel would have sworn she heard Emily whisper, "She's in my room, watch her," but decided the pain had gone to her head. She waited for her kiss, but Emily danced to the door.

"Hey, Em. Me, too?"

With a martyred sigh, Emily came back and kissed Rachel, while Rachel felt like a world-class loser mom. "Is it a Monday?" she asked the room, a little defeated. "Because it sure as hell feels like a Monday."

"It's Wednesday, Mom," Emily said in a humor-the-idiot voice. "Bye!"

Garrett followed her to the door, then turned to Rachel. "Call me if you need anything." And with a nod to both Ben and Adam, he was gone.

Adam straightened, his now sorry-looking bouquet in his hands. He set them by Rachel's bed, where they drooped in a way Rachel sympathized with. "I've got to run, too," he said. "I've got a client." He glanced at Ben before leaning down and kissing Rachel on the cheek, setting her file down by the flowers. "In case you want to see that everything is in order. Can I bring you dinner?"

"Oh, Adam, how sweet. But don't trouble yourself."

"It's no trouble."

AT ADAM'S OFFER of dinner, Emily stopped short in the hallway, then raced past a startled Garrett and peeked her head back in her mom's bedroom. "Mom, Dad's doing dinner tonight. I forgot to tell you." She added a smile because in her experience, a smile always aided her cause.

Bless her dad, he didn't blink, much less call her a big, fancy liar.

God, she loved him.

"Oh. Well, then." Adam kissed Rachel again, gave her a smile Emily was quite certain her mother thought sweet, and finally, *finally* he left.

Emily again glanced at her father. *Yes!* He had a little frown on his face, and was watching Adam go from the doorway. Yes, yes, yes! He didn't like that Adam had kissed her, either! So maybe her parents weren't falling all over each other as she'd hoped they'd be by now, but this was only day two.

Still, she'd have to work fast. Her luck, Adam would do something stupid like...propose. Her stomach sank. "This time I'm really leaving." Without a wave, she raced down the hall, ignored the muted puppy whines she could hear from her room—holy smokes she still had to deal with *that*—hopped onto the pole and leaped down into the living room just as Adam came down the spiral stairs. Opening the front door for him, she walked him out. "Thanks for checking on my mom," she said.

"You don't have to thank me, Emily. I like to see her."

*Well, duh. That was the problem.* "My dad is here now though, so he can check on her."

Adam searched her features, then slowly nodded. "I see."

"You do?"

"Yes." A small smile touched his lips. "You'd like me to vanish."

She flushed. "Well, I didn't want to hurt your feelings or anything."

With a grim smile, he pushed up his glasses. "You want them back together. Of course you want them back together."

Okay, that took her back. She'd been very sly about this, so... "How did you know?"

"My parents were divorced. Let's just say I recognize the desperation."

"Oh." She winced, thinking he was awfully nice for her to be wishing him so dead. Maybe he could just go far, far away.

"Emily, you know your parents have been apart a very long time now, and—"

"It could happen! They could get back together."

He closed his mouth. Looked at her with that same gentle smile that speared her with guilt and nodded. "It could."

"So, you'll stop kissing her?"

Adam let out a laugh. "I'll tell you what...if your mom wants me to stop kissing her, I will. Okay?"

She looked into his kind eyes and felt a little bit of what her mom must like about him. Which made him a bigger threat than she'd imagined. And what could she say? It would have to be good enough.

Besides, surely after another day or so, her mother would want her dad to be kissing her and no one else. After all, her dad was irresistible.

As she was walking back inside, the house phone rang. She grabbed it up, for a minute hoping it was Alicia, her new e-mail pal. They'd "met" a few weeks ago in her school's homework chat room, even though Alicia didn't go to her school. Sometimes kids from other schools hacked in, which she was glad for because she didn't like the kids in her school. Anyway, they'd decided to be best friends and Alicia, who lived in Los Angeles, had been promising to call so they could talk for real.

"Hey, baby, how's your mom?"

Aunt Mel. Jeez, Emily must not have been that convincing earlier this morning when she'd called Mel to keep her away. Looked like she'd have to try harder. "Hi! Like I said, Mom's great. In fact, she was just saying again how she didn't want you to take any more time off work because she's doing so great."

"Really?"

Emily could hear the skepticism in Mel's voice. "Really," she gushed. "She got out of bed all by herself." Her father came into the room with the puppy under his arm and gave her a long look as he took Patches outside. Emily winced, but kept up the flow of Mom's-doing-great chatter.

"So, how's school?" Mel asked when Emily had finally wound down.

She winced again. School was a deep, dark pit of hell. She had no friends there, no one who cared. "Sucky."

Mel laughed. "If your mother hears you use that word, it'll be suckier."

"Yeah." Her dad came back in, gave her a thumb's-up sign over Patches's head, which meant the puppy had done her duty. But then Patches saw Emily and barked with excitement before her dad could stop her. "Aunt Mel, I gotta go or I'll be late for school," she said quickly. "But honest, things are—"

"Great?" Mel said with a smile in her voice.

"Yeah! So stay there and…" *What was it Mom would say?* She needed to sound grown-up. "You know. Live your life."

Aunt Melanie laughed. "Sounds good."

The puppy barked for the second time, looking quite pleased with herself.

"What was that?" Mel asked.

"Nothing. The school bus. Gotta go!"

Oh man, she'd just lied to her aunt. *Again.* It was accumulating on her. This morning alone, she'd lied to her father, Adam and her mother, too. That must be a record of some kind.

Ben covered the puppy's mouth and with another long look at Emily, took her back upstairs.

Hanging up the phone, Emily put her forehead to the wall. Being twelve was harder than she thought.

# CHAPTER EIGHT

RACHEL NEVER DID manage to get herself dressed that day. When the party finally left her bedroom, she crawled back into bed, both defeated and depressed at her exhaustion level. She fell asleep and was haunted by dreams of strong, loving arms, by whiskey-colored eyes that saw her, really saw her, and by some miracle loved her anyway, and her own feeble, weak fear of letting herself return that love.

Awake now, she lay there staring at the ceiling. Her stomach growled and she could have sworn she'd just heard a dog bark, but that had to just be a lingering dream. She told herself it hadn't been weakness or fear that destroyed her and Ben so long ago, but cold, hard facts.

He'd had to go.

She'd had to stay.

Simple. Besides, that had been long ago. They'd moved on. Maybe they had to deal with each other again now, but the feelings they'd once shared were long gone.

Her door opened. Ben came in, carrying a tray with hot oatmeal and buttered toast. He set it on her lap, grabbed the chair in the corner of the room, spun it around and straddled it. Steepling his fingers, he peered at her over the top of them. "Eat up. We have a physical therapist appointment later, you'll need your strength."

As if she could eat with him watching her like that. "I'm not really that hungry—"

Her stomach growled loudly into the room.

"Yeah, not hungry," he said dryly. "Eat, Rachel. I'm not budging until you do."

With that incentive, she ate the entire bowl.

"You feeling any better?"

"If I say yes, will you get on a plane?"

He smiled. "Probably not."

She had to smile back. "It was worth a shot."

"Yeah. Eat."

And good as his word, when she'd finished, he left her alone.

AT DUSK Emily came in with another tray that held some heavenly scented soup and more toast. Behind her stood Ben, his face solemn, and if she didn't know better, tentative.

Was that from earlier, when she'd fallen asleep on the way back from her particularly brutal physical therapy appointment? He'd carried her inside, set her on her bed, then kissed her softly.

She'd let their lips cling for one moment, and then shocked at herself, had turned away, cowardly feigning sleep.

They hadn't talked since.

"Mom, guess what. Dad taught me how to cook soup." She positively glowed as she sniffed proudly at the steaming bowl. "Yum, right? It smells better than all that canned stuff you always make us use. Hey, maybe when you're better, he can teach you to cook, too."

Rachel eyed Ben, who was either wise enough not to smile or didn't find the humor in the fact Rachel had never taken the time to learn to cook much past the very basics.

"Want some company?" Without waiting for an answer, Emily set the tray on Rachel's lap and sat on the bed. It was the first time that Rachel could remember seeing her without the laptop attached like an appendage to her arm.

"Come on, Dad." Emily patted the bed. "Sit."

Ben straightened from where he'd been holding up the doorjamb and shook his head. "No, I—"

"Dad! Mom hates to eat alone. Come on over. Right here, next to me. She'll share. Won't you, Mom?"

Ben looked at her as he moved closer, and indeed sat on her bed, carefully, slowly, clearly being considerate to not jar her.

And all Rachel could think, inanely, was that they were on the same bed.

"Now I know how to make mac and cheese *and* soup," Emily announced, then frowned. "Dad, what else can you teach me to cook? Pizza?"

Ben lifted a brow. "Well, we could talk about that, soon as you tell your mother about Patches—"

"Oh, wait!" Emily interrupted and cocked her head. "Yep, that's my computer beeping. Sorry, gotta go."

"I didn't hear it," Rachel said, but Emily was gone, having raced out of the room like a tornado was on her heels, leaving just the two of them.

Rachel stared at her soup.

"Thank you." With him this close, she had to fight the ridiculous urge to burrow under the covers and hide.

"Don't thank me until you eat up." Picking up the spoon from the tray, he scooped a small bit of the hot liquid, then held it up to her mouth.

"I can feed myself."

He merely nudged her lips with the spoon, and the warm, heavenly-tasting broth slid into her mouth.

He waited until she swallowed. ''Well?''

''Amazing,'' she admitted, and he smiled and scooped another bite.

''Really, I can do it.''

''Rach...you're still exhausted.''

She looked away, but he gently reached out and touched her chin, until she turned back to him. ''Is it that bad having my help?'' he asked quietly. ''Really?''

God, his eyes were deep. His meaning even deeper. ''No,'' she whispered, then closed her eyes. ''Not compared to say...I don't know...getting a root canal?''

Now he laughed, as she'd intended, and yep, the sound was still low and sexy, still made her stomach tingle. Then he brought her another sip of soup. And another...

''You're still good at the kitchen thing, I see,'' she said after a few minutes, her belly getting nice and full.

''Yeah, well, when you grow up having to put it together yourself or go hungry, you learn quick.''

The broth suddenly stuck in her throat, the picture his simple words created breaking her heart—a young boy, terminally hungry. How many times had she suspected his foster home was not a good place? But no matter how many times she'd asked, he'd never opened up about it.

She wouldn't ask now, she couldn't afford the intimacy that would require. She waited for the awkward silence to drift over them. Oddly enough, the silence didn't seem awkward at all.

''Rach?''

She jerked upright, realizing she'd actually started to fall asleep right in front of him. ''I'm sorry—''

"Hey, you're tired, no big deal. You had a pretty brutal physical therapy session today." Setting aside the tray, he helped her into the bathroom, where she brushed her teeth and got ready for bed.

Afterward, she fell asleep with the image of Ben on her mind. In the middle of the night, she came awake again, her heart heavy, her body aching. She flipped on her light with the clapper Emily had insisted on, a gadget she'd thought so stupid until now, when she didn't have the energy to do anything but very weakly, very quietly, clap once.

She stared at the pad of paper by her bed, a pad she usually filled with new ideas for *Gracie* when she couldn't sleep.

But the comic strip that had been so important to her before the accident now seemed…frivolous. Just a bunch of stupid drawings, whereas other people were actually doing things to help people in the world. Taking action to make a difference.

Like Ben.

"Rach?"

Speaking of. He was a tall, dark shadow standing in her doorway. He took one step into her bedroom and the glow from her lamp bathed him in yellow light.

"Are you all right?" he asked.

He wore only sweat bottoms, low slung and untied, as if hastily put on. Closing her eyes, she tried to lose the image of him nearly nude and so magnificent that she wanted to gobble him up. "Define *all right*," she said.

"Do you need help into the bathroom?"

So intense, so serious. Did she look that bad? Yes, she decided, she probably did. "I'm fine."

"Do you need water? Have you been drinking enough—"

"Truly. I'm fine. I just…can't sleep," she admitted. "And I can't draw to save my life." She managed to sound calm about that.

"Oh." He scratched his chest, looking around, clearly unsure how to help her with such an intangible problem.

"Don't worry," she said dryly. "I won't ask you to sing and dance to get me back to sleep."

"I could read you a bedtime story," he offered, losing some of his intensity and actually smiling.

Good God, that smile was lethal, and could disarm her unhappiness at having him here. She didn't want to disarm anything. "I'll just read to myself."

"You sure?"

What she was sure about was that he needed to leave the room. Now. "Positive. You can go."

Wistfulness crossed his features. "Rach, you know I can't yet—"

"I meant for right now." But how nice to know that he was even more eager than she to get out of here.

With a slight nod, he turned away.

"Ben?"

His shoulders tensed, making her realize she wasn't the only uptight one tonight. "Thanks," she whispered, then waited until she was alone again before reaching for the historical romance lying by her drawing pad.

One of the nurses in the hospital had given it to her, and she hadn't known how to say she didn't typically read romances. Now, in the middle of the night, she opened the only book she could reach and lost herself in a story about a lusty pirate and his wild and sexy prisoner…

WHEN SHE WOKE NEXT, it was morning and her biggest heartbreak was standing at the foot of her bed staring at her grimly, looking as alive and virile as ever.

He was leaning against one of the bedposts, his hands in the pockets of soft, worn jeans. He wore a dark-blue T-shirt that made him look both tough and sexy, an image complemented by the silver earring shining in his ear.

Her pirate, she thought with an inane urge to giggle, and shot the historical romance on her chest a dark look.

Ben stepped close and picked up the book, which happened to be opened to a scene that had steamed her reading glasses last night. He read a few lines silently and his brow shot up his forehead, disappearing into the hair falling over his eyes. *"Throbbing manhood?"*

"Romance novels are empowering," she said primly.

"I'll bet they are." His voice sounded a little strained as he read a bit more. "Wow."

"Are you here for a reason?"

"Yeah." He set the book aside and let out a careful breath. "You need any help getting up?"

She pictured his hands on her, the way his breathing always shallowed when he helped her get dressed, and how her body reacted. "No, I'll be fine."

"Let me at least get you into the bathroom."

"I said I'll be fine." Her voice came out far sharper than she intended, but he was messing with her head. "Please. Just…go."

His jaw was granite. "We've already established I won't."

But he had once. Damn him, she had the insane, juvenile urge to punish him for that still, to make him want to walk away now, again. But one thing she knew about Ben Asher was that he was quite possibly the most stubborn man on the planet. He'd promised to stay, for now at least, and because of it, he wasn't budging.

Instead of leaving, he hauled off her covers, exposing her in the silky bathrobe she'd managed to get herself into the night before. Before she could so much as draw another breath, he'd slipped his arms around her and scooped her from the bed. "Bathroom first?" he asked calmly, as if he held her every day. "Sponge bath? Or just clothes?"

He had one arm around her back, his fingers curled just beneath her breast. The other arm beneath her thighs.

Did he know she wore nothing beneath it, nothing at all?

"Sponge bath," she managed. "But—"

"Let me guess. You can do it yourself." Striding into her bathroom, he set her on the closed commode, then turned on the tub. "Stay."

Did she have a choice? She wondered why on earth she'd thought a nurse such a bad idea. A nice female nurse would have been good right now. She could have stripped off her robe in front of a female nurse, sat gingerly on the edge of the tub with a female nurse, maybe even could have gotten in—

"Here." He was back, once again hunkering in front of her. He had plastic trash bags and duct tape, and before she knew what he meant to do, he'd jerked open her robe to the tops of her thighs.

"Hey—"

"You're going to be thanking me soon enough when the warm water hits your body, trust me." Without looking away from his task, he slid one of the bags over the cast on her left leg, smoothed it around her thigh with his big hands, then secured it with duct tape. Leaning forward, he used his teeth to rip off the duct tape.

She stared down at his head between her legs, feeling his hair brush over her flesh, and didn't know whether to splay her thighs open farther or kick him.

*Kick him,* she decided, because she was quivering and not just from the pain.

With a surprised yelp, he fell to his butt on the tile. Watching her with a wary eye, he came back up on his knees and put his hands on his hips. "You feel better now?"

"Um, yes," she admitted. "Sorry."

"No, you're not." He gently pushed back the flowing sleeve of the robe and gave her left arm the same treatment as he'd given her leg. "There."

Around them, with hot water running into the tub, the bathroom became steamy. Closed in.

Standing, Ben let out a tight smile. "So. How are we going to do this? The easy way or the hard way?"

She clutched the robe to her chest. "I can manage from here."

"The hard way, then," he muttered. "Great." He tossed her the pretty pink loofah hanging from the shower head and turned his back to her—his broad shoulders, wavy, wild hair and attitude all mocking her. "Manage away."

She glanced at the full bubbling bath and the loofah in her hand. She could just dip it in and wash her body, and it sounded like heaven. But… "Not with you standing right there."

With a long-suffering sigh, he dropped his head between his shoulders, defining an irritated male. "My eyes are closed."

"Yes, but—"

"But nothing, Rachel. You want to wash or not?"

She looked at the glorious steam rising from the tub. Did she want to get clean? Only more than her next breath. "Yes."

"Then do it. You're shaking like a damn leaf on the first day of autumn." He craned his neck and looked at her. "And no, I'm not leaving. I want to make sure you don't fall."

Concern filled his eyes. She wondered if he even knew it. "Just keep your eyes closed." She managed to pull herself up to a stand and dropped her robe, watched it pool at her feet. Black dots danced in her vision, but she blinked them away, imagining her hair soft and silky from a real washing, her skin smooth and clean from the tip of her head to her toes. Naked, anticipating, only a few breaths away from collapsing, she went to sit on the edge of the tub.

But it was terribly awkward, and put too much pressure on her healing ribs and pelvis.

"What's the matter?" His back was to her, eyes still closed.

She knew this because she kept peeking at his reflection in the mirror to make sure he wasn't cheating. "Nothing." She tried again, and wanted to cry. Damn it, only a month ago she was in the finest shape of her life! "Ben…"

He whipped around so fast she got even dizzier, and as if he already knew, Ben grabbed her. Embarrassment chased anger, chased a bombardment of sensations…like *did the man's hands feel good on her body,* which brought her back to anger because they were *Ben's* hands, and it wasn't sexual, it was survival. He had her naked body plastered to his fully clothed one, and was completely supporting her weight. She felt her face heat, felt her throat heat, felt everything heat.

He had one arm across her back, one lower, across her bare butt, his hand gripping a cheek. *"Ben."* She lifted her face, and found her mouth an inch from his. But it wasn't their proximity that backed her breath up in her throat. It was the look in his eyes. Dark, intensely speculative and so hot she couldn't have drawn air into her lungs to save her life. "You…can let me go now," she said in a funny feathery voice she hardly recognized.

"Yeah." But she would have sworn his arms actually tightened, including the hand on her butt, before he slowly released her, sitting her back on the commode. "You okay?"

No. No, she wasn't. "Fine," she said through clenched teeth because her body had reacted without permission. Her nipples were two hard tight points and her legs had gone mushy, not to mention what was happening between them. A shiver trailed over her skin as his breath tickled down the side of her neck, and she let out a sound that shocked her with its neediness.

Further shocking her, Ben nibbled in the exact spot he'd breathed on, nuzzling the side of her throat and the curve of her shoulder until her bones liquefied. "Should I close my eyes again, Rachel?"

Her heart jerked, then again as he dragged his mouth over her flesh. "Yes!"

He didn't. In fact he kept them wide-open and all over her. He slid one hand up her hip to her waist, then a little higher, gliding his thumb up and down over her skin, on the heavy underside of a breast. "I've seen it all before."

"A long time ago." She felt like a marshmallow, a

melting marshmallow over a slow, perfect flame. "Close 'em."

"You're even more amazing now than you were then, and I remember you as pretty damn amazing."

She crossed her casted arm over her breasts and tried to not think about the parts he could still see quite clearly. "Is...that supposed to make me feel better?"

"Well..." He let out a low, nipple-hardening laugh. "Looking at you is making *me* feel better."

"Close your eyes," she said through her teeth. "Or find out how hard a cast is over your head."

He tilted his head and studied her while his hands took another slow pass at the flesh plumped out beneath the cast. "So you're going to ignore the fact that every time we're within two feet of each other we nearly spontaneously combust?"

With great effort, she lifted her bag-covered left arm warningly.

His eyes stayed right on hers instead of the breasts she'd exposed. "You're a glutton for punishment, babe." But he sighed and closed his eyes. "Okay."

*Babe.* He hadn't called her "babe" in...well, thirteen years.

More steam escaped from the tub, swirling around them, creating an ambiance of intimacy. Ben stood right there, a breath away, hair falling over his forehead, eyes closed, a sexy little smile curving his lips. Inviting. Beguiling.

All it would take was one word from her, even a touch, and he'd jump in without looking, jump right into a relationship with her again, or at least a *sexual* one.

But she never jumped without looking, and certainly not with a man with a foot already half out the door.

All she had to do was get better and he'd be gone,

she reminded herself as she soaped her body. So that's what she'd do, she'd get better, fast as she possibly could.

THE RESTLESSNESS was going to kill her. Early dawn light filtered in Rachel's room as she struggled to get herself out of bed the next morning. She reached for her wheelchair, then hesitated.

Her various aches and pains seemed to be lessening every day, albeit slightly, and she decided today was the day she tried to go without the dreaded, hated chair. She wanted to walk, damn it, and determined to do just that, she grabbed the cane she'd gotten from the physical therapist yesterday, the one who planned to torture her today as well.

Carefully, holding her breath, she stood. Wobbled, but held her own. So far so good. She felt unsteady and weak, ready to collapse at the slightest breeze.

But upright was upright and she'd take it. The early morning was silent as she made her slow, painful progress to the bedroom door. Opening it, she saw the hall was still in shadow. The only light came from a glow from a night-light in the hall bathroom. Shuffling her way down the hall she peeked in. On the counter sat a dark blue toothbrush. Not Emily's.

Ben's.

Funny how just one piece of plastic could cause such conflicting emotions. Late last night when she hadn't been able to sleep, he'd come into her room with a deck of cards and had taught her naughty card games he'd picked up in Nigeria. Or somewhere.

The man was something. He'd had her laughing. *Laughing.*

She made it to her studio for the first time since the

accident. Just walking in here used to set her creative juices flowing. She'd yank open her shades on the wall of windows, grin with pure joy at the sight of South Village in full swing far below and go to work.

She waited for some of that joy to hit her. Even just a little.

Nothing. Nothing but a tightening in her chest that suggested panic. And exhaustion from the exertion of getting here.

Her easel was set up, with a blank sheet of paper on it. Just as she'd left it on the day of the accident. There was a note on the pad, with her own words *teachers versus administration* written on it. She stared down at it blankly, knowing she'd written that before being slammed by a car, before hitting the pavement at thirty miles per hour, knowing the words should signify what she intended Gracie's next strip to be about... But for the life of her she couldn't remember writing the words, much less what she'd intended.

It didn't matter anyway...it was just a cartoon.

Helplessness and uselessness had become old friends since that day, and they hit her again now. Suddenly she wanted to do something new, something...important. She thought of Ben's work, and how many people he'd helped, and closed her eyes. Frustration choked her. She wondered how long someone could live with so much frustration before just blowing up.

She weaved, her muscles violently trembling with the strain of being upright, forcing her to sit in the love seat. She gripped the cushions at her sides and refused to give in to defeat. How she was going to get back up and to her room without asking for help was beyond her—especially since that help would probably come in the form of a tall, sleepy, sexy man—but she wouldn't ask.

She'd stay right where she was, thank you very much.

Staring around the room that used to be her favorite haven, she fought tears and wondered how her life had come to feel like a prison. Nothing was the same. Not her job, not Emily, who didn't seem to need her anymore, not her house, not anything she'd counted on to be constant and calming and hers.

Certainly not with Ben's undeniably demanding presence. A presence she should be grateful for, as she knew what it cost him to be caged here. But because of him, even her relationship with Emily had changed. She'd watched her daughter turn to someone else for comfort and love. The loss of their closeness, which was all Rachel seemed to have at the moment, left her on shaky ground, and she covered her face with her hands.

"Rachel."

Jerking her head up, she faced the one man who'd always shattered any control she'd had. Too bad she had none left to shatter. "Damn it, you went away once. Why won't you go away now?"

"You going to start with that again?" He pushed away from the doorway and came toward her. From the look of his messed-up hair, bare chest and low-slung sweats, at least one of them had been sleeping last night. Irrationally, she resented him for that, too.

"How did you get here?" he asked.

"Walked."

"You did?" He looked shocked. "You should have called for me to help you. You working?"

"Yeah." With a bitter laugh, she gestured to her empty easel. "Working away."

"Rachel—" He broke off when the phone rang, and since it was right by his elbow, he grabbed it without so much as asking if she minded.

"Hello?" His face went tense. "I thought you were going to call me back on my cell— Yes...you've got a lead on him?" Ben glanced at Rachel, eyes grim, jaw bunching, and went quiet as he listened. Given how his eyes narrowed, the news wasn't good.

"Who is it?" she asked, only to be completely ignored. *"Ben."*

He actually put up a hand silencing her. She glared at him, furious, but somehow her gaze ended up on his chest, then his flat, ridged belly, and the way his sweats sagged nearly down far enough to see—

"I'll be right down," he said, disconnecting with deceptive calm while danger rolled off him in waves. "I've got to run," he said, one hundred and eighty pounds of carefully controlled temper.

"Who was that?"

"Tell Em I'll be back for breakfast."

"Ben—"

He was already at the door, but with an oath, he came back. Cupping her head with incredibly gentle hands, he tipped her face up. "It'll be okay," he said making a heartbreaking promise she didn't understand but wanted to.

"Ben—"

"Shh." He let his lips meet hers in a sweet, clinging kiss. "I'll be back."

Yes, but how to tell him that's what she was afraid of?

She brought her fingers up to her lips and watched him go, wondering why she'd let him kiss her.

Because she'd lost her mind, that's why. He'd been trying to distract her, and damn it, it had worked.

Struck by an overwhelming curiosity, she picked up the receiver of her phone and checked caller ID.

Unavailable.

Rachel lifted her head and stared at the door where Ben had just vanished.

From downstairs she heard the front door shut.

He was gone. Gone to meet someone…unavailable.

She hit star-six-nine to dial the number back. As it started to ring, her heart began to pound.

"Agent Brewer."

Rachel stared at the phone.

*"Hello?"*

With a stammered apology, Rachel hung up and wondered what the hell was going on. Who was Brewer and what was the big secret?

## CHAPTER NINE

BEN GOT CAUGHT in traffic on the way to meet Agent Brewer, delaying their meeting. The lead on Asada turned out to be a known accomplice, who'd been picked up in South America and was being detained and questioned.

"What did he say about Asada?" Ben asked.

Brewer shook his head. "He's not telling. Not yet. But that he was picked up in South America is an excellent indication Asada is still there. They'll find him. Soon."

But Ben wanted more than just a promise. He wanted... Hell, he wanted this over. Unaccustomed to such fear, as he rarely got involved this personally in a story, he didn't know what to do with it all.

But this wasn't a story—this was his life. Emily's life. Rachel's.

At the thought of her, his mind took him places he wasn't prepared to go. Like back to the sponge bath incident from the day before. Rachel had stood in that bathroom nude, wet, glorious...and glared at him. Hadn't mattered, not when he couldn't tear his eyes off her curves, shimmering and molded by the water streaming down her tall, lithe body.

He was just a man, and a weak one at that. How was he supposed to maintain any sort of mental distance under these circumstances?

Thinking about Asada on the loose helped. "Soon could be too late."

Agent Brewer, a twenty-year veteran and dedicated to his job—evidenced by the various awards on the walls of his small office—nodded. "I know your fear. But we're doing all we can."

Ben would be impressed only if Asada was caught. "If Asada's still in South America, with his old contacts and in terrain he knows like the back of his hand, he can hide forever."

"Better than being the States, hunting you down."

"He could have men here. Men willing to do his bidding."

Brewer sighed. "We've been reviewing tapes from L.A. International near the date of Rachel's accident." He pushed play on the remote on his desk, and images rolled across the TV on the wall, showing two dark-skinned men carrying briefcases, leaving a terminal at LAX. The date stamp was from six and a half weeks earlier. "These two men arrived from South America. We're trying to track them down. Just wanted you to know what they look like."

Terror sat in the pit of Ben's belly like a rock. Terror and guilt. He'd brought all this on Rachel. The hospital stay, the pain, the limitations, everything...*his fault.*

The weight of that crushed in on him, making him stagger, then sink to a chair. "So why aren't they making another move on either Rachel or Emily?" he asked hoarsely.

"Our theory is that with most of Asada's assets seized, they can't. He's just watching, biding his time."

And the cat-and-mouse game continued.

BY THE TIME Ben left Brewer's office, South Village was well on its way to another prosperous day. Having lived elsewhere for so long, it was hard to reconcile the obvious wealth here with the world he knew, which could be full of suffering and hunger.

Stuck in traffic gridlock, he used his cell phone to set up some work for himself, writing a few stories he'd been collecting for a rainy day. He could do this from Rachel's house during the day. Had to do this, in order to maintain his sanity.

"A home base?" his editor asked in joking horror. "You mean you'll actually have an address? A land line?"

"Hard to believe, huh?"

"Well, this I've got to see. Stay in touch."

Ben promised and turned onto Rachel's street. Blissfully unaware of his world and all it contained, Emily sat on the top step of the house. She wore black jeans with a hole in one knee and a snug T-shirt that invited him to Take a Hike in the Angeles Crest Mountains. She had Patches in her lap, sleeping, and the laptop precariously balanced on her knees. Her head was down as she concentrated, her fingers flying over the keys. He could see the twenty-five-foot phone cord attached, running beneath the front door and back into the house.

Was it possible for his heart to squeeze any tighter? How could it be that this beautiful, sweet creature didn't have friends except for her computer? The urge to hide her, to protect her from the big, bad wolf of life was overpowering, and for a moment he simply watched her, feeling such an ache he didn't know what to do with himself.

When she noticed him standing there, she closed her computer and grinned, and just like that, his aching heart tipped on its side. God, he loved her. And except for the grace of God it could have been *her* Asada had gone after. Could still intend to go after.

That hardened him, made him determined to see that nothing, *nothing,* happened to this child of his heart. He came closer and scratched the groggy Patches on the head. He got his hand licked for his effort.

"I tried to tell Mom about Patches," Emily said. "But she's always sleeping. Or grumpy."

"She's hurting. Emmie, don't wait outside for me."

"South Village is a safe place, Dad."

"Please, Em."

"Jeez, okay."

"And about the dog. You tell your mom today, or I will."

"Man. You've gotten strict." She glanced at her purple sparkling watch. "We don't have enough time for artery cloggers."

Strict? He was strict? Hell, he hardly knew how to be a dad and she thought he was *strict?* She didn't know the meaning of the damn word. "How about McDonald's on the way to school?" he asked.

She put her face next to Patches—who'd been scrubbed in the downstairs bathroom and brushed until the puppy practically shined—wordlessly asking for a sloppy doggy kiss. Patches obliged happily. "Mom hates McDonald's."

"So, I'll pick her up something disgustingly healthy on the way back."

She let out a slow grin that went a long way toward dissipating the chill he'd had since the early morning phone call. "Okay."

"Seriously, though, you're going to have to tell her about the puppy, Emily. I'm tired of hiding her."

From smile to frown in a heartbeat. "I know." She kissed the puppy right on the mouth, making him wince.

"Now," he said.

"Oh, Dad. I can't tell her now, she's sleeping again. But I promise to do it first thing this afternoon." For added effect she blinked her big, huge, adoring eyes at him.

Ah, hell. Strict? That was a joke. He was a sap, a complete sap. "The minute you walk in the door."

"Promise. Dad?" She tilted her head and studied him more closely than he usually let people study him. "You care about Mom, don't you? You know, like you used to, when you first had me?"

He'd been long gone by the time Emily had been born, though he'd come back right afterward for a rare visit to South Village. Rachel had refused to see him, but even now he could remember standing in front of the glass partition of the infant nursery, hands wide on the glass, nose pressed to it, staring at her, his baby. "Emily—"

"Because I know you used to love each other. I can see it in the picture Mom has."

He blinked. "She has a picture?"

"In her jewelry drawer, beneath her ring box. You guys look really young, and you have your arms around her. She's laughing." Her gaze went wistful. "She's laughing really hard and you're looking at her like you really love her."

Rachel had kept a picture of them. Hidden. Why would a woman who'd told him to go far, far away do such a thing? It made about as much sense as Emily hoping they still loved each other. "That was a long time ago, Em, you know that."

"But that doesn't mean your feelings have to change. Did you love me when I first was born?"

"Very much."

"Do you love me now?"

Ben closed his eyes. "Of course I do. Em—"

"See? It could happen. You guys could make it happen, if you wanted."

He sat down next to her, his long thighs brushing her shorter ones. Patches put her little head on his knee and looked at him with hero worship that matched his daughter's. "Emily, I'm only here because—"

"Because I called you," she said earnestly. "And I know I kinda fooled you, but you came. You came really fast. That means something, Dad."

Ben thought of why he'd *really* come, and of what he'd learned this morning. "And I'm staying." For as long as it took, no matter how badly he needed out. "I'm staying to help you both out. But that's it, Em. That's it." *Liar.*

Emily's eyes told him the same thing.

BALANCING THE squirming puppy, some sort of green cucumber protein shake, and a container of a very unappetizing-looking soup that the pretty redheaded owner of Café Delight had sworn was Rachel's favorite, Ben walked toward Rachel's front door. He'd dropped Emily off at school and now needed to face Rachel with the knowledge of what he'd done to her burning a hole in his gut.

And he wasn't talking about just the damn puppy, which he somehow had to keep quiet for a few more hours.

The front door was unlocked, which just about stopped his heart. Damn it, he'd talked to her about this, about being careless. He dumped the puppy on the foyer floor. "Stay," he said firmly, and rushed through the house toward the murmur of voices in the kitchen.

Rachel sat at the table looking whole and unharmed, and Ben stopped short, drawing an unsteady breath. "You unlocked the front door, damn it."

"Oh, I did that." Adam came in from the walk-in pantry holding an old-fashioned, decorated tin. "Cookie?"

Ben stared at Rachel's accountant. "No." He turned to Rachel. She was dressed in a long slip of a sundress he imagined she probably could have gotten on herself with effort, but he couldn't help but wonder if the saintly Adam had helped her.

If so, had her pulse raced the way it had when Ben had had his hands all over her? Had her lips parted, inviting his?

Goddamn it, it didn't matter. And he had to make this quick before the puppy did something more stupid than Ben had done leaving the thing alone in the foyer. "You can't just leave the damn door unlocked."

Rachel's face was utterly closed off to him. "Would that have anything to do with your phone call that had you rushing off at dawn?"

He stared at her for one long beat before Adam came to the table and set the tin in front of Rachel. "And anyway, she wasn't alone." Adam smiled. "Did you know this is actually a very low-crime district?"

A headache began right between Ben's eyes. Asada didn't give a shit about low crime districts; all he wanted to do was destroy Ben. Nothing could do that except by bringing more pain and suffering to Emily or Rachel. *Again.*

Not that Rachel understood that, because he hadn't

told her, and honest to God, the depth of his own deception was going to bury him. "Look, Adam, I appreciate that, but—"

"You appreciate that?" Rachel marveled, pure fire in her eyes.

Whoa. Had he thought her emotions closed off to him? She was furious. At him.

What had he done now?

"Why do you *appreciate* that, Ben?" she almost purred. "You don't own me, you don't even belong here. You don't have responsibility over me at all."

Ben carefully set the food he'd brought in front of her. Put his hands on his hips and tried to figure a way out of this mess.

But there was no way out.

Inanely, he wondered what the puppy was up to and how much damage she could cause in the two minutes she'd been alone.

Adam opened up the containers from Ben and smiled at Rachel. "Your favorites. Maybe now you'll eat." He looked up at Ben. "She's lost weight."

Given that Ben had had his eyes and hands over every single bare inch of her body only yesterday, he thought she was pretty damn fine. But he was going to forget that, forget the feel of her, the scent of her. Everything. "Adam's right, you should eat." He went to the swinging doors to recapture the loose puppy. "I'm outta here."

"You always have one foot out of here," she said. "You've had one foot out of here since the day you showed up."

Wasn't that the truth? It was ironic, he thought, to be using Adam as an excuse to vanish, when just days ago he'd wanted to knock Adam's socks off for kissing Rachel on the cheek. Even more ironic when one considered what Ben himself had done to Rachel since he'd been back.

A lot more than a kiss on the cheek.

Ben glanced back. Rachel had her casted leg up on the adjacent chair, casted arm resting on the table. The bruises on her face were fading, but the scar over her left eye was not. She wore a handkerchief on her head but he knew that her hair, while still a beautiful light gold, had barely begun to grow back. For that alone, he hated himself. She'd suffered so much because of him, and suddenly he couldn't even stand to be in the same room with her. He didn't *deserve* to be in the same room with her, and pushing through the doors, he left the kitchen.

Once in the living room, he scooped up the errant puppy, who was cheerfully chewing on a black sparkly sandal he figured to be Emily's. He brought both the ruined sandal and Patches to Emily's room. "This afternoon, your secret is out," he warned. "Until then, you'll go outside when I take you, and sleep when I tell you. No trouble, no messes, no accidents, you hear?"

Patches panted her agreement.

Emily had made a dog bed out of a box and an old blanket, but he knew Patches preferred Emily's bed. Only problem, she wasn't big enough to climb up by herself. She stood on the floor at the side of the mattress doing flips to try to get up, to no avail. When she saw Ben looking at her, she started in on the aren't-I-adorable wriggle, her entire hind-end moving back and forth so fast she could hardly walk.

"Let's hope Rachel finds you half as cute as you think you are." Ben squatted down to stroke her head.

She fell to her back, exposing her belly, madly licking

Ben's hand and wrist, tail waggling back and forth at the speed of light. When he stood and moved to the door, she followed.

"Oh, no," Ben said with a laugh. "I'm not getting between mom and daughter, I'd be crazy to. You're Emily's news, dog."

Big puppy eyes blinked sadly.

"Hey, you're just lucky Rachel isn't on top of her game, because believe me, if she was, you'd be Dead Puppy Walking."

Yeah, when Rachel was sharp, nothing got past her. Not a single thing. And if she'd made her mind up about something, forget it.

Abruptly he remembered his last day in South Village all those years ago. He'd been sent a plane ticket, had his assignment and his bag packed. More than anything, he wanted to leave South Village far behind, but still he'd hesitated.

He couldn't leave without seeing Rachel one more time.

With pride weighing him down, he'd marched up to the Wellers' house. It'd been so big he'd figured fifty people could live in there and never cross paths.

He could still turn around and walk away, and no one would ever know he'd come to beg her to want him, the way no one had ever wanted him.

Pathetic. He was pathetic, but before he could take off, Mrs. Wellers answered the door, a glass in one hand, her other gripping the doorway as if she needed a lifeline. Far younger than his foster parents, it was odd to see how alcohol and careless living had aged her. She'd looked right through him, not recognizing him, even though by then Ben had been in Rachel's life for six months.

"It's Ben, Mrs. Wellers. I need to talk to Rachel."

She'd hiccuped, then with a wide wave that sent her vodka or gin or whatever she was drinking sloshing over the edge of the glass, she shook her head. Tossing back her well-tended hair and downing the rest of her drink, she'd swallowed hard and said, "Rachel doesn't want to talk to the likes of you."

*The likes of you.* Par for the course for Ben Asher, aka no good son of a bitch. In school, out of school, every-damn-where he'd been a no one from nobody and no place.

He didn't remember running out of there, but the bus ride to the airport had been interminably long. He hadn't taken a good deep breath until he'd met up with his new peers on the other side of the world, where he'd been treated like an equal. Like a somebody.

God, he needed a damn walk, he thought, shrugging off the old and unwelcome memories. Needed air. He glanced at Patches, who had fallen asleep on her back, and carefully shut Emily's bedroom door.

He could still hear Adam in the kitchen, talking to Rachel in that gentle voice that made the peace-loving Ben want to clobber him.

What the hell was wrong with him? Adam was a good man who obviously relished taking care of Rachel. Ben should be thrilled she had someone like that. It would make leaving all that much easier.

Yeah. He should be thrilled. And he would be when they located Asada.

Figuring Rachel was safe enough for the moment, Ben let himself out. He'd like to hop on a plane but a walk would have to do.

He walked past the market, past the art gallery. Kitty-corner from Rachel's house was a small park, lush and green, where he found an intense game of three-on-two basketball in the middle court. The men looked to be in their thirties, and given the amount of swearing, illegal moves and outrageous fouls, they were quite serious about the game. The three players were shirted, the two players against them had stripped to the waist. One was tall, dark and had the meanest jump shot Ben had ever seen. The other was average height, and had a carrottop to go with his temper, but he moved like lightning.

Something about them drew Ben closer, then closer still, and he pulled his ever present camera off his shoulder. He'd just gotten a great shot of a layup when he was stopped by the redhead.

Chest heaving, sweat running down his face, the guy jerked his head toward the court. "We're short a player."

Ben pulled his face away from the lens. "Yeah?"

"You any good?"

Ben had been born naturally athletic, but couldn't say if the gift had been inherited, since he knew nothing about his genes. He'd played ball in high school, but since then had only played in makeshift courts in any given Developing Nation, with people he'd had to teach. "I'm okay."

"Then ditch the camera, we need you."

Ben ditched the camera and his shirt. And played the most cathartically vicious basketball game ever. By the time it was over, they'd won by the skin of their teeth and one basket.

The other team took off. *Limped* off. Ben had learned the redhead was Steve, his partner Tony. Slouched against a brick wall, nursing various injuries and sucking down water, Ben also learned his teammates were a lawyer and a cop.

"We beat the shit out of each other three days a week, if you're interested," Steve said, swiping at a bloody lip.

Ben had released quite a bit of tension in the past hour. He had hated this town and all the people in it. No one had ever looked at him in this town.

But these guys were looking at him now. "I'm not here for long…" He *hoped* he wasn't here for long.

"We'll take what we can get." Tony smiled grimly. "Because damn, you're a tough son of a bitch."

Ben glanced at the refurbished firehouse he hadn't let out of his sight during the game. "Yeah." Some of the weight he'd just played off was coming back. He *was* a tough son of a bitch. But tough enough to take on Asada?

God, he hoped so.

# CHAPTER TEN

AFTER ADAM LEFT, Rachel took the elevator up to her studio, where she crashed in the window seat. It frustrated her to be so weary, but at least she hadn't had to use the wheelchair today. *Baby steps,* her physical therapist reminded her constantly.

Her gaze wandered to the park on the corner and found the basketball game. She couldn't take her eyes off Ben, not during the game, and not now as he crossed the street, heading back. Even when she knew she should move away from the window rather than risk him catching sight of her there, she stayed.

From the crosswalk, he paused, sending a wary glance toward her front door. His broad shoulders sagged slightly, as if he held the weight of the world. He looked beat, drained. Human.

Then he looked up and caught her. She'd been ogling him, his messy hair and damp body.

Especially his damp body. Eyes right on her, he slowly lifted a hand, waggled his fingers at her.

She closed her eyes, and when she opened them, he was gone.

She was reminding herself that was a good thing when he appeared in the doorway of her studio.

"You okay?"

Concern. Always concern, no matter how furious, how anything he was, concern took precedence.

Well, she was damn tired of concern. Tired of being weak and vulnerable, when what she really wanted was to toss him right back out of her life on his fat, sexy head.

Then his eyes fell to what she had in her lap…the sleeping puppy. She'd found the dog in Emily's room the other day, and had been waiting for someone to confess ever since.

He winced. "Found her, huh?"

"Did you think I wouldn't?"

"Emily said—"

"Emily said what, Ben? That I wouldn't mind the both of you lying, hiding her behind my back?"

With a grimace, he scrubbed his face. "Look, she gave me the big green eyes, okay? She said you wanted a puppy. She said you'd like her."

"If I'd really wanted a puppy, why would Emily hide her from me? For *days?*"

He winced again. "Okay, I'm shitty at this whole dad thing. We both know it."

That stopped her, along with the misery on his face, and she swallowed whatever angry retort she'd had ready. "You think you're a bad dad?"

"I know it. For God's sake, I live on the other side of the world."

"Yes, but you call. You e-mail. You see her."

"Once every couple months doesn't cut it. I have no experience with good parenting, but that's no excuse. You didn't either, and look at you. You're a great mom."

It was one of the few times he'd brought up her childhood and she hadn't gone defensive on him, but she didn't feel defensive, she felt…protective. And surprisingly enough, she felt it for him. "We are who we are,

Ben. And I'd say we've both done the best we could under the circumstances. As for Emily...I think you're amazing with her.''

He laughed, a short, bitter sound.

''You are,'' she said softly, wanting him to believe her. Odd to be the comforter for once. Odder still to like it. ''She loves this time with you.''

''But...? I think I heard one at the end of that sentence.''

''*But* I worry how she'll miss you when you leave.'' She looked down at the puppy, trying to remain neutral. ''Because you are leaving. Eventually. You'll have to. It's in your blood. We both know that, too.''

''Yeah.'' He came all the way into the room, one hundred percent pure, frustrated, hot, half-naked male. ''I'm sorry about Patches.''

Rachel stroked the soft puppy and melted again, as she had from the very first moment she'd found her crying alone in Emily's room. ''Are you?''

''She was homeless, Rach.''

Well, if the look on his face combined with the way he said it didn't tear her heart right out. She took a good long look at the man she'd always wanted to think of as selfish.

But in fact, there wasn't a single selfish bone in his entire body. The needy had always drawn him. In high school he'd readily given away anything he had to kids less fortunate, and there hadn't been many. He'd followed the same path in his career, using his talents to help others by bringing their plight to the masses, forcing people to see what they might have chosen not to see otherwise. He would give a perfect stranger the shirt off his back, and had.

She eyed his naked torso. Things hadn't changed.

"I'll pay for all her stuff."

"It's okay, Ben."

Now he just looked adorably confused. "Why?"

"Why?" She nearly laughed at his expression but instead felt the absolutely inexplicable need to hug him, which would be like hugging a resting but half-starved leopard. Not exactly good for her health. "Because you made Emily happy. You made her happy in a way I can't seem to lately."

She ignored his surprise because that tore at her, too. Did he think she was completely heartless? Yes, of course he did. "Why were you talking to some Agent Brewer about me, Ben?"

His easy, open smile faded, and he turned away, his sleek, smooth back tense. His shoulders lifted in a shrug before he turned back to her. "He's an FBI agent. I was worried about you."

She wished he'd put his shirt back on. His chest, still damp, was damn distracting. "What does an FBI agent have to do with my recovery?"

"I'm talking about the hit-and-run part of your accident."

"I don't understand."

"I didn't realize the investigation had stalled until I got here. Ever since, I've been after the authorities to rush it, make it a priority."

Even here, far from work, he was concerned with justice. God, to have that drive, and the ability to see it through. She admired him for that and, as she glanced at her empty easel, wished for a fraction of his courage.

Ben was looking at the flowers on a windowsill, another gift from Adam. Sweet, even-keeled, kind Adam. She could say she was extremely fond of him, that he made her smile and was easy to be with. She could say she'd been contemplating doing as she knew he wanted and taking their relationship to the next level.

Until recently. Until Ben. She wouldn't admit this under threat of death, but from the moment she'd seen the two men standing next to each other, one so dynamic, larger than life, charismatic...the other paling a little in comparison, things had changed.

Not that she wanted Ben instead.

Okay, maybe she did, secretly, *extremely* secretly. She'd have to have ice in her veins not to want him. But she didn't *want* to want him, which in her mind changed everything.

"It's time to get into town for your physical therapy appointment," he said, checking his watch.

She hadn't yet figured out how to get out of him driving her to her physical therapy appointments. Frustrated as they both were with the circumstances, those times alone in the car with him were far too intimate for her peace of mind. "I'm ready." Gently, she pushed the puppy out of her lap. Her legs had fallen asleep in her stagnant position, and getting up turned into an exercise in futility and frustration.

"Hey, *hey*," he said, rushing over, scooping her up when she might have slipped out of the window seat. "You can't just do that, you can't just move that fast, you've got to—"

"What? Not move? Not think? Not breathe? Well, you try it and see how fast you go insane."

"Hmm. Grumpy again." He carried her down the hall to her bedroom, where he sat with her on her bed, his back to the headboard. One leg on the floor, one bent on the mattress, he tipped his head up and closed his eyes, as if forgetting she was sprawled in his lap.

"I thought we had to go."

"Yeah." But his arms just tightened on her.

The puppy had followed them and let out a happy little bark.

"You can let me go," Rachel said. "I'm perfectly fine—"

"Rachel?"

"Yes?"

"Please shut up. Just for a moment."

Yes, but if she shut up, then all she could do was feel, and what she'd feel was the warm, achingly familiar strength of him surrounding her. She could get used to that, very used to that.

Too bad Ben couldn't. "Look, you only came here because Emily called you. She said I needed you. But we both know what that was about, and I don't think we need to discuss it further."

His eyes were still closed, his body relaxed beneath his. "You're right about that."

"Damn it, Ben, I *know* you want out. I don't buy the promise to Emily anymore. I don't buy any of it, so tell me the truth. You want to go."

He was silent.

*"Ben."*

"Yes," he admitted softly. "I want to go."

She realized her hands were fisted against the hot, hard flesh of his chest and she jerked them loose. "Then why won't you?"

"Because I did promise. Whether you buy that or not is up to you." His voice was low and clearly angry. She'd insulted his sense of pride and integrity. Maybe later she'd stop to feel bad about that, but right now she needed his hands off her because they were bringing her body to life in a way she couldn't deal with.

"Bottom line," he said. "You do need me."

"I have other people who could help me—"

"Like Adam," he pointed out helpfully. "I suppose he could have helped you with your sponge bath?"

That closed her mouth.

His hands slid up her body to cup her head, turning her to face him. "I'm not going anywhere, not yet."

Not yet. The words raced like a promise, a threat, through her mind. Not yet.

But he would go.

His thumb slid over her lower lip and parts of her body leaped to life, hoping for more. But she'd already kissed him. A huge mistake, as the memories of that particular kiss, combined with the memories of what could come after those mind-blowing kisses, were already keeping her up at night.

Ben Asher had destroyed her once in this lifetime, and once had been enough.

His eyes were on hers, letting her see his thoughts, and what he was thinking made her melt even without the kisses.

"Ben," she whispered shakily as he lowered his mouth toward hers. "Doesn't this terrify you?"

"You mean the way time stops when you look at me? Hell, yeah, it terrifies me. But then again, everything about you does, it always has."

Another stroke of his thumb over her mouth, and her knees trembled. "We…can't."

"*Can't* isn't in my vocabulary…."

"Then *I* can't."

He froze at that. "You…can't."

"No," she whispered.

"Same old story," he whispered back. "Fine. You can't." With that he helped her up and into the car. The ride to and from the physical therapy appointment was interminably silent…and long.

Afterward, he insisted on helping her up to her room. He'd just helped her back on her bed, had leaned over her with a look on his face that had her hormones jerking to attention, when from below, the front door slammed, making them both jump.

Emily's voice called out hopefully. "Dad?"

With a groaning laugh, Ben scooped up the wildly wriggling puppy who'd become frantic at the sound of her beloved Emily's voice—and set her on the bed.

*"Dad?"*

Rachel closed her eyes to the happiness in her daughter's voice, the happiness that had come from Ben's presence, but jerked them open again when she felt Ben come close again. Hand on either side of her hips, he leaned in, brushing his mouth over hers, smiling a sexy little smile when her lips clung of their own accord. "Now *that's* better. Did you know you lose your grumpiness when we kiss?"

Patches barked joyfully, right in their faces.

*"Dad!* Where are you?"

"We're not finished," he said softly.

"We were finished thirteen years ago."

Still looking at Rachel, he called out, "Up here, sweetness." When Emily danced into the room, he smiled grimly when she jolted to a stop at the sight of Patches in her mother's room.

"Uh-oh," she breathed.

Ben stood up and kissed Emily's forehead. "Own up to your mistakes, kiddo. Always." And then he left them alone.

"You, uh, found Patches." Emily winced, resembling Ben so much it almost hurt to look at her at all. *"Oops."*

"This is bigger than an 'oops'."

"Mom, she was homeless!"

"But you lied to me."

"No, I didn't. I never said I didn't have a dog in here." When Rachel just looked at her balefully, Emily caved and sagged to a chair. "I know. I lied by omission."

"Yes, you did. Emily, a dog is a big responsibility."

"I can handle it, Mom. I'll train her, I'll feed her, I'll do everything for her."

"Yes, you will."

Emily brightened. "Then I can keep her?"

"On a couple of conditions." Emily looked guarded again and Rachel wanted to touch her so badly. What had happened to her baby? When had she grown up and needed her independence so fiercely? Why did it have to be this way? "One, you're right—you'll train her, clean up after her and feed her."

"I will, I promise."

"You'll also earn the money it'll take to train and feed her by adding to your chores."

"Okay," she said, slightly less enthusiastic. Emily liked her hard-earned money. She liked it a lot.

"And three…" *I love you, baby.* "You won't ever hide anything like that from me again. Deal?"

Emily stood up.

Rachel's heart cracked. She was going to walk away. Be snooty. Be…distant.

But her daughter smiled, walked over and wrapped her arms around Rachel so tightly she could hardly breathe.

"Deal," Em whispered and squeezed harder.

Which was good, because breathing was overrated

anyway. Rachel blinked away tears and hugged her back.

Patches barked in joy.

TWO DAYS PASSED while Rachel thought about what Ben had said, dreamed about it.

*We're not finished.*

Adam had brought her some books earlier, but neither they or Adam himself had been able to hold her full attention. When Garrett had come by with her mail, she'd been able to do little more than smile her thanks.

Her thoughts were concentrated on one thing, and one thing only. Ben.

*We're not finished.*

Sleepless late one night, she grabbed her cane and hobbled down the hall, ignoring the pain in her leg from overuse. She was tired of the wheelchair. Tired of not moving under her own steam.

Tired of everything, she had to admit.

She was ready to get better, and refused to understand what was taking so long.

In Emily's room, she watched the moonlight dance across the bed. Beneath the covers, her precious daughter sighed in her sleep. On top of the covers at the foot of the bed slept Patches.

God, she missed this, coming in here to kiss Emily good-night. With a little smile she turned in a slow circle, taking in the comfortable disaster that was Emily's room, grateful to be able to touch the slim sprawled-out form. She straightened the wildly strewn covers the best she could with her one good arm, inhaling the smell of bubblegum-scented shampoo and soap, looking at the mess that never ceased, the laptop that was open and—

Open and online. Moving closer in the dark, Rachel

sighed, the smile gone. She turned to the bed. "You're not sleeping."

She got a soft snore.

With a disparaging sound, Rachel shut the computer and disconnected the phone cord. "It's late and it's a school night."

No movement, but at least the fake deep breathing had stopped. Rachel stroked the pixie cut sticking out of the covers and let out a breath. "Good night, baby. Love you."

Still no answer.

She nodded to herself, trying not to hurt over that, and made her way back to her own room. She moved to the window with muscles that were now throbbing. It wasn't just stubbornness that kept her from taking a painkiller, but the fact that she hated the grogginess in the morning. She'd rather hurt.

On the street below, a police car turned the corner. An unusual sight. Even more unusual, it came to a slow crawl right in front of her house. While she frowned, the officer looked the place over with what seemed like extreme caution. After a long moment, he drove on.

Unnerved, Rachel got into bed. Stared at the ceiling.

And worried that some crazed criminal was on the loose. No, that couldn't be it. He'd only looked at *her* house, none of the others.

She wanted to talk to someone. She could call Adam—he'd come in a heartbeat. But he wasn't looking at her as her accountant; he was looking at her differently now—no, wait. That wasn't true.

*She* was looking at *him* differently.

And then there'd be the look she'd get from Ben if Adam showed up in the middle of the night.

And then there was Ben himself. Just down the hall,

in one of her spare beds... It wasn't talking she wanted to do with Ben. She wanted... Oh, boy, what she wanted.

Diversion, she needed a diversion and quick. Shaking, she reached for the phone. Mel. He sister had always said Ben wasn't good enough for her. Mel always told Rachel about what a womanizer he'd become, how he never asked about Rachel, how he seemed so relieved not to have to deal with her.

Yep, her sister would talk her out of this insanity. She dialed as fast as her fingers could go.

"Hey," said Mel in a breathy voice.

"Mel, thank God." Rachel rushed out. "Quick. Talk me out of going down the hall and—"

"Leave a message, sexy," Mel continued in a throaty murmur. "And I'll get back to you, I promise!"

*Beep.*

*Really bad time to be gone, sis.* "Hey. It's me." She let out a shaky sigh. "Look, it's no biggie, don't worry about calling me back. I'll just..." Rachel's voice hitched, giving her away, damn it. "I'll just talk to you later," she added quickly, before she lost it, and disconnected. Then she curled up in bed the best she could, and did her best to fall asleep.

She finally managed, but not before the sun finally started its rise over the horizon.

# CHAPTER ELEVEN

Dear Ben,
Do you think you've paid enough?
Don't stop watching, waiting…
I surely won't.

FOR TWO WEEKS, Ben worked overtime—writing articles, picking small freelance pieces he'd never had time to do before—trying not to go out of his living mind. Every day that passed watching Rachel struggle to get on with her life, to get back to work, to be a good mom, to deal with his presence, killed him. During that time the various agencies involved worked overtime as well, trying to get a lead on Asada.

They traced the hit-and-run car to the previous owner. The guy's story was that he'd deserted it two months ago when the engine blew, but the truth was he'd sold it for cash to a couple of immigrants from South America who had no papers. He identified the men as the same ones on the videotape from LAX. It was now believed that Asada had never even stepped foot inside the States, but had his hired men do the deed.

Ben held his latest letter from Asada. Through the paper, he could feel the hatred, and knew he would be staying in South Village for some time to come, stifling or not.

He wrote his articles. He played basketball with Steve and Tony, attempting to lose himself in the organized chaos of a good, hard, vicious game. It worked.

Until one day during a particularly cathartic game when he happened to glance across the street and once again caught Rachel watching him from her studio window.

With sweat running down his chest and his heart pumping, time stopped for one long beat. Then Rachel turned away, breaking the spell, and Ben went back to some serious ass-kicking. But nearly a month into this caretaking thing, he almost wished Asada would make his move so he could be caught, so Ben could be released from this hell, so he could get on a plane and put ten thousand miles between him and South Village.

But Asada didn't make his move. No one did. Which left Ben good and stuck until further notice.

MELANIE HAD IT ALL. She was quite certain of it. She had a fab job buying clothes for five linked upscale boutiques in Santa Barbara. She had a brand-new red Miata that had put a serious dent in her retirement fund but drove like a sweetie. If she chose, she could have a date every night of the week and her mirror assured her she had the best shape of any thirty-three-year-old around.

Too bad her boss was a jerk, the guys out there were all cheap pricks and, in the past few years, she'd had to pay big bucks for a local surgeon to keep her beauty in check.

Ignoring the speed limit, she headed out of Santa Barbara, making the two-hour trek to South Village for the first time in a month, since right before Rachel had gotten out of the hospital.

Cranking the music, she puffed from the one cigarette

a day she allowed herself—not because it was bad for her, hell everything good was bad for her—but because she was getting lines around her mouth from holding the cigarette between her lips. Couldn't have that, not when surgery cost so much.

Slowly the music started to grate on her and her smile faded, because really, what did she have to smile about? Justin had turned out to be married. After an attack of conscience, he'd broken it off with her, which really bit the big one. No one broke up with her. *She* did all the breaking up, thank you very much.

Ah, well…he'd been too quick with the trigger in bed anyway.

The truth was, she'd be out on the town tonight, on the prowl, if it hadn't been that late-night message from Rachel a couple of weeks back. She didn't know why, but in a far too rare moment, her baby sister needed her. God, she loved to be needed. So much. And that it was Rachel doing the needing filled a void deep inside her.

She'd have come sooner, but last weekend had been the boat races, and the weekend before that a fashion show she couldn't miss, and besides every time she called, Emily kept saying everything was good. But it was time to get down there now and see her sister, the only person in Mel's entire universe who always accepted her, no matter what stupid stunts she pulled.

And there had been some pretty stupid ones.

Parking in South Village was always a challenge and today, a Friday, was no exception. She cruised the block three times before finding a spot within walking distance—which couldn't be that far given her high-heeled sandals. Why in the world Rachel chose to live on one of the busiest pedestrian blocks in the entire state was beyond her.

Mel wanted wide-open spaces and the beach. And unlimited parking so she could wear pretty shoes that were invariably uncomfortable.

Once out of the car, she paused to toss back her hair and glanced into the side-view mirror to touch up her lipstick. She also practiced a smile to lay on Rachel, a smile that wouldn't reveal her shock at her sister's appearance.

That had been the hardest part at the hospital. She hadn't been prepared to see her baby sister lying so still in the hospital bed, a woman who'd never been still in her life. But worse than that had been the casts, the bandages, the horrible bruising and scarring.

And my God, the loss of her glorious, golden hair. Mel hadn't been able to get past that, not until Rachel had noticed her discomfort and joked that she could always grow her hair again, but if she'd been six feet under…that would have been hard to fix.

Horrifying them both, Mel had burst into tears.

Mel lifted her chin now, determined to be as brave as her sister, who was the bravest woman she'd ever known. Then her gaze connected with the man sitting on the front steps of the refurbished firehouse. Of all the people in the world, he was the last she'd ever expected to be sitting there so quietly. Ben Asher wore basketball shorts and nothing else, looking lean, rugged and deliciously sweaty.

God, she loved lean and rugged and sweaty men, and before she could curtail it, need gushed through her. Ben Asher was everything she enjoyed in a man—tall, dark and gorgeous. Not model gorgeous, but a rough-and-tumble magnificent, a man who didn't mind getting down and dirty. He was a rebel at heart, a man who knew what he wanted and knew how to get it.

He sure looked mighty fine. Young enough to still be a hard body, old enough to know what to do with it. He was propped back on his elbows, biceps and forearms nicely delineated. His damp chest was dusted lightly with dark hair from pec to pec. A line of it ran down, swirled around his belly button, vanishing tantalizingly into his shorts, as if in invitation for her hand to follow, to discover the treasures beyond.

And she had no doubt there were treasures. On a man like that? Oh, yeah, there'd be treasures. My, my, he was something. He hadn't shaved today, maybe not yesterday either, and her thighs tightened thinking about that rough stubble running over her body.

She'd seen him at least once a year since he and Rachel had split. She'd brought Emily to him whenever and wherever he'd asked, mostly just to get a good look at him. Nothing wrong with a look.

But deep, *deep* down, she knew Ben had hurt Rachel more than he'd ever realized and in spite of her active hormones, her loyalties—misguided as they sometimes were—were always to her sister. So yes, she enjoyed looking at the man. Who wouldn't? And maybe to make herself feel better about that, she'd lied a few times about him to Rachel—saying that he was a slut, that he sneered when Rachel's name came up…whatever popped into her head to make her look better for lusting after the one man her sister had ever cracked her cool facade for.

And besides, Rachel never talked about him, never asked, so what harm could it all be? The very slight little crush she'd once had on him would hurt no one.

She supposed she should feel guilty, especially since Ben had always, *always,* asked about Rachel without a sneer. Maybe a better woman would have been truthful, but she'd never claimed to be good.

As she strutted her stuff across the street, walking the walk and smiling the smile, making sure he caught both, her gaze caught on the man in the yard next to Rachel's house.

It was Garrett—dentist, Good Samaritan, and all-around Goody Two-shoes. He was raking the lawn, wearing simple jeans and a T-shirt, nothing special, certainly no Greek God. And yet when he glanced over and saw her, for a brief second, he went still.

She did, too, right in the middle of the street, instantly forgetting about Ben, frozen with the memory from last New Year's Eve. She'd come to visit Rachel, who'd fallen asleep before ten o'clock. Bored and lonely, dangerously so, Mel had taken herself out to a bar not far from the house. She'd gone looking for trouble, and had found Garrett instead.

In a moment of insanity, she'd danced with him.

In a second moment of even more insanity, she'd gone home with him, for one long, glorious night. They hadn't spoken since.

*Because you've snubbed him each time he'd tried*, she reminded herself.

"Mel," Ben said in that low, gruff voice of his as she came into the yard.

She sought one last glance at Garrett, which made her stomach leap. "Ben." She forced herself to relax as he slowly uncurled his long body and stood with the grace of a lean tiger. Forced her mind off Garrett, the man who didn't matter. "What are you doing here, sexy? Taking Emily off on some exotic trip? I would have brought her to you."

"I'm here for Rachel."

Huh? "She...called you?"

He laughed at that, a low, sensual sound that she imagined could make a nun want to purr. Out of the corner of her eye, she caught Garrett watering his flowers. He did it with the same concentration he gave everything and knowing she'd been the focus of that concentration once, her stomach leaped again. What the hell had gotten into her? She had no idea. She'd had sex recently and had only last night pulled out her handy-dandy vibrator.

"No, she didn't call." Ben's slight smile still played around his firm mouth. "Have you ever known your sister to call for help?"

"Uh...no," she admitted with a smile of her own, a real one this time. "So then...?"

"I'm here to take care of her, which again, is a bit tricky, since according to her, she needs no one and nothing." His mouth twisted ironically. "Things haven't changed much in that direction."

"You're here to take care of her," Mel repeated slowly. "But Emily said she'd hired a nurse."

"Was that the story you got?"

She stared into his laughing eyes and shook her head. "Oh, no. She didn't."

"Oh, yeah, she did."

"And you came running." To save the day. To save Rachel. "How very...sweet of you." She tried to think if she'd ever been with a man who'd drop everything, his career, his life, to come running for her. From another part of the world, no less.

No. No, she hadn't.

She purposely kept her gaze off the man on the next yard, the man who'd never even told a soul he'd wanted her at least once.

"She's doing better," Ben said, and if Mel was the blushing kind, she might have blushed for getting caught not asking about Rachel's health, for being more worried about herself and her inexplicable need for a man she wasn't even acknowledging.

"I'll just see for myself, I suppose," she said, and by habit sent him a come-hither smile, the one that usually rendered men stupid, just to see what would happen.

Immune, Ben opened the door for her, and utterly without permission, her heart tugged. Why didn't the men she slept with open doors for her?

Well, actually, Garrett had, that long-ago night. But she wasn't going to think of him again.

"Rach?" Ben, moving to the pole in the living room, called up. He turned to Melanie. "I left her in her studio an hour ago, she was going to try to work."

"She's up to that?" The last time she'd seen her sister, she'd looked like death warmed over.

"Nope, but we've already established she's stubborn as hell. Maybe you can talk her into lunch. She's been eating like a damn bird."

Mel followed him and shook her head. He hadn't even glanced at her carefully painted mouth, or run his gaze down her body, even though her little white sundress— accent on the *little*—was spraypainted to her body.

Was she losing it? She looked down at herself and had to say…she looked pretty damn hot.

Had Garrett checked her out thoroughly? She hoped he'd swallowed his tongue.

Not that she was thinking of him.

They took the stairs. At the closed door to the studio, Ben turned back to face her and smiled. "Ready to get your head bitten off?"

She jerked her thoughts off Garrett. "Why?"

"Well, she probably doesn't snap at you every time you look at her, but—" with a low, soft laugh, he scratched his chest and looked a little sheepish "—Rachel and I…we seem to bring out the extremes in each other."

That he hadn't said "the worst," but the "extremes," stopped her cold. What, exactly, had been going on here? She put a hand on her hip. "You two doing something stupid, like knocking it out again? I sure as hell hope you know how to use condoms correctly these days."

The door whipped open. Rachel stood there, propped up by a cane, glaring at the two of them.

"Hi, honey," Ben said sweetly. "I'm home."

Rachel narrowed her eyes at him, and then turned on Melanie. "You want to ask me something to my face?"

Oh, boy. She made the mistake of glancing at Ben.

"Don't look at him," Rachel demanded. "Look at me. I'm standing right here. *Standing,* thank you for asking, and yes, it hurts like hell."

"Hey, sis. You're looking…great." Melanie decided to smile. It usually worked, though it appeared she was batting below average today.

Rachel let out a rude noise and turned away. She stared at her easel, which was conspicuously blank.

"Rach…" Ben moved into the room and shocked Melanie by putting his hands on Rachel's shoulders, one of which was in a sling supporting her casted left arm. "Come on, babe. Let's go downstairs and grab some grub. Em made those disgusting healthy cookies, remember? You've got to eat them before she gets home in an hour or she'll worry."

"*You* eat them."

"Well, darlin', I would, except they taste like dirt. And I have to say, I'm not overly fond of dirt."

Rachel laughed. *Laughed.* Ben laughed, too, that same soft, sexy sound that tickled over Mel's good spots.

Ben smiled down at Rachel, then reached out and stroked her cheek.

She blushed.

And while Mel stared at them, Ben ran his hands lightly down her sister's arms, up and down, meeting Rachel's gaze with such warmth, such affection, such… heat and intensity, it completely stole Mel's breath.

"My God," she said with a laugh that sounded shrill to her own ears. "Times *have* changed. Last time I checked, the two of you couldn't be in the same time zone, much less in the same room. Now look at you, so cozy."

Rachel turned her face away and stepped clear of Ben so that his hands fell to his sides. "We're merely cohabitating to appease Emily, Mel, so don't go making any big deal out of it."

"Cohabitating…or commingling?"

"Knock it off, Mel," Ben said with more heat than she was used to from the king of laid-back city.

Well, didn't he have some nerve! For years she'd been doing his bidding, taking Emily to the ends of the earth to meet him. Granted she always jumped when he called because she didn't object to looking at him for a few days a couple of times a year, but where was the gratitude? "Okay, then," she said lightly, when oddly enough, her throat burned. "But I can't imagine why I risked my job to race down here. Oh, wait…yes, I remember…because Rachel called me in tears."

Ben whipped his face toward Rachel, his eyes dark and intent. "You were crying?"

An irrational jealousy choked Melanie at the way he looked at Rachel. His silver earring gleamed, his hair fell over his forehead and nearly to his shoulders. His hard body hadn't come from any gym, but from years of using his muscles the old-fashioned way. Everything about him screamed rebel, trouble seeker, black heart.

Didn't Rachel get it? A man like that was tailor-made for a woman like...well, like *Mel*.

Not Rachel. She needed quiet, calm, sweet and kind. She needed stability and security.

Ben didn't know the meaning of those words. Damn it, seeing the two of them standing there staring at each other was like a fingernail scraping down a chalkboard. Because whether they admitted it or not, there was such a shimmering connection between them, she could practically reach out and touch it.

She wanted to reach out and touch it, all right, but she wanted it for herself.

"I was not crying." Rachel tipped her head back, stared at the ceiling. "I was just...I don't know. Feeling sorry for myself. End of story. And anyway, it was weeks ago. You know what? I'm ready for those dirt-flavored cookies."

Ben shook his head. "You should have come to me."

"You playing the hero now?" Melanie laughed into the silence. "That's *my* job this weekend, bud. So..." She clapped her hands together and tried to look hungry. "Let's go get the cookies and see if we can't doctor them up. Say with chocolate syrup. Something fattening."

She'd need something fattening to get over the hot, intensive looks Ben kept shooting Rachel. She'd need an entire bakery.

EMILY PLOPPED DOWN on the crowded school bus. As other kids walked by, she clutched her backpack in her lap and stared straight ahead, deciding she didn't care if anyone sat down next to her. She didn't care one little bit.

She hated school. She hated her teachers, though they'd be shocked to hear it. They loved her because she knew the material, because she was quiet and never gave them any trouble.

But they didn't *see* her. No one at school did. She'd thought it wouldn't matter, that this year she was old enough, mature enough, not to care that she was different. Turns out she could be wrong.

"Can I sit here?"

She looked up. And up. It was the tall, skinny kid from her history class. He kept to himself and was a brainiac, too. She'd wanted to ask him about that, ask him if he felt as out of place in this school that seemed to favor athletes over scholars, but she'd never had the nerve.

"Emily? Can I sit here?"

*He knew her name.* "Uh..." Tongue-tied? She was tongue-tied? How new and awful was that? She settled for lifting a negligent shoulder, biting her lip when he sat.

"I'm Van," he said, tossing his backpack to the floor at his feet. "We have history together."

"Yeah." *Yeah?* Was that all she could come up with? She clunked her head back on the seat and wondered if a thunderbolt could just strike her dead and get it over with.

Van had a disk in his hand, which meant he could operate a computer, and her heart started to pound. She started to sweat, too, which really grossed her out. *Please, don't notice.* Trying to swipe at her upper lip without catching his eye, she managed to knock his disk out of his hand and onto the floor.

"Oh!" She dived for it. "I'm so sorry!"

He bent, too, and they clunked heads hard.

"Ouch," he said, rubbing his forehead, but he was smiling.

She wasn't; she wanted to die. She brushed the disk off on her jeans, going beet red as the two girls behind them started to snicker.

It was official. She was a loser with a capital *L.*

"It's no biggie." In spite of the red spot over his eye, he kept smiling. "It's just a copy."

Just then the bus made a sharp turn, and she plowed into him. Her shoulder to his chest this time. *Ohmigod, could it get worse?* Mortified, she looked up into his face, but his smile turned into a grin.

She found herself grinning, too. Helplessly. *Talk to him. Ask him about the disk. Mention your computer. Say something, say anything!*

It took her five minutes to figure out what to say. She'd decided to ask him if he ever went to the computer lab after school, but the bus stopped and he got off.

*Loser.*

*Double loser.*

She had three more stops before she could drown her sorrows in chocolate milk with Patches. Unzipping her backpack, she reached in and cracked her laptop open enough so that she could just barely read the screen. She couldn't get e-mail yet, but she could reread what she'd downloaded this morning.

Alicia had written her, lamenting that her parents sucked, school sucked, life sucked.

Amen to that. She hit reply, and glancing around to make sure no one was looking at her—as if!—she began to type: "Alicia, Yeah, everything sucks here, too."

She didn't want Alicia to feel left out. Besides, school did still suck, but at home, things were…interesting. She'd been working on her parents, who still hadn't figured out they were supposed to be together. Jeez, talk about two stubborn people! They were circling each other like caged bears, but there did seem to be a lot less snarling.

And her dad did get really grumpy whenever Adam-the-accountant showed up, which always made Emily want to laugh and hug him at the same time. Her mom, though…she wasn't trying as hard as her dad to get along. Emily was really mad at her for that.

But it just didn't feel cool to admit such things. Emily didn't want to get ditched for being such a wimp as to want her parents married.

But God, she wanted that, so much. She'd done everything she could, including not going to her mom in the mornings when she'd called out for help, biting her fingernails to the stubs in guilt, but relaxing when she'd hear her dad go running instead. Twice she'd "accidentally" hung up on Adam when he'd called rather than bring the phone to her mom. Best yet, she'd managed to convince her aunt Mel, who was coming down today for the weekend, to take her out to the latest DiCaprio movie tonight, which would leave her parents alone.

What she'd planned would add to her crimes, but she didn't care. If it worked, it'd be perfect.

She hoped.

The bus pulled up on her street. Excited, she shut the

computer, zipped up her backpack and got off the bus, and didn't even stop to glower at a single kid.

RACHEL LEANED AWAY from the easel and drew out a careful breath. The paper was still blank, pathetically blank. Ironic, given that today she actually felt good enough to skip all her pain meds.

Which meant she was on the road to recovery.

Good.

But she'd apparently lost her ability to come up with a *Gracie* cartoon to save her sorry life.

Bad.

It wasn't just work, she had to admit. It'd been a rough day all around, starting with this morning when Emily hadn't wanted to get out of bed. Rachel knew she'd stayed up too late on her damn computer, but pointing that out had only started a feud.

Ben had stepped in, sweetly coaxing his daughter out of bed with the promise of McDonald's on the way to school. When Rachel had suggested that maybe he could try something other than bribery, as in her opinion, Emily needed to learn responsibility, the feud had turned to all-out war.

Ben's eyes had gone a little hard as he'd backed off, and she could mentally smack herself now, because she understood she'd inadvertently undermined his authority in front of Emily, but damn it, she wasn't used to sharing the day-to-day responsibility of raising their daughter.

Wasn't used to anything when it came to Ben, including the way he always seemed to touch her, look at her.

Kiss her.

Naturally, Emily had leaped to her father's defense and, between the dog yelping for attention and Emily yelling and Ben's extremely loud silence, Rachel had ended up with a headache.

She was getting tired of wondering when Ben's wanderlust would get the best of him. She'd seen him writing, muttering, playing with his camera. She'd seen him reading the world events in the newspaper, seen the wheels turning in his head. She'd heard him on the phone just yesterday, talking about some future job in Siberia or somewhere. And he'd been pacing in his bedroom at night like a caged mountain cat.

Always when she woke up, she figured this would be the day he'd be gone.

But he hadn't left.

Soon, though, she had no doubt. Soon he'd leave and she'd take her first deep breath since he'd shown up on their doorstep. Yep, he'd be gone, and she'd be glad. Just a matter of time now.

She'd go on with her life, maybe take it in a new direction....

The phone rang, drawing her out of the reverie and firmly into the present.

"Doll!" Gwen Ariani, her agent, spoke in her rough voice that was the result of smoking for thirty years. "How's it going?"

Her blank easel mocked her. "It's not."

"No? Well, it's soon yet. You still have an entire month before you have to start cranking out again. Thank God you'd worked so far ahead of yourself, huh?"

"Gwen..." Rachel closed her eyes and admitted what she'd been wanting to admit for a good long time now. "I don't know if I want to 'crank' out the strip again. I'm thinking about ending *Gracie*."

"Hold on, doll. Clearly, I'm losing my hearing."

"No, you're not."

"Then I'm having a heart attack."

"I just wanted to start something new."

"Another strip?"

"No." Rachel ran a finger over the new laptop she'd had delivered. "I'm thinking of starting over. Completely over. And writing instead of drawing."

Dead silence for a long beat. "You mean, walk away from the biggest cash cow of your life? Can't you just write a little on the side now and then?"

Rachel had expected resistance. *Gracie* made them all a lot of money. "I'm not talking a little hobby, Gwen. I'm thinking of writing a book."

"You're still on meds, right?"

"No."

"Come on, Rachel, people don't walk away from a gig like this. You only draw one strip a week, for God's sake. Hello! Cakewalk!"

From under the closed studio door came a slip of paper. Eyes narrowed, Rachel moved slowly, using her cane. "I'm sorry you don't understand, Gwen, but—" She unfolded the typed sheet of paper and silently read the note. "It's time for a truce, past time. Meet me in the gardens at eight. Dinner on me."

Rachel frowned. Ben wanted a truce? What did that mean, exactly? That he'd go away? She hadn't known the man to give in on anything in his life.

But a truce...

"Rachel?"

She fingered the note. "Gwen, I've got to go."

"Wait—"

"I'm sorry, I'll call you next week." She hung up and stared at the words on the paper again, wondering what on earth that man was up to.

BEN WAS ALSO looking at a note, one that had been slipped under his door. "It's time for a truce, past time. Meet me in the gardens at eight. Dinner on me."

Rachel wanted a truce? That was new to him. She certainly hadn't shown a weakening in those ten-foot walls she wore around her like a cloak. Nope, whenever he wanted in, he was forced to bash them down one brick at a time. A touch seemed to work, as did kissing her.

But those things were far more dangerous to him than to her, and besides, he wearied of the constant battle.

Now this, a truce. Did *he* want one? Hell, no.

Would he go to the garden and stare at her beautiful face? Hell, yes.

# CHAPTER TWELVE

AT EIGHT O'CLOCK that night Rachel opened the sliding glass door to the back garden. It had been an interesting afternoon. Gwen had called back twice, trying not to show her panic over the impending loss of *Gracie*. Their online server had gone down for several hours sending Emily into a tailspin over the lack of e-mail. Adam had called wanting to take her out to a new downtown dinner theater. Mel was acting pissy about God knew what. The puppy was going to be the death of her if she so much as chewed one more thing. And her doctor had told her she'd be a little longer on the casts.

All in all, a shitty day. But at least Melanie had taken Emily out for a movie and the puppy was sleeping. A few moments of peace. Maybe. She made her careful way outside, and at the sight before her, all her thoughts scattered like the light evening wind.

Candles burned everywhere, on the brick path, hanging from the trees, on the table that had been dressed up with her fancy linens and best china. And sitting at the table, looking at her with those dark eyes and sexy mouth curved in the slightest of a smile, was Ben.

Uh-oh. Thinking about resisting him and everything he made her feel was one thing when he wasn't actually in front of her, but Ben in the flesh was something else entirely. Her heart clutched, her stomach quivered. Her palms went damp. The entire visceral reaction was more than a little disturbing.

Had she forgotten that this man, and this man alone, had once destroyed her? Had she forgotten he already had one foot out the door, and that when he left it would likely be another thirteen years before she saw him again?

He stood up and came toward her, wearing jeans and a plain white T-shirt beneath an open, long-sleeved, blue chambray shirt. "Hey," he said.

"Hey yourself."

He took her hand and guided her to the table. She eyed her best china, the three daisies in a small vase in the center of the table, the utter care that had gone into the setting and then realized he was studying her. *"What?"*

"You look beautiful," he said so simply she wanted to believe him. Wanted a lot of things, actually.

"Ben…about earlier. I'm sorry about getting mad over the McDonald's bribe. It's just that I'm used to handling her all by myself, and—"

"You handle everything by yourself."

"I didn't—" She let out a breath and blinked at him. "What?"

"You handle everything by yourself—your injuries, your house, your hopes and dreams and fears. Your daughter."

"She's your daughter, too."

"I know that, I'm just not always sure you know it."

Whoa. This didn't sound like a truce to her. "Ben—"

"Look, all I want to say is, don't apologize for something you're not really sorry for."

"I…okay." She blew out a careful breath. "You're right."

"And be honest. You like routine, you like to get your way and when I wasn't here, you had both whenever you wanted it."

"Yes," she agreed tightly. "And when you're gone, things will go back to normal. They'll have to. So I'd appreciate it if you didn't spoil Emily while you were here."

He let out a little laugh. "You act like I'm already half gone."

"Aren't you?"

Still standing, they stared at each other, at the same old impasse. The thirteen years might not have happened at all, Rachel thought bitterly, and wondered how she'd ever let herself dream things might be different this time, even if those dreams had only been in the deep, dark of the night. "You could try to deny it," she whispered, horrified at what she was revealing by even saying it, but unwilling to hold back.

He stared at her for a beat, then grimaced. Shoving his hands through his hair, he turned in a slow circle, then faced her again. "Rachel." Just that, just her name, in a voice as tortured as her insides felt.

"Forget it," she said, inhaling deeply. "Just forget it."

"You know I had to leave back then. I had the offer of a lifetime. You *know* that. But I never meant to do it without you, it never occurred to me that I'd have to. That you'd send me away."

She knew her eyes were shining with unshed tears. Knowing that her heart was in her voice, she said, "And it never occurred to you that I had to stay, every bit as much as you had to go."

"Rach," he whispered again and stepped closer. He slid his fingers along her jaw, beneath the straw hat she

wore over her extremely short hair. His thumb gently
glided along her cheek. "I'm sorry. I'm sorry I hurt
you."

"Me, too," she said softly, and meant it. So sorry.

He let out a slow breath. "So."

"So," she repeated, and had to let out a little smile.

His returning smile stole her breath. He hitched his
head toward the table. "Think we can manage?"

"We can try."

"Good." He slipped his arm around her bad side,
gently pulling her snug against him so that as they turned
toward the table and started walking, he was her cane.

"What's cooking?" she asked, trying not to think
about how hard he felt from shoulder to thigh, how
warm. How positively solid. She concentrated on something else instead—the itching beneath the cast, the re-
sidual heat of the day.

"Well, now." He tipped his head down to hers, his
mouth curving into a smile. "I was going to ask you the
same thing."

He sat her down, scooted her chair in for her then
moved to his side of the table. Shrugging out of his long-
sleeved shirt, he set it over the back of his chair and sat
as well. "Hungry?" Before she could answer, he pulled
the lid off the steaming platter. Mac and cheese.

Not that Rachel wasn't grateful for any meal that she
didn't have to cook, but she knew Ben's culinary skills
and had to admit to surprise over the simplistic menu.

"Looks great," he said, and smiled one of his killer
smiles.

In spite of herself, she laughed. "Didn't it look great
before?"

"Before?"

"When you cooked it, Ben."

His smile froze a little. "But I didn't cook it."

"But...I didn't either."

"Sure you did. I got your note." He pulled it out of the pocket of the shirt on the back of his chair. The piece of paper looked suspiciously like hers.

She stared at it in disbelief, then pulled out hers and handed it to him.

After reading it, he tossed his head back and laughed.

Rachel, who didn't think this was funny in the least, sat back. Her daughter had struck again.

Ben just laughed some more. "You have to admit, she got us."

"Oh, she got us. And I'm going to get her."

"How can you not find this funny?"

That was simple. Everything in her life was out of her control, including this, and she deeply resented that. With a shiver, she imagined what could have happened tonight if the truth hadn't been discovered, if she'd continued to believe Ben had set this all up himself. She shivered again, and with a frown Ben stood up and grabbed his shirt from the back of his chair. "Here," he said, and draped it over her shoulders.

Encompassed in his warmth, she closed her eyes when his hands lingered over her shoulders, gently squeezing and massaging the tightness of her muscles there.

"Rach..." His mouth was by her ear so that she could feel his warm breath against her sensitive skin. If she hadn't learned the truth, she'd probably have melted back against him, let herself get lost in what he was so silently offering, lost in a way she hadn't allowed herself since...*him*.

Damn it. Straightening away, she grabbed her fork.

"All right." He pulled away with a low chuckle. "I can take a hint."

"If I'd been hinting, I'd have picked up the knife."

He smiled and served them both. Lifting the crystal water glass, he toasted her. "To our ingenious daughter."

"Should we really toast her antics?"

His eyes were warm and laughing, and yet behind that was something else, something that took her breath with its heat and intensity. "Oh, yeah," he murmured. "And here's to something else, Rach. Here's to us."

"While you're here."

"While I'm here," he agreed.

She ignored the hitch in her heart and nodded lightly. "Okay. Then here's to us not killing each other for the duration."

He grinned.

Suddenly starving, she leaned into the table to eat. In the breast pocket of Ben's shirt a paper crinkled, poking her through the material. Thinking her daughter had been meddling even further, she pulled out the folded paper, opened it and read what was on it. "Dear Ben, Do you think you've paid? Don't stop watching, waiting...I surely won't."

Ben came out of his chair the moment he saw what Rachel had, but it was too late.

She lifted her head and pierced him with horror-filled eyes. "What is this?"

Cursing himself would do no good, lying to her even less, though Ben considered both. Would have done either if he could have gotten away with it, but Rachel would have seen right through him.

Still, he might have tried if it wasn't for one thing.

He *owed* her the truth, probably should have given it to her long ago. Carefully he took Asada's letter back, folded it again and put it in the pocket of his jeans.

"Ben." Her voice shook. "Are you in trouble?"

He scratched his jaw and considered that. "Aren't I usually?"

*"Ben."*

"Yeah. I'm, uh, thinking about how to start."

"From the beginning," she suggested, her voice a little thin. "Who wrote that letter? My God, is someone stalking you? Are you in danger? Could you be hurt?"

He stared at her, stunned by the realizations that she was shaking, pale, terrified...for him. She thought *he* was in danger...

Planting her cane, she went to rise out of her chair, but he stopped her, and went to his knees before her so that their faces were level. "I'm sorry you found out like this."

"Just tell me," she begged. "Tell me what's going on."

"Yeah, okay." He put his hand on her casted arm, imagined himself being struck by the car that had hit her. Imagined the pain, the fear, the subsequent nightmare of the long hospital stay. Imagined all she'd been through since, and tried to figure out how to tell her that the true hell could be just beginning. Oh, and that it was his fault.

"About six months ago," he started. "I was looking for a new story."

When she nodded, silently urging him on, clearly still worried about *him,* he felt sick. "I found an American retreat based in Brazil, where the so-called minister raised money there for what he called his missions of hope. He solicited unsuspecting, generous patrons from all around the world, raising millions."

"I read that piece," she said. "Instead of building and

feeding villages with all that money, he pocketed everything, right?''

She'd read it. She'd followed his work. Probably not the smartest time for him to be both blown away and flattered by that.

"You exposed the international scam," she continued. "And the guy went to prison."

"Manuel Asada, and yes, once in prison, he lost everything. His people, his empire, everything. He..." Ben drew a deep breath. "He vowed revenge on me for destroying his world."

Her eyes were huge on his. "And...?"

"And during his extradition to the States, where he would have stood trial for bilking a bunch of rich Americans out of their spending cash, he escaped."

"And...?"

He smiled grimly. Emily hadn't been just randomly blessed with brains, she'd gotten them from this woman sitting before him, her eyes sharp on his. "And now he's vanished."

"And wanting your head on a platter."

"Not mine exactly...just those I care about."

She went utterly still. "My God, Ben..." She stared at him for another breath, then pushed to her feet with her cane. When he tried to help her, she shoved his hands away, stared at him some more, then paced away from him the best she could. Thinking. Putting it all together.

When she whipped back, he thought he was ready.

"So you didn't come here to South Village for me, for this...." She gestured to her casts and cane. "You came out of some misguided notion you had to protect Emily."

"And you."

"But why would Asada think you cared about *me?*"

"Because I do," he said tightly.

Again she froze. Stared at him with numbed horror. "The accident."

"Yeah. Only I don't think it was much of an accident at all. God, Rach…" How to convey the guilt, the sorrow, the regret? The murderous rage swimming inside him without an outlet? He went to her, took her shoulders in his hands, felt her trembling. "I didn't mean for this to happen, I'm so sorry." She let out a sort of choked sob that stabbed at him. "If it could have been me instead," he said in a hoarse voice. "I'd do it in a heartbeat. Anything, *anything,* to have kept you safe."

Her eyes filled and she covered her mouth. "It could have been Emily. Our baby—"

Unable to hold back in the face of that, he slid his arms around her, holding her close. For a moment, she clung to him, and he lost himself in the familiar feel of her, her scent and shape beneath his hands feeling so overwhelmingly like…home.

Then with shocking strength she once again shoved free. "I thought you were home because…that you…" She let out an embarrassed sound and covered her face. "I want you to go," she said from behind her fingers.

"I can't."

"Won't, you mean."

"Damn right. I'm not budging until Asada is found."

She dropped her hand from her face and stared at him with those big, expressive, hurting eyes, making him hate himself all over again as he watched emotion after emotion chase across her face. "I knew there had to be something tying you here," she said quietly. "Something more than us."

He hadn't imagined he could hurt more than he did,

but her words twisted the knife. "I'm sorry," he said again, the words pathetically inadequate.

She turned away. "So am I. Just promise me something."

"Anything," he said rashly.

"The minute it's safe, you're gone."

He stared at her slim spine and all the courage and strength shimmering around her like a beacon, and closed his eyes. Then he gave her the words that would seal their fate, words he'd wanted to utter more than anything, so he had no idea why they stuck in his throat. "I promise. Soon as it's safe, I'm gone."

In Brazil, night came suddenly, viciously, without warning. One moment the birds were singing, the bees humming, then the next—utter and complete black silence.

Manuel had always loved that, but now he dreaded the shifting of the clock, hated when the sun fell out of the sky, because it left him hiding out like a mole until morning's light.

There was so little left for him here. Only a few people hustling around to do his bidding, securing the compound. Just a few minions who had nowhere else to go otherwise he was quite certain he'd be completely alone.

Reduced to this, hiding out, depending on others for everything, was slowly driving him mad. Night or day, he had nothing to do but think and torture himself with what-ifs.

What if he'd killed Ben Asher before his story had hit?

What if he hadn't been caught unaware and jailed before he could stash away his assets? What if he hadn't had to spend so much to bribe his way back through the jungle to his compound?

What if, what if…

The need for revenge was a burning hunger that drove him to live each day. He would rebuild. He'd once again have people eating out of the palm of his hand and paying for the privilege. And he would have his empire back. He'd be even bigger this time, and no one would get the best of him ever again.

No one.

## CHAPTER THIRTEEN

BEN STOOD on the balcony watching the night go by. He'd figured that this would be preferable to being in bed where all he'd been able to do was stare at the ceiling.

But being out here turned out to be no different because watching the people winding their way through the streets, all he could really see was Rachel's face as the truth had sunk in about why he'd come back.

He wondered if, when he'd been in the Brazilian jungle taking pictures of Asada's compound, had he known what havoc his article would wreak, would he still have done it? Would he still have snapped those pictures and written down all the facts for the world to see?

Rachel's silent and strong grief tonight had nearly brought him to his knees. Watching her piece together the puzzle, seeing her understand what danger he'd put her and Emily in had been nothing short of torture.

Grimacing, he rubbed his eyes with the heels of his hands, but nothing changed. He was still scum. He'd still brought an element of his world to his daughter and the woman who'd once brought him more joy than anyone else ever had.

Pulled by a sudden overpowering need to see them, touch them, assure himself they were safe, he moved inside. He died a thousand deaths when he opened Rachel's bedroom door and found her bed empty. She wasn't in the bathroom, wasn't in her studio, though Mel was, fast asleep on the couch against the far wall.

Palms damp, heart cold, he ran to Emily's room. At what he found in her bed made him sag against the wall in weak-kneed relief, though he didn't deserve that relief.

Her daughter was there, sideways, covers tossed to the floor, arms and legs sprawled wide.

Safe.

Next to her, in the smallest corner of the bed, turned on her good side, facing Emily, was Rachel.

Also safe.

How was it possible just looking at them made him want to smile and cry and run like hell all at the same time?

It took a long moment for his heart to settle. He tugged the covers back over her and, unable to resist, bent close to press his lips to her temple. In her sleep, she snuffled, mumbled something inarticulate, then sighed back into a deep slumber.

God, she was sweet. And his. He moved to Rachel's side, covering her as well, yet he didn't dare touch her. She was sweet, too. So sweet. But not his. She never would be; his own actions had guaranteed that.

He didn't leave the room for a long time, wanting to watch over these two pieces that made up his heart. Nothing, *nothing,* would hurt them. He'd willingly die seeing to it.

RACHEL HAD DEALT with a lot of blows in her life. In fact, dealing was a particular forte of hers. So with little fanfare, she handled the new nightmares since her little "date" with Ben two nights ago. She handled the shock and horror of the accident all over again, knowing now it hadn't been an accident at all, but the insane revenge of a madman.

And she'd handled the real reasons Ben was here, despite the fact that for a little while she'd actually thought Ben had wanted to be with her.

In any case, certain things made better sense now. She consoled herself with that. The police drive-bys, for example, which the FBI had arranged since in all likelihood she and Emily were being stalked by an international criminal on the run. The way Ben personally locked up the doors and windows every night, making sure he was the last one to bed.

That thought brought her back to his presence here and she still cringed when she considered it. Had she really believed he'd come back of his own free will, aided by Emily's helpful manipulations?

Yes, pathetic as it was to admit, she'd really believed it.

"Mom." Emily bounced into her studio. She'd just walked the dog with Mel and was back, healthy and safe.

Rachel had never thought of South Village as a dangerous place, especially on a Sunday afternoon...until now. She'd never thought a lot of things until now, with Ben back.

God, he needed to get out of her life. "Hey, baby." Unable to help herself, she held out her arms, holding her breath until Emily walked into them, letting Rachel hug and kiss her for a long moment. Ben had assured her that Emily was as safe as she could be, but Rachel doubted she'd ever relax again. She'd ordered Mace to keep with her and, holding Emily, her precious baby, she wished she'd bought a gun instead.

In her arms, Emily squirmed and reluctantly Rachel let her loose.

Pulling away, Emily grinned, one of those open and fancy grins Rachel hadn't seen in a while. "Guess what, Mom?"

"You planned another embarrassing fake dinner date?"

She had the good grace to blush over that. "Um, no. That sort of idea shouldn't be repeated."

"Thankfully."

"I'm going to stop bugging you to homeschool me."

This was a first, and a moment that should have been cause for joy. But Rachel had been considering doing exactly that, homeschooling Emily, until Asada was caught. "Why the change of heart?"

"Okay, don't freak."

Uh-oh.

"There's this boy…"

A boy. She'd been so locked up in the unbelievable nightmare of her life, she'd forgotten…Emily's life hadn't changed. "Is he cute?"

*"Mom!"*

"What?"

"We're just friends! Jeez!"

Rachel laughed. "Friends is good."

"Oh, goody! Are we talking boys?" Melanie walked into the studio wearing a pair of black hip-hugging jeans and a red bandanna as a top. "But I gotta tell you, sugar, boys make really crappy friends." She caught Rachel's long gaze over Emily's head. "What? They do. Never trust a guy," Mel said to Emily. "Never."

The phone rang. With a sigh, Rachel punched speaker. "Hello?"

"So…how's *Gracie?*" Gwen's gravelly voice boomed into the room, so gravelly Rachel could almost smell the cigarette smoke. "I was thinking I could come by and pick her up."

"Gwen, I...don't have anything for you." Rachel sighed when both Mel and Emily looked at her in surprise. She couldn't blame them, she'd been disappearing into this very room every day, even today, a Sunday. If she wasn't working on *Gracie,* what was she doing?

She had no idea.

"Rachel, you're not still entertaining that silly notion of giving up on *Gracie* are you?"

Rachel rolled her eyes heavenward. "I'll call you, Gwen."

"But—"

Rachel disconnected. Smiled shakily at Emily and Mel, who were still staring at her.

"You're giving up the biggest paycheck you've ever had?" Mel asked. *"Why?"*

"I didn't say I was giving it up."

"Mom, I thought you loved *Gracie.*"

"Oh, for God's sake." Rachel forced a laugh. "You're all talking about *Gracie* like she is real."

*"Mom."*

Rachel sighed. How to explain that she was no longer creatively stimulated by the very thing that used to be her life? That she wanted to go in a new direction, that she had this deep burning desire—a desire she hadn't felt since Ben had been in her life way back when—to make a difference?

He did that to her, she knew now. He fed her passion.

Damn him. "Sometimes," she said carefully. "A person has to stretch herself or move on."

"But..." Emily looked confused. "If you stop working, what will that mean? Will we have to move?"

"No."

"Don't be stupid, Rach. You're not giving up *Gracie*," Mel said. "That's just crazy."

Rachel ignored that and reached for Emily's hand. "The truth is things aren't the same for me anymore. I don't know what I'm going to do, but nothing will change for you, okay? No moving."

"Em…" Melanie was watching Rachel as if she were a live cannon about to go off. "Give your mom and me a minute."

"You just want to talk about something good."

"Emily."

"Fine. Whatever! Don't include me, I don't care." The door slammed behind her.

"That'll cost you," warned Rachel.

"I can deal with her. What I can't deal with is you being skimpy on the details."

"Mel—"

"Friday night at the movies, Em told me about her little stunt. Getting Ben here without either of you knowing. Keeping him here by binding him to a promise to stay until you're better. And she told me about the dinner date that night, too, the little weasel. Good thing she's so cute." She looked Rachel over very carefully. "So…you didn't say all weekend…how did that go?"

"What?"

"Cut the innocent crap, sis. The dinner with Ben. It's Sunday. I'm leaving in a few. The least you can do is tell me how long it took you to figure out you'd been set up by a twelve-year-old."

"Longer than you might think, actually."

Mel raised a carefully plucked brow. "You really thought he'd set up a date with you?"

"And he thought the same of me," she said, feeling defensive and unhappy about it.

"So what happened? You guys take a stroll down memory lane or what?"

Rachel thought of the things that had taken her down memory lane. The embraces, the kisses. The yearning for more. "Uh…"

Mel gaped. "My God. You're blushing. What the hell did the two of you do anyway, knock it out right there in the garden? Hope you were smart enough not to break the condom this time."

"Mel!"

"Sorry." She actually looked it, too, which was a shock. "I guess I'm just floored the two of you are getting along, when for years I've been doing the traveling between the two of you, taking Em—"

"I know." Rachel covered her tired eyes with her fingers. "I know," she said again, more softly. "And we're grateful—"

"You're even speaking for him now, huh?"

Rachel had no idea what had caused this mood of Mel's, but she didn't have time for it. "Do you want to know what happened between us or not?"

"Sure, if you were stupid enough to do anything with the man who walks around here shimmering with resentment and dying to get the hell back to whatever far corner of the earth he came from."

If that didn't put it into perspective… "There are mitigating circumstances."

"Do tell."

Careful to keep all personal details out of it—including the numerous mind-numbing, bone-melting kisses—Rachel told her about Manuel Asada. About the extradition, his escape. Her accident. The letters, everything.

"Holy shit," Mel kept saying over and over again. "Holy double shit."

"So now you know why he's here," Rachel said. "And it's not out of a misguided attempt to pick up where we left off, so stop referring to it that way."

"Holy shit."

"You've said that."

"I'm not leaving."

"Yes, you are. You'll lose your job if you're not back for work tomorrow. I'm fine here. I'll see you soon."

"Yeah." Mel got to the door, then came back for a long, bone-crunching hug. They'd never said the words *I love you*. They didn't say them now, though that wasn't really surprising, as Rachel had never said those words to a single soul except Emily.

Not once…

When Mel had left, Rachel looked around the room she'd once loved and wondered…what held her back? What always held her back? Fear? Or an inability to share herself? Both, maybe.

Not liking what that said about her, she shrugged it off for now. They were things more important than love at the moment. Far more.

To get rid of the terrible tension within her, she needed a run. Not going to happen, but her physical therapist told her she could start walking. She went out into the backyard. It was big for South Village standards, and until the accident, she and Emily had spent a lot of time out here. Since she'd been unable to get down on her knees and rip out weeds, the place had become overgrown, but a few casts weren't going to stop her anymore, nothing was. Pulling weeds had always been a particularly soothing therapy, and she could use some therapy now.

She walked to the back corner of the property, where she had a small fenced-in vegetable garden. She maneuvered the stone path slowly. It was a bit slippery, but she'd just decided to let nothing stop her.

Except her own stupidity. When the cane slipped out from beneath her, so did her casted leg and, without warning, she hit the ground hard enough to rattle her teeth.

For a moment she sat there in the dirt taking stock. She'd lost a sandal and her straw hat. Her sunglasses were on her chin. Her butt hurt, but that was to be expected as she'd landed on it. Her casted leg and arm seemed to have been properly protected, but she'd scraped up her knee and elbow. Amusing, really. She'd been hit by a car and hadn't felt a thing for days. She took a tumble in her garden and wanted to cry.

Laughing at herself at that, she went to get up…and found she couldn't. Her casted leg was at such an angle on the slight uphill grade that she couldn't get it beneath her to push to a stand, not without support, and her cane had fallen out of her reach.

If that didn't fry her already stinging butt. She refused to yell for help to Em, who was upstairs listening to CDs. Nor would she yell for Ben who, the last time she'd seen him, had gone into his makeshift dark room, aka her downstairs bathroom. With a lot of huffing and puffing, and quite a bit of inventive swearing, she rolled and grabbed her cane. Then, and this took a while, she managed to get her leg in a position where she could roll to her own good knee, which was now quite a bit bloody.

While she kneeled there in the dirt trying to figure out how to stand up on her own, she listened to the birds sing, the bees buzzing around, and realized life went on. No matter that she couldn't draw, that her daughter had become an alien, that her ex-lover was in the house giving her looks that took her breath…life went on.

And so would she. Suddenly, she felt lighter and less angry than she'd felt since the accident. Gritting her teeth, she used her last bit of energy to stand up. She'd done it, all on her own, and was a wobbly, shaky but grinning mess when Ben appeared.

With the sun behind him, all she could see was his dark outline towering over her, and he did tower. His hands were on his lean hips, his hair wild.

"What happened?" he demanded.

"Well, I fell, and—"

"Are you all right?"

"Besides bruised pride and a sore butt? Yes."

"You just can't accept your own limitations, can you?" He reached for her. "No, not you. You have to go out and prove they don't exist, because heaven forgoddamn-bid you allow yourself to lean on someone once in a while."

"Gee, I guess you're not going to kiss my boo-boos all better."

He didn't bother to respond to that as he checked her over. His face was utterly impassive, but she had a hard time feeling the same. His fingers checked her ribs—each and every one. His knuckles brushed the underside of her breasts and apparently her libido was in full working order because her nipples hardened. She looked at his face to see if he'd notice. "I said I'm fine."

He might as well have been a stone wall for all he responded as he brushed dirt from her clothes. Then his eyes met hers. At the inferno of heat she saw there, she swallowed hard. Had she thought he hadn't noticed her?

He'd noticed. And he was barely holding back. "Guess I owe you a thank-you—"

This ended in a gasp as he bent and lifted her in his arms.

"Ben, don't be ridiculous, I can walk, it just took me a while to get— *Ben*."

Ignoring her, he headed toward the house.

"Okay, listen. I—"

"You're bleeding."

She looked down at the abrasions that were minor in comparison to her other problems and had to laugh. "Just scrapes." They were almost at the house now. "Ben, for God's sake, I'm fine."

He didn't stop until he'd carried her into her bathroom and set her butt on the counter. Rifling through her cabinets, he wet a washcloth and proceeded to clean the dirt out of her cut knee.

"Ouch!"

Still silent, he hit the spots with first-aid spray.

Gritting her teeth, she glared at him. "Double ouch."

He didn't speak as he covered the abrasions with bandages, but his fingers lingered on her skin, her first real sign of any softening in him. She stared up at his granite features and remembered what Melanie had said about Ben resenting being here. His anger would certainly reflect that, she supposed...but in spite of his intense silence, she didn't feel his resentment. No, what she felt was far more devastating. She felt his fear, his palatable fear. And guilt. The last broke her heart. "Ben...thank you."

His thumb stroked over her jaw, removing a smudge of dirt there, and something in his eyes softened. "You're the most stubborn person I've ever met, you know that?"

"You've mentioned." And suddenly, she felt his searing hunger as well, an unfed passion.

From deep within her came an answering hunger, an answering passion. Even knowing this was temporary, that he'd be gone soon enough, she felt it. It consumed her, even as it terrified her. "If I'm the most stubborn person ever, where does that leave you?"

In a move that seemed to surprise him as much as it did her, he leaned in and touched his lips to hers. "It leaves me frustrated as hell, babe." He scooped her up again and carried her to her bed, where he stood back and shoved his hands in his pockets as if he didn't quite trust them. "Now, be good and stay there. Stay right there while I walk away."

"Ben—"

"I'm walking away, Rachel," he said hoarsely. "No matter what I see in your eyes. I have to." And without another word, he turned and did exactly that.

For a week, Ben felt like he was on pins and needles. It was too busy in the city, too crowded. He was angry at his own inability to keep his emotions in check, but he couldn't admit that to anyone, especially the woman who hadn't chosen to have him here in the first place.

Being with Rachel was breaking his resolve to keep an emotional distance. Watching her struggle to put meaning to her life, seeing her be a mom to his daughter, it was bringing it all back, why he'd fallen for her in the first place. She'd always made him want to be a better man, and that hadn't changed.

God, he needed to go. The desperation to do just that was nearly as strong as when he'd been a young boy trapped in this same town.

Eventually, he promised himself. Eventually it would end. The authorities had assured him just today that they honestly believed Asada had gone underground and didn't plan to resurface. If that was true, Ben could go, and soon. Knowing that, he spent time with Emily, taking her to breakfast every morning before personally dropping her off at school, before making her promise to get directly on the bus afterward, where he'd be waiting for her at home. This always made her roll her eyes, but he could tell it pleased her. It pleased him too, oddly enough, doing what he'd imagined were mundane things with his own flesh and blood. But he truly enjoyed her company and, while Emily appeared to feel the same, she still carried her laptop everywhere, still referred to her online buddy Alicia as her only real friend.

When he wasn't writing, he took pictures, mostly to entertain himself. He continued to play basketball every day at lunch, keeping one eye on the house where he knew Rachel sat in her studio, chasing her own demons.

Today he came back inside, sweaty and exhausted, his mind still overcharged. He knew Rachel had gone to a late breakfast with Adam, who would then take her to the doctor's appointment Ben had wanted to take her to. He made a face as he went up to the stairs. Immature of him, but there it was. Pulling off his shirt, he strode toward his bedroom, passing Rachel's…and stopping so short he nearly plowed into the wall.

She sat on her bed in nothing but two towels, one around her head, the other around her body. Her damp body.

Galvanized by the sight, he didn't move. "I thought you were with Adam." Horror struck him. "He's not in your shower?"

She let out a short laugh. "No. He went to his office to get my files. I've…been in my studio."

"Working?"

"Still not making much progress in that area."

*Run,* his head told him. *Run like hell and never look back.*

Instead his feet, directed by the part of his body in charge—and it wasn't his brain—took him to the foot of her bed, where he looked her over hungrily, broodingly, wondering where exactly she and the good Adam stood, and wishing he didn't care. Then all of those thoughts flew out of his head as... "Your leg and arm casts are off."

She lifted the named body parts with a little smile. They were thin and white and shaking from exertion, but she looked so proud he felt his heart swell inside his chest.

"What do you think?" she asked.

"What do I think?" That he wanted her so badly he was the one trembling. That he was shocked at the ferocity of that wanting, and that he was terrified it had gathered even more strength this time around.

Once upon a time he'd loved her—wildly, fiercely, with everything he had.

He couldn't allow it to happen again. He couldn't. but he was terrified the matter had been taken out of his hands. Slowly, he pulled her to her feet. It was driving him crazy, having her so close yet so far. Tired of that distance, he actually reached for the towel around her, with some half-baked idea of yanking it off, tackling her down to the bed and reminding her how good it could be to toss their differences right out the window, if only for a few moments.

He felt her start to melt against him, and she wasn't the only one. He was melting, too. He had his fingers curled in the front of her towel between her two lush, warm breasts, when she slowly shook her head. "Ben, we can't do this."

"Speak for yourself."

"Okay, fine. *I* can't do this." She took a big step back and he suspected an even bigger mental one. "I have a meeting with Adam in twenty minutes."

"Ah." He nodded. "Right. This wasn't on your day planner for today. Probably because it's an unscheduled emotion, right? I know how you hate those." Feeling nasty, feeling mean, feeling frustrated and hard and horny as hell, Ben stepped back, too. And right out of the room.

If only he could get her out of his head so easily.

*Dangerously caged*, that's what he felt after a month and a half in South Village. Dangerously caged and brooding, not a good combination.

He took a good, long hot shower, then grabbed his camera bag and headed to the downstairs bathroom, where he had set up his darkroom. He'd lose himself in developing film.

But that turned out to be a farce too, because when his pictures came to life on paper, they were of Rachel sitting at her drawing table, looking as hauntingly beautiful as ever.

And as tortured as he.

# CHAPTER FOURTEEN

HER NEXT FREE Saturday morning, Melanie drove back to South Village. She told herself she was entitled to two days away, that she wanted to see for herself how Rachel was doing and wanted to hang out with Emily. *Girl time,* she told herself. She needed family girl time.

Lies.

She wanted to see if Garrett glanced at her. It was a matter of pride now, as she hated how much she thought about him. She had no idea why it had been over between them New Year's Eve before she'd even gotten her panties back on.

Maybe she just needed sex.

She needed sex.

Her sister did not. She never had. In fact, it seemed bitterly unfair that it was possible Rachel, her almost virginal sister, was getting it on with one of the sexiest men alive, while Mel churned and burned.

Garrett wasn't out front when she parked. Fine. Good. She didn't need to see him anyway.

She let herself in Rachel's house.

Given the tense silence she found between Rachel and Ben when she entered the kitchen, she figured they couldn't have done it yet. Not with her sister acting as tightly self-controlled as ever. God forbid she allow anything as mundane as lust to shatter that control.

Or had she?

Melanie took a good hard second look and found herself dumbstruck. Appeared that the reason for the so-thick-she-could-cut-it tension in the room most positively wasn't temper after all.

Yes, Rachel had two high spots of color on her cheeks, but she wasn't meeting anyone's eye. A sure sign of guilt if anything, and Mel should know. Furthermore, her sister's blouse wasn't tucked in, a huge fashion no-no in Rachel's book—and the bandanna on her head looked slightly askance, revealing short, spiky strands of blond hair going in every direction.

Hmm.

Ben himself was no better off. His shirt hung open, though he'd hastily buttoned it when Melanie had entered. His hair had either been attacked by migrating birds or a set of hungry fingers.

*Double hmm.* "Don't tell me you two have forgotten how badly things turned out last time," she said into the silence.

Rachel closed her eyes. "Melanie."

"Well, they did! You guys were over the moon about each other." She pointed to Ben. "But when she said go, you did. And you..." She looked at Rachel. "You let him. Hello, people...what does that tell you? That you aren't meant to be, okay? I mean, why be stupid enough to try again? Especially when you're only together due to a madman on the loose."

A muscle in Ben's jaw ticked, which was really sexy as hell, damn him. "You told her," he said to Rachel.

"I had to." Using her cane, Rachel headed for the door, nearly plowing over the tall, yummy neighbor standing there looking extremely sorry to be doing so.

Mel's heart drummed against her ribs, but she plastered a bored smile on her face. Garrett held out a stack of mail to Rachel. "I'm sorry to intrude," he said softly.

"You're not intruding." Rachel tossed the mail to the table. "Not at all, but if you'll excuse me—" Without waiting for an answer, she vanished.

Ben shot Melanie a long, talk-to-you-about-this-later look that made her feel about five years old, and followed Rachel out.

Which left Garrett standing there alone—tall, dark, brooding. And yummy. What would he say? They hadn't spoken much since their hot, animalistic tryst, and never about what had happened between them. But they also hadn't been alone in all this time.

They were now. Would he bring it up? Or maybe reach for her with those sensual hands, and—

"Why did you do that?" he demanded in a harsh whisper. "Bringing up the past, *their* past, like it's any of your business?"

Shocked at his accusatory, furious tone, she laughed, but Garrett didn't even crack a smile in return so hers slowly faded. "My sister's past *is* my business."

He pushed away from the doorway and moved across the room with grace and strength unusual in a man so tall. That she knew exactly how graceful and strong he was in minute detail, really burned.

"Not when you're being purposely hurtful, it isn't," he said.

"I wasn't." She watched him reach into the cupboard for a mug, then pour coffee into it as if he belonged here.

She knew her sister considered him a good friend, but that she'd never managed that kind of relationship with him bugged the hell out of her. Was she such a bad person? And she resented how at home *he* was in Rachel's house, all while acting as if the two of them hadn't once been naked and wild together. "Not that I should have to explain myself to you," she added, her words coming to an awkward halt when he handed her the steaming mug of coffee. She stared down at the drink.

"Don't you like coffee?"

They were fighting, she thought, confused, and yet...he'd offered her a drink. Oh, wait. She got it. He wanted her again.

But nothing in his dark-blue eyes suggested sexual invitation.

What was wrong with him anyway? Men were always thinking about sex, always planning their next conquest.

Weren't they?

"It's not poisonous," he said lightly, while she continued to look suspiciously into the mug.

"I take sugar and milk."

Silently he doctored the mug, then poured himself his own. Black.

"I care about my sister," she said a bit too defensively when he just looked at her. "I don't want to see her hurt again."

"If you care about her as you say, then you'd see that she's glowing, *glowing,* for the first time in far too long."

He let her stew about that while he drank. In his big hands the mug looked so small, so dainty, and she got sidetracked remembering how small and dainty she'd felt in his arms. How warm and safe. Damn him.

"I think it's clear she's glowing because of Ben," Garrett said. "So excuse me if I'm being too forthright for you, but wanting to destroy that doesn't seem like a caring, sisterly thing to do."

She stared at him. A dentist. A *nobody*. "Did you just call me a bad sister?"

Considering, he drank some more coffee. "Do you really care what I think?"

She didn't face such blunt honesty often. Her boss was never honest, her co-workers far more interested in furthering their careers than being truthful. She didn't have a lot of close friends…okay, she had no close friends. As for her lovers, she was rarely up-front with them, or them with her, for that matter. "Look…"

"Garrett," he reminded her, a little smile playing around his lips.

She knew his damn name! "You know what? You're right, I don't care what you think of me."

"Then you won't care that I think you're trying to get between them for purely selfish reasons."

Melanie stared at him. How often did a man talk to her so…so openly? Certainly, she'd never been called on the carpet like this, and she had to say it was shockingly…arousing. He wasn't going to lie, he wasn't going to bullshit.

Oh, man. She wanted him again. She really did. And she wasn't the sort to deny herself. With a toss of her hair she smiled. "You think you know it all, don't you? Well, isn't it your lucky day."

He cocked a brow. "Really? Why?"

"Because it just so happens I like a guy who knows it all."

A little smile curved his lips. "Is that right?"

Oh, yeah. Males were so pathetically easy. Thank God.

He nodded once, agreeably, and…turned away? He went to the sink and washed out his mug, replacing it in the cupboard before heading toward the door.

Melanie watched the lines of his sleek back, his nice tight ass, and was reminded that his body made her mouth water.

But he was still walking away from her. "Garrett?"

"Not this time, Melanie."

She couldn't have heard him correctly. "Um... what?"

"A one-night stand isn't going to be enough for me. Not with you. If you ever want more, you know where I live." Then the cocky bastard walked out on her.

ON MONDAY, Ben picked Emily up from school. He liked to do that when he didn't have to get Rachel to a doctor's appointment or if he wasn't busy taking pictures or writing. He liked picking her up in person, if only to spend an extra twenty minutes a day with her. In the car with him was the wriggling Patches pacing the passenger seat, waiting hopefully for the center of her universe to join them.

The middle school sat on a relatively quiet street of South Village, and like so many others it was a historical building. It had been one of the first schools built here in the late 1800s, though it'd been redone three times due to fires. Now a brick building with white trim, mock verandas and vines crawling up the sides, it seemed like a place out of time. Ben might have sat there in 1890 in his horse and buggy waiting for his daughter.

But then the bell rang, and kids—all pierced and dyed, wearing hip-huggers, bell-bottoms and leather, carrying laptops and cell phones—emerged from the building in droves. He had to laugh at himself, as his daughter was right in the middle of them, looking decidedly twenty-first century.

She walked out alone, but halfway down the path, someone called out to her.

Ben tensed when he saw it was a boy about her age. He wore jeans and a plain T-shirt—nothing tattooed, torn or slashed. A normal kid. He said something to Emily, to which he got a shrug as a response. After a few more moments of trying, he gave up.

Emily kept walking.

The boy watched her go with an expression on his face Ben knew all too well. Rejection. Not knowing a thing about the kid, Ben's empathies were firmly in his court.

Emily, oblivious to the heartbreak behind her, looked up and saw Patches waiting for her. With a squeal, she tossed her backpack into the car and followed it in, grabbing the puppy and hugging her close. A love fest ensued, with lots of girl smiles and puppy kisses.

"Hey, sweetness." Ben knew better than to lean in for his own kiss. Public displays of affection were equivalent to the torture rack for twelve-going-on-thirty-year-olds. "Don't look now, but he's still looking."

She rubbed noses with the puppy. "Who?"

"The boy you were talking to."

Horror crossed her face. "You were watching me?"

"No, I was waiting for you."

Given her expression, she didn't see the difference. "Dad, just drive away. Quick!"

But he couldn't drive away. The street had come to a standstill, thanks to an accident in the intersection one hundred yards ahead. "We're not going anywhere." He turned off the engine. Since they were still at the curb, he pocketed his keys and got out of the car.

"Dad!"

Walking around, he opened her door. "Want to show me your classroom?"

"No! I can't!"

"Can't what?"

"I can't walk around with you at my school!"

"Why not? Hey, let's take some pictures. You've been wanting to learn how to use my camera, right?"

"Yeah."

"Well, now's a perfect time. We have a captive audience." He clipped a leash on Patches. Grabbing his camera, he tugged his daughter free of the car and handed her the leash.

On the grass around the front of school sat hundreds of kids, waiting for their rides, socializing, reading, talking, with a few even studying. A perfect place for a man fascinated by people and the way they looked through his lens.

"*Dad!*"

He'd started walking and grinned—wisely with his back to his daughter—when he heard her and the puppy scramble to keep up with him.

There were a group of cheerleaders on the grass practicing. On the steps sat four guys disagreeing about some game they'd seen that night before on television. Kids of every size and color, all doing their own thing, walked the path. Feeling lighthearted for no reason other than he had his daughter with him, Ben started snapping shots, explaining to Emily why he focused on certain things as he went. They'd been at it ten minutes when a man in a suit stood at the double doors to the school, squinting at him.

"Excuse me," the man called. "What are you doing?"

"Taking pictures." Ben hoisted the camera.

The man squinted some more in disapproval that wasn't anything new for Ben, but then suddenly he blinked. "Ben? Ben Asher?"

While Ben just looked at him, wondering who the hell knew him and why, the man grinned and thrust out his hand. "Ritchie Atchison."

"Ritchie." High school. Skinny runt with an even lower profile than Ben had had.

"Yep." Ritchie, balding and wearing reading glasses, laughed. "It's me. I'm principal of this joint. What do you think of that?"

"That you moved up from The Tracks."

Ritchie laughed again and slapped him on the back. "You know it. Now I'm torturing the kids of the kids who tortured me." He sighed in bliss. "Nothing better than that. So…I've enjoyed your articles and pictures over the years. You hit it big. What are you doing taking pictures here?"

"I'm Emily's father." He put his hand on Emily's shoulder, wanting to grin when he felt her tense. Oh, yeah, he'd definitely turned into a dad, one who was talking to the enemy. "Traffic isn't moving so I thought she could show me around."

Ritchie nodded to his camera. "Maybe you'll share some of those with our yearbook committee. For old times' sake."

Ben didn't do anything for old times' sake, but he did love taking pictures, and the kids lounging around spitting attitude and spunk drew him. He glanced at Emily, who was saying don't-you-dare with her eyes. He grinned.

She shook her head and narrowed her eyes at him.

"Love to," he said in tune to her loud sigh, which he

ignored. "Here, hold this, sweetness," and handed her his light meter.

Over the next hour she became his apprentice assistant. She started out silent, resentment pouring off her in palpable waves, but he kept asking her to hand him something, or her opinion on which shot to get, so she had no choice but to get involved.

"What do you think about them, Em? Should we grab the pic?" He pointed to a couple sitting side by side, nose to nose, lips to lips. Had he ever been that love-struck?

Oh, yeah, he had.

"They were homecoming queen and king," she said. "He helped me reach a book in the library once."

"So, let's give them a shot at fame and fortune." He took the picture to Emily's smile.

God, he loved her smile. Wished she'd always smile.

Startled at the click of the camera, the couple looked up. He waved. When they waved back, Emily groaned. "Dad—"

"Look," he said. A group of basketball players in jerseys sat on the brick planter, huddled over what looked like a play book. He moved closer, tugging Emily with him. She still held Patches, who let out one "hello" bark.

"I'm taking people shots for the yearbook today," Ben told them, and lifted his camera. "Picture?"

They tossed their arms around each other and yelled "Cheese," hamming while he snapped a handful of shots.

"Uh, excuse me?"

He and Emily both turned and faced a tall, gangly kid who nodded toward a group sitting on the grass. "Chess Club. Can you get us, too?"

Ben looked at Emily. "What do you think?"

She bit her lip and looked over at the group, where the boy who'd tried talking to her earlier sat. He looked up at her. Smiled.

Emily went beet red. "Your call."

"Nope. It's an assistant call."

The gangly kid looked at Emily with new respect. "Emily? Please?"

She hadn't taken her eyes off the boy. "Okay," she whispered.

"So…" Ben leaned in. "What's his name?"

"Who?"

He laughed. "You know who."

"Oh. He's Van."

"Should we get him in the picture?"

"I don't care."

"*Em*. Should we get him in a picture?"

"Yeah." Then she giggled. *Giggled*. His heart lit at the sound.

By the end of the next hour, Ben had used up eight rolls of film, the kids were in hog heaven, and Emily had been transformed into Lady Popular and looking at Ben with hero worship. He loved that she'd come out of her shell a bit, which had been his goal. He loved that he'd brought joy to a few kids with nothing more than his camera.

But the hero thing… He was no hero and never would be. He brooded over that on the drive back. "Em…" He turned down their street and by some miracle got a spot out front of the house. He stared up at the red brick and felt the noose tighten around his neck. "Your mom is getting better every day."

"Yeah."

"Soon she'll be without the cane entirely."

"Her hair is still short."

"That's not exactly a handicap, Em."

She turned to him, a surprising resentment in every line of her body. "You want to go."

Beneath the resentment was hurt; he'd be an idiot not to see it. Damn it. How was it he could be nearly thirty-one years old and still be such an idiot? "I don't live here, sweetness. You know that."

"I hate her!"

Ben blinked. The intricate workings of a twelve-year-old mind had completely escaped him. "What? You hate who?"

"Mom! She's making you want to leave! I hate her!" She grabbed Patches and slammed out of the car, running up the walk.

God, how had he managed to screw *this* up? Ben ran after her and the puppy. "Em, wait." Of course she didn't, and by the time he caught up with her, she'd run up the circular staircase, and was heading straight for Rachel's studio. "Hold on a sec," he said, catching her shoulders. "Hold on. We need to talk about this."

"Why?" She set down Patches and took off her leash. "You're not doing anything wrong, *she* is."

"No—"

"It's true, Dad." She straightened. "You came here, you've done everything you needed to do, and all she's done is shove you away at every turn and make you want to go—"

The studio door opened to a pale Rachel. She looked at Emily. "I'm guessing you have something to say to me."

"Yeah." A sullen expression replaced Emily's earnest one. "Dad wants to go away and it's all your fault.

You make it obvious he doesn't really live here, that he has to go the minute you're better.''

"There are circumstances you don't understand—"

"I understand! You're selfish and mean and I hate you!"

Rachel drew back. "Well. That's new."

"I mean it!" But Emily's eyes were wide and filled with tears. "I hate you."

"Em—" Ben's heart pinched at the look on Rachel's face, but she held up a hand halting his words.

"Let her finish."

"That's all. That's all I have to say." Emily crossed her arms over her chest. She added a shaky little hitch of breath. Ben guessed she was one beat away from meltdown.

"Okay, one thing at a time." Rachel drew a shaky breath. "You know your dad doesn't live here, you also know he has to go back at some point. If he wants to go now, there's nothing holding him here."

"But there is," Emily cried. "Me. *I'm* holding him here!"

Ben's throat went tight. "You know I love you, Em, but it's true. I don't live here. I have to go."

"But why? I'm here. What else could you want?"

Ben took her hand and tugged her closer, then cupped her soft, sweet, hurting face. "Yes, you're here, which makes this house one of my very favorite places. But I'll see you. I'll call you."

"That's not how a real family works."

"Not all families live together, you know that. And you're old enough to understand why."

"Because Mom doesn't love you."

Yeah. Rachel didn't love him. Hadn't that always been the problem? "As your mother said, there are circumstances you don't understand, and no, we're not going to explain them to you. But one thing I can and will tell you, Emily Anne, is that the way you talked to your mother just now is unacceptable—''

"Ben—"

Now he held up his hand to halt Rachel's words. "It's okay to be mad at someone you love," he said quietly to a now sobbing Emily. "But it's not okay to be cruel."

Emily buried her chest in Ben's chest and unable to do anything else, he wrapped his arms around her. Putting his mouth to her ear, he whispered, "I love you. Your mom loves you. You have it pretty good right there, Em, trust me. I'm sorry we can't give you the rest."

She squeezed him so hard she nearly stole the life right out of him, and he closed his eyes as he listened to her cry, his daughter, his blood, his only family, the best part of his heart.

Then she pulled back, sniffed, and shoved her hands into her pockets. Looking at her toes, she said to Rachel, "I'm sorry I said I hate you. I don't, not really." Then she took off running toward her bedroom.

The door slammed hard enough to rattle the windows.

Patches whined.

Ben let out a shaky breath. "Whew. Twelve is fun, huh?"

Rachel stared down the hallway for a long moment. "If you've truly got one foot out the door already," she said quietly. "Then get the rest of the way out."

"Rachel—"

"No more buts, Ben, this is killing us. Killing all of us. I understand the *possible* threat of Asada—"

"He's more than a possible threat."

"We both know that threat lessens every day that

passes. Yes, there's Emily, and obviously she wants you to stay, but we both know that isn't going to happen.''

"We're...bonding," he said, feeling oddly desperate.

"So finish bonding."

"I don't know how to tell her I'm going." He felt bare, stripped down to the soul.

"She already knows."

"She's hurting." *I'm hurting.* "She's only twelve."

"She more mature than you give her credit for. Tell her. Tell her soon."

"Rach—"

"Dragging it out, Ben? How unlike you."

Yeah. He probably deserved that. "I need a little more time."

"Fine. A little more time. Take it. Then go, just go." And with as much grace as ever, she walked away.

A headache started right between Ben's eyes.

The puppy watched her go and let out a pathetic little whimper.

He scooped her up and got himself licked across the mouth for his effort.

*Just go, Ben.*

How many times had he heard that now? Damn it, he never stayed where he wasn't wanted.

Never.

Patches whined again, more softly now. "Yeah," he whispered, holding her close. "I know the feeling."

# CHAPTER FIFTEEN

ONE NIGHT shortly after Emily's blowup they played Scrabble, just the three of them. Rachel sat on the couch in the living room, with Emily and Ben on the floor around the coffee table. Patches lay asleep on Ben's feet.

Emily, tongue between her teeth, holding back a smile, carefully laid down the letters *D-A-D*, then beamed at Ben.

With a grin, he added the *D-Y*, making the word *daddy*.

Rachel looked down at her letters, the ones that seemed to dance around and mock her with their uselessness. "How come I always lose at this game?" she asked as she put *E-S* to Ben's *Y*, making the word *yes*.. "Woo-hoo, look at me get the points."

"It's all in your attitude," Ben said.

Emily nodded in agreement and used the *S* in *yes* to spell *bestest*.

"That's not a word," Rachel protested.

"See, negative attitude." Emily tsked and added up her points.

Ben laughed. "Sweetness, are you cheating?"

"She always cheats." Rachel glared at her daughter. "It's why she always wins."

"Fine." Emily took away the *E-S-T* and left *best*. "Happy?"

"I will be if I win," Rachel teased.

Ben sprawled on the floor and smiled up at her. Beside him, Emily was positively glowing, happier than Rachel had seen her in a while.

The moment was so good, so bittersweet, she wanted to freeze-frame it. A perfect snapshot in time, with everyone's hearts light and happy.

Ben cocked his head, then sat up and put a hand on Rachel's arm, looking into her eyes. "You okay?"

"I am," she said, and it'd never been more true. "I really am."

He smiled again, and went back to the game.

But left his hand on her arm.

AT THE END of the week, Ben was still there and Rachel didn't know whether she was sorry or relieved. They'd had coffee together every morning. Lunch, too, at the house if she didn't have a therapist or doctor appointment, or at a café if she did. They had dinner together as well, with Emily, the three of them somehow finding things to talk about.

Or argue about.

But things were never dull. She'd gotten rather used to his presence, shockingly enough, to listening to him talk, laugh, watching his tall, lean form play basketball as if he were sheer poetry in motion, hearing him mutter to himself in his darkroom, seeing him with Emily. Every part of having him live in the house was both a comfort and a nightmare.

When he left, her life would go back to "normal," to what she'd built for herself and Emily, and it was a great life. She had her daughter, her house, her career…well, maybe not her career, but even so, she had no real regrets.

And yet, when it came to personal relationships…

she'd be alone. She was alone now, no doubt. But with Ben's presence she could almost imagine how it would be if he ever settled down and stayed in one place.

The weekend arrived, and per her usual Saturday morning routine, she sat in the kitchen with a cup of tea and the newspaper. Her leg ached today, so she had it elevated with cool packs. She sat there telling herself it was okay with her that Ben had managed to get her lazy daughter out of the house at dawn for a hike.

She told herself she enjoyed the peace and quiet of the empty house, but the truth was…she would have enjoyed the hike more.

Even if she didn't have the strength for it.

But neither of them had asked. She held her cup of tea and looked around her, as always in quiet moments like this, experienced some lingering uneasiness about Asada. She hated that she still felt the urge to peek over her shoulder, and chastised herself for her paranoia.

The FBI had reassured them over and over that with every passing day their chances increased that Asada wasn't ever going to make a move. Which meant Ben was in all likelihood free of any obligation.

A good thing, Rachel decided. A very good thing.

Suddenly the door opened and Melanie bounced into the kitchen with unaccustomed energy for a Saturday morning. Shocked, Rachel stared at her. "Hey."

"Hey." Mel tossed her keys on the table and plopped herself down. She was made up and dressed to kill with a leather skirt, halter top and do-me heels. "Thought I'd visit."

Rachel eyed the difference between the two of them— she in her loose, gauzy, shapeless sundress, hair undoubtedly wild, feet bare, no makeup—and had to laugh at the two extremes. "Last I checked, it was a Saturday. A day you traditionally reserve for sleeping past noon, getting a manicure and catching a movie."

"Oh. Well, maybe I'm all movied out."

"Uh-huh." Rachel narrowed her eyes. "What are you really up to, Mel?"

"Me?" Mel dumped three tablespoons of sugar into her tea, then after a moment's hesitation, went back for a fourth. "Just wanted to see how you're doing, that's all."

"You just saw me last weekend, plus you called three times this week." Rachel cupped her fingers around her tea, still needing to be warm all the time in order not to stiffen up. Her life had forever changed, there was no doubt of that, but she refused to let others change their lives because of what had happened to her. Leaning in, she put a hand over her sister's. "Mel, you don't have to give up your life for this. For me. I'm doing fine."

Her sister shrugged. "Maybe I don't believe you."

"Why?" Rachel had to smile as she lifted her arms. "Don't I look fabulous?"

"No." Mel didn't smile to soften the blunt word. "You look miserable. Like you're hurting, and I don't mean physically."

"That's ridiculous." Rachel stared down into her tea and lied. "I don't know what you're talking about."

"Yeah, that's because we're discussing you. If we were tearing apart *my* life, which we've done often enough, then you'd know exactly what I was talking about."

"Mel—"

"Look, I know I'm a screwup, but I don't expect it of you."

"And just what am I supposedly screwing up?"

"Seen Adam much lately?"

"A little."

"Because of his busy schedule?"

"Uh…no."

"Because you've been ignoring him?"

Rachel looked at her fingers. Specifically her fingernails. Which were ragged and hadn't seen a nail file or polish in months.

"You know, before the accident, I'd have sworn you were this close to sleeping with him." Mel held up fingers only an inch apart. "Maybe even considering marrying him."

"The accident changed everything."

"The accident did…or Ben?"

Rachel's gaze jerked up to Mel's before she could stop herself. "Don't be ridiculous."

"Is it ridiculous that you never sleep with anyone? Is it ridiculous that if you did, you'd fake an orgasm rather than tell them they're totally inept with the female anatomy…or that you can't seem to relinquish that last little bit of control?"

"Mel—"

"Admit it, sis. You don't know how to let someone be that close to you."

"Like *you* know!"

"Hey, I know how to climax." A smug smile crossed her well-glossed mouth. "Often." She flashed a look to the man who'd just let himself in and was now leaning back with lazy ease against the doorjamb, unabashedly eavesdropping on what Rachel figured to be her most embarrassing moment. She wanted to crawl in a hole and die— Right after she killed Melanie. "Where's Emily?" she asked, striving for cool, calm and collected.

"Bathing Patches, who seems to have a thing for

jumping in puddles." With a wry smile, Ben lifted his leg to examine the bottom of his jeans, which were mud splattered. Then he leveled Rachel with one of those classic Ben looks that made her pulse scramble and her skin feel too tight. "Don't let me interrupt."

"To not interrupt you'd have to be on the other side of the closed door," Rachel muttered.

Melanie grinned. "Talking sex makes her grumpy."

"Not me," Ben offered.

And Mel, still grinning, nodded. "Me, either. So Ben...we're taking a survey...do you ever fake your orgasms?"

"No, ma'am."

"Me, either." Melanie cocked her head. "It just seems like if someone was going to fake it...then they'd fake it the other way. You know, like they *didn't* get one."

Given Ben's wide grin, he agreed.

"That way, you'd get another," Mel reasoned. "Maybe even two, depending on how fast you can come."

"I'm with you." Ben looked at Rachel and the temperature shot up in the room to boiling point. "Orgasms are good."

Melanie laughed. *Laughed.* "Yeah. Well, if Ms. Prude here would get off her duff and call Adam over here, maybe she'd figure it out."

Ben's smile faded at that.

Not noticing, or maybe not caring, Mel jumped down off the counter and headed for the door.

"Where are you going?" Rachel demanded of her sister.

"Off to watch my niece bathe a puppy. Don't do anything I wouldn't, sis." A sly smile crept over her features. "Oh wait…I don't have to tell you that, you won't do *anything*."

"Come back here—" She let out a breath when Mel let the door shut behind her. "Traitor."

Ben sauntered his way toward her. "Interesting topic of conversation." He walked around the back of her, trailing a finger over her shoulder and bringing a set of goose bumps to the surface of her skin. "Orgasms."

Did that require a response? Suddenly, she could hardly breathe, much less think of a brilliant way out of this particular topic. "H-how was your hike?"

"Fun." Then he leaned in over her shoulder, putting his mouth right beneath her ear, against the sensitive skin there. "Is it true, Rach?"

"Is wh-what true?"

His breath was soft and warm against her skin, his jaw rough with a day's old growth. The contrast liquefied her bones. "Do you fake your orgasms with your lovers?"

"I—" His fingers trailed upward, over the back of her neck and she fought to keep her eyes open.

"Rachel?"

She closed her mouth. "I don't want to discuss this with you."

"I bet you don't." Shifting around so that they were face-to-face, he ran a finger over her cheek. "So let's cut to the chase."

"Ben—"

His hand slid around the back of her neck to cup her head, holding her gaze steady with his. "Did you fake with me?"

Trying to pull away did no good, he was strong and, though his hold was gentle, he couldn't be budged. "We were seventeen!" she said, exasperated on all counts.

"We had no particular skills in that area and you know it."

He brought their faces even closer together. "I did the best I could back then, but yeah, we were young. Young and inexperienced. I'm sorry if I wasn't any good for you."

Remembering what they'd shared brought a flush to her cheeks. Truth was, inexperienced or not, it stood unrivaled to this very day as the hottest, most erotic, most touching experience of her life.

And he was apologizing for it.

"But I promise you," he said softly, still holding her gaze prisoner. "If you sleep with me now, I'd prove there's no need to fake anything."

She stared at his mouth, wide and firm, and yet she had reason to know it felt soft and tasted like pure heaven.

"Rach...?"

She actually leaned toward that low, sexy voice making promises she thought she just might be interested in. Then she thought of the actual physical action required to do what he was suggesting.

He'd get naked. No problem there.

Then she'd have to get naked—big problem there. He was perfection, and she... "No."

Ben let out a soft, rude noise and dared her with both his eyes and his voice. "Chicken," he taunted softly.

"Just being realistic."

Another man would have conceded defeat and walked away. Another man would have hidden his thoughts.

Ben stood there, right there, only inches away, and let her see everything he felt. Annoyance. Heat. Frustration. *Heat.* "You're really not going let me prove it?"

"No." She looked away. "I'm not interested."

"Ten minutes," he promised silkily. "I could rock your world in ten minutes."

"Go away, Ben."

No big surprise, he did.

BEN SHOVED OUT the front door, slowing down only to lock it behind him. Asada was long gone, everyone kept telling him that, but he couldn't break the old habit of watching his back.

And Emily's.

And Rachel's. Damn her.

She'd kicked him out. Nothing new. Stepping out the front gate, he joined the early Saturday morning shoppers, of which there were many, and lost himself in the streets. They were as different from the mean, hustling, dangerous streets he'd gotten used to as they could get. These were clean and tantalized with mouthwatering scents from the cafés. They were busy, but also easygoing and safe. No need for this terrible tension and aggression, and no outlet for those feelings, either.

Stalking along, blindly window-shopping, he was torn between wishing he was on the other side of the world, and wishing Rachel would have let him fulfill his promise. It would kill them both, of course, being together like that again. Or at least it would kill *him*, but—

"Ben!"

Oh, and now he was hearing things. Rachel's soft voice above the crowd. As if she'd be chasing him down, as if she could—

"Ben, wait!"

Whipping around, he stopped short in shock. Rachel, in her loose, gauzy sundress and sandals, using her cane as she chased him down at an alarming speed. She was going to stumble and take a fall, was his first heart-stopping thought.

She looked frantic to catch him. Him, Ben Asher, the man she'd just shoved out her door.

"I'm sorry," she rushed, still coming at him. When she was within two feet, he held out his arms, completely without thought.

She walked right into them and fit like she belonged there.

At the slight tightening of his arms and his lack of smile, hers faded. She swallowed hard. "Oh, Ben."

The two words spoke volumes and yet didn't tell him a thing. "Did you want to finish talking about orgasms?" he asked a little hoarsely.

A woman walking by, arms loaded with shopping bags, looked over with a lifted eyebrow.

"Uh, no." Rachel smiled apologetically at the woman. "I was hoping we could talk about...other stuff."

"I'd rather give you an orgasm."

This time it was a man walking his hundred-pound Saint Bernard who overheard, and he shot them a comical second glance while Rachel closed her eyes. "*Talk,* Ben. Can we talk?"

"If that's all you've got."

"That's all you're getting." She pointed to a sidewalk café a few buildings down. "Hungry?"

*For you.* "Sure."

When they were seated, Rachel ordered an iced tea, set her menu aside, and looked at him across the table.

"What?"

"Don't brood."

"Why would I brood?"

"I don't know."

He nodded. "Are you sleeping with Adam?"

She sighed.

His heart kicked once, hard. "Are you?"

"You have such a one-track mind."

"*Are you?*"

"You know that's none of your business."

He answered with a very impolite one-word expletive and she sighed again. "No, I'm not sleeping with Adam."

She wasn't sleeping with Adam. Thank God. "You're right," he said primly, folding his hands. "It's none of my business."

Across the table, she groaned and cupped her face in her hands. "You're such a jerk," she said, muffled.

"Yeah, it's a special talent of mine." He took in her confusion, and disgust filled him. *Self* disgust. What right did he have to want her single?

It was possible that by this time next week he'd be gone, so far gone.

The waitress brought the iced teas. To keep them there, at the same table, talking, even if the air was filled with tension, Ben ordered a large brunch.

"Tell me something," Rachel said, playing with her straw. "What are you in such a hurry to get back to?"

"A personal question, Rach?"

She put lemon and sugar in her iced tea. Took a sip. Pushed the drink aside and looked right into his eyes. "Yes. Maybe it's because I'm older. More mellow—" She glared when he laughed. "I am," she insisted, and lifted a shoulder. "I'd really like to know. Tell me why you can't stand being tied to one place for longer than it takes to do a load of laundry, when there's no place in particular even waiting for you. No place and no one."

"Hey, I've done my laundry here. Quite a few times. I've even done *your* laundry. I like your pale-peach satin panties, by the way, and that black lace bra…"

She rolled her eyes. "You know what I mean."

Yeah. Yeah, he did. And because her curiosity was honest and not bitter, because she obviously really wanted to know, he found he could try to admit some of what he thought of as his secret shame, the one thing he'd never told another soul. "Staying in one spot, making roots…it infers you've found your home, found yourself."

"Yes," she agreed.

"But I don't even know who I really am. I can't seem to find myself."

She sat back, looking a little stunned. "But you know who you are."

"Who I am is a man with no idea who his parents were or where I came from."

Her eyes softened. "I didn't know that."

"Because I never told you. I couldn't."

"Oh, Ben. Were you always in a foster home?"

"Yes. It was 'Christian duty.' They liked to say that."

"That's so wrong!" Her voice was thick, emotional. "No child should ever feel that they weren't wanted. I hate that for you."

"Don't," he said a bit harshly, unable to take her pity. "I'm just trying to explain."

"You were never given any information about your past at all?"

He downed half his glass of tea for his suddenly parched throat. "All I know is that when I was about two days old, I was found in a trash bin in Los Angeles, nearly dead of exposure and starvation."

She covered her mouth with her fingers, fingers that

shook, he noted. No, it wasn't a pretty story, but she'd asked. "So yeah, I always knew I belonged nowhere, with no one."

"How cruel! How could a foster parent, someone trusted with a child, do that? Make you feel that way?" she cried.

"Hey. Hey, it doesn't matter now," he said, a little surprised, and touched, at the tears shimmering in her eyes. He put a hand over hers. "I'm trying to make you understand, that's all. Why I don't like it here."

"Why didn't you ever tell me all this before?"

"I never told anyone." He could hear the hurt and shock in her voice and for some reason, sought to alleviate both. "I just pretended it wasn't so bad. And when I was with you, it wasn't." He smiled into the face of her tears. "Look, Rach, the point of all this is, I always planned on getting out of South Village, only I couldn't do it until I was eighteen. My entire childhood and adolescence, I was stuck. Held by circumstance, poverty, disregard, whatever. So the minute I graduated—"

"You got the hell out," she finished softly.

"I got the hell out," he agreed.

"You never said. I never knew. I never understood."

"I wasn't real great at sharing that side of my life. I was so full of frustration and rage and the need to get out, I didn't know what I wanted—other than to go, of course—or even what I'd do with myself when I did."

"But you found out."

"Yeah." He thought of all the places he'd been, how in each one he'd learned something new, and had added it to the stack, accumulating experiences and emotions in a way he hadn't been able to growing up. "I loved it. I still love it."

Her eyes were immeasurably sad, and yet full of

something else too, a new understanding. Finally, she understood him.

Why was that the most bittersweet thing of all?

She turned her hand over in his and held on. "Ben? I want to tell you something. Something I should have told you a long time ago, too." She bit her lower lip. "I didn't belong anywhere, either."

"You belong here in South Village."

"I didn't always. You know we moved at the drop of a hat while my father raided and pillaged corporations."

"Yes."

"Until we came here, until I found South Village, I never had roots or a real home, either."

"And yet we ended up on opposite sides of the fence."

Her eyes filled again. "I never saw it that way before...but how I feel about my home...that's how you feel about your travels. My God, and all this time I thought we were so different."

"I know." His throat felt raw, talking to her like this. Sharing. Feeling it all over again. Chest aching, he leaned forward, wanting to be closer. "Want to hear something shocking?"

That got a short laugh. "After all this?" she asked. "Please. What else would shock me?"

He let out a sheepish smile. "Truthfully? It's not so bad waking up every morning to view the sunrise from the same porch. Not so bad having a tangible address in a full but clean and happy city leaping with life... I can admit that much, even if I can't share your love for it."

One lone tear slowly spilled over, slipped down her cheek. "Oh, Ben."

His gaze dropped to her lips to watch the words come out.

Her gaze dropped to his lips, too.

"This hasn't changed, has it?" He leaned close over the table, so that her breath mingled with his, making him shiver in anticipation, awareness. Need. "This physical attraction."

Her tongue darted out, wet her dry lips, making him groan. "It always was crazy," she agreed in a hushed whisper. "Always uncontrollable, this…this…"

"Need. We need each other, Rach. It doesn't change anything about who we are, but damn, I'd really like to hear you say it."

"What, that I need you more than my next breath, in a way I don't want?" Her eyes were big on his. "Well, I do. God, Ben, I do."

"Good." They were so close it seemed like the most natural thing in the entire world to close the gap between them and capture her lips with his.

With a low sound in her throat, she pushed even closer. Ben shoved the things cluttering the table out of his way so he could get more of her mouth, more of her. It was good, and he angled in for even more, which she gave, until a shattering crash of glass had them both pulling back, blinking like moles coming out in to the daylight.

Rachel stared at the ground at their feet, where one of them had knocked over her iced tea. "Was that us?"

He laughed, but it backed up in his throat when she licked her lips again, as if she needed that last taste of him. "Maybe we should get out of here," he suggested, thinking somewhere…like her bedroom.

She let out a low laugh that was so innately female, so sensual, it revved his engines all over again. "Oh, no. We're not getting out of here. This is not leading back to the question of my…" She blushed.

"Your orgasms?"

"Uh, yes." She stole his tea and sipped. "We're staying right here. Out of temptation and trouble."

"For how long?"

"As long as it takes to cool off."

*Great.* "More iced tea, please," he said to a passing waitress.

## CHAPTER SIXTEEN

THE CODED KNOCK came before dawn. Manuel made his way carefully through the dark, damp cellar. He still didn't dare risk using a generator at this time of day, so a small flashlight was all he had.

Specs of dirt and dust danced through the air in the beam of light, but he couldn't focus on that or he'd lose his mind. He answered the door eagerly, too eagerly, but he couldn't help that, either. *Everything* hinged on this.

"Did you get it?"

"The raid got a little bloody," came the hesitant answer. "The villagers fought back."

"Did you get the money?" Manuel Asada repeated with dangerous calm.

"Y-yes."

Everything within him relaxed. Finally. The tide would turn now, because with the money they'd stolen tonight, it was a start. Money was power, and with power he could do anything.

Like destroy the man who'd brought him down.

FOR RACHEL, the next few days fell into a rhythmic pattern of continued physical therapy, attempting to connect with her daughter and a silent, intense, arousing sort of dance with Ben. The longing, the hunger was unmistakable, but she knew it would be so much worse if they gave in.

So she did her best to ignore the sensual, earthy humming inside her body—and Ben's promise to ease that humming.

Always in the past, work had been her savior, but *Gracie* continued to elude her. Instead, when she sat at her easel, she ended up with a sketch of...Ben of all things. Ben on his knees, his arms around Emily, who was not only smiling as she always had in the good old days, she was cradling the well-behaved—*ha!*—Patches.

A fantasy. She pulled the sheet off, tossed it aside and started again, this time ending up with a sketch of South Village's joyful, exuberant nightlife, the refurbished firehouse and the street where she lived in the midst of the scene.

Did she really see her life here like that, joyful and exuberant?

Possibly...lately. She'd be a fool to not admit Ben did that for her, made her feel...alive. Shockingly alive.

She wanted him. She could admit that since he was leaving. He wanted her, too. They could easily fall into a pattern of sharing their nights together before he moved on. Would it really be such a mistake? That she was even thinking it made her reach for the phone for a reality check. "Mel?"

"What's up?" her sister asked, mercifully answering her cell.

"Nothing much."

"Uh-huh. You let Adam give you an orgasm yet?"

"No."

"Don't tell me you let Ben do it."

"Mel. You make him sound like a...toy."

"You did, didn't you? You did Ben."

"I did not. *We* did not."

"Well, whew."

Rachel stared at the drawing of him on the floor. Even two-dimensional, he looked so vibrant. Charismatic. "Why do you say it like that? Like it would be such a bad thing?"

"How quickly they forget," Mel muttered. "Remember your past with him? The fact that he destroyed you, and has the ability to do it again with one little 'good-bye'?"

"I haven't forgotten," Rachel said softly.

"Good. Keep repeating it to yourself like a mantra until your hormones are under control. Or if you must do something about them, call Adam."

"I can't."

"Why not?"

"He called me last night…told me he wasn't going to contact me again until I made a decision on what I wanted with Ben."

"Ouch."

"Yeah, ouch." But not as painful as she'd thought it would be.

"Well, call him back, tell him you've made your decision and Ben is leaving."

"Mel—"

"Oops, I've gotta run, psycho boss alert."

"*Mel*—"

Click.

Rachel set the phone back on its base and sighed. She'd gotten her pep talk. No sex with Ben. Determined to forget it, she turned back to her easel.

EMILY SAT on the backyard deck, laptop on her thighs. Her concentration was on the brilliant colors in the sky as the sun went down, her screen forgotten. She loved this house so much, loved the backyard, her bedroom, the elevator, the fire pole, the easy access to shopping and food…she loved everything about it.

But she wasn't a little kid anymore. She knew her home was special. And expensive. Everyone who saw it oohed and aahed.

And because she knew it, she also understood something else. She was lucky, very lucky. Bending for the puppy asleep at her feet, she pulled the warm, little body close. Patches let out a soft, sleepy puppy sound and yawned so wide she nearly turned her mouth inside out, making Emily smile before she buried her face in Patches's neck.

Above her came two quiet voices, her mother's and…her father's? They must be on her mother's deck, watching the same sunset.

Together.

Her heart hitched, but she reminded herself that they'd been together all this time now and, despite her best efforts, they weren't making wedding plans. In fact, her father had tried to tell her he was going soon. She'd pretended not to understand, but she knew she couldn't put him off forever. He wanted to say goodbye.

She just didn't want to.

How could he walk away from them, when lately she'd felt things softening between him and her mom? It wasn't just her hopeful imagination. Her mom smiled more often, at him. And he often simply watched her in return, something in his eyes making Emily sure he cared.

"Not a bad sunset," came her dad's voice. "For a city offering."

Her mother laughed. *Laughed.*

Emily strained to hear more, but all she caught was

her father's answering deep chuckle and a husky, low reply.

They were laughing together. Talking. They were— Wait a minute... If they were sitting on that particular balcony together, it meant they'd been together in her mother's bedroom.

Maybe they'd...done it. *Ewww!* But realistically, they'd already done it at least once, she was living proof. Torn between disgust and hope, she grabbed her laptop and the puppy before she heard something she didn't want to, and took herself inside to give them privacy.

With renewed hope, she sat at her desk to work out her next move in her plan of attack of making them fall in love.

WITH NO IDEA her daughter sat just below her planning on a miracle Rachel couldn't imagine, she was enjoying the sunset on her bedroom balcony. She sat on a lounge chair, wishing she had the energy to go get a pad and her pencils to capture some of the beauty before her.

Then a deep voice from the shadows said, "Not a bad sunset, for a city offering."

She laughed even as she felt a catch in her chest. Looking up, she found Ben propped up against the double French doors of her bedroom, just watching her. "That's why we have smog and pollution, to give such brilliant color to our sunsets. Just for you, Ben."

He grinned at her.

Her heart fluttered. "What are you doing?"

Pushing away from the doors, he came toward her in his easy, graceful, confident walk, the one that always reminded her of how comfortable he was in his own skin.

What she would give to be half that comfortable.

"What am I doing?" he repeated thoughtfully, sitting next to her even though there wasn't really room for the both of them. It left her plastered to him thigh to thigh, arm to arm, intensifying the connection between them.

"I guess I'm just being," he said. "With you."

In the past, when they'd been young and full of lustful hormones, there had been no just...sitting and being. He'd always had his hands on her, and though it had been a new and frankly terrifying experience sharing such easy affection, she'd grown quite dependent on it.

In the years since, she hadn't allowed herself much of that. When Ben had first showed up on her doorstep again, she'd felt the jolt of awareness all the way to her bandaged toes, and had wondered how she'd ever manage to ignore him and his blatant sexuality.

They were older now, and supposedly far more mature than they'd been at seventeen, so one would think it would be easier. After all, they'd decided there could be nothing between them, and certainly they could control themselves.

But here in the dark, on a warm, tempting late-spring night, with the stars far above and the city lights around them, with his warm strength and familiar scent...God, she needed. She needed him. "Just sitting, just *being,* is a bad idea," she whispered. "You know that."

"Yeah." The chair squeaked as he leaned in, touched her face. Stroked his thumb over her lower lip and started a set of delicious shivers racing down her spine. "But being here with you is making me want in a way I haven't in a good long time. Since you, actually."

She laughed. "Don't tell me there's been no other women."

His thumb covered both her lips now, halting her

words. His soft, wry chuckle brushed over her cheek. "Do you really want to talk about other women? Now?"

Through the dark she met his eyes. He'd shifted closer, with a hand on either side of her, so that she felt surrounded by him. And liking it. Thinking about him doing this with someone else was a problem. She shouldn't care, she knew that. It had been a long, long time, and someone as naturally sensual as Ben would never have gone a year without a physical connection, much less thirteen. "No," she whispered. "I don't want to talk about other women."

In the dark, he smiled, slow and long. "Good, because there's not room in my head for anyone but you." He nudged even closer. "Right here...with you." His mouth nuzzled along her throat. "What do you think?"

"Think?" With his hands gliding up her body, his mouth making its way toward hers... "I *can't* think."

"Because I'm touching you?"

"Yes." She had no idea why, but she lifted her face and covered his mouth with hers, swallowing his surprised inhale, sighing with pleasure as he hauled her against him.

Then he surged to his feet, and her world tilted. Gasping, she threw her arms around his neck for balance. "What are you doing?"

"Finishing what you just started." He kicked the French doors shut behind them and set her on the floor next to her bed. "Be sure, Rach." He waited, quivering with barely restrained control as he let her make the decision.

The power of that made her dizzy. "Ben—"

He put his finger to her lips. "Yes, or no."

She stared up at him, feeling as if she stood on the very edge of a deep cliff. Jumping, even with a parachute, would be bad. But not jumping, not living, was no choice at all. "Yes," she whispered, and reached for him.

The only light in the room came from the sun just sinking below the horizon. Long shadows slanted across the floor and bed. Ben took her face in his hands and tilted it up. Then he kissed her, stealing what little air she had left in her lungs. His mouth felt as firm as the rest of him, and just as sexy, as giving…as male. Everything within her trembled, and she clutched at him for support. She could feel his heat, his strength, and it was so familiar and yet so new, her heart skipped a beat. By the time he lifted his head and looked at her, she was a goner. Being in his arms like this was both heaven and hell. Yes, there were a hundred reasons this was a bad idea, a thousand, but as he sank his fingers into her hair and lowered his face again, she couldn't think of a single one, could think of nothing but *more, please more.*

"What's under the robe?" he asked hoarsely, nuzzling at the opening at her neck.

"Uh…" As his mouth made its way to her shoulder, nudging off the robe as he went, she struggled to put a thought together. "Not much."

"Not much is good," he whispered reverently, and slid his hands inside, parting the tie, letting the thing fall open. With characteristic bluntness, he looked his fill, which suddenly made her want to squirm. She knew what she looked like, still a little too thin, scarred…and unlike him, far from perfect. "Ben—"

"Oh, Rach, I've missed this body, I've missed you." With those stunning words, he lowered his head, splayed his hands wide across her bare back, urging her closer, and opened his mouth on a breast.

Shocked at the immediate clutching of her body to his, at how she felt as if she was burning up from the inside out, she could only hold on. She hadn't felt this flash of heat and need and desperation in thirteen long years, an eternity. Far in the back of her mind, she heard the horrifyingly hungry whimpers she let out as he nibbled at her, but couldn't help herself—she was on fire, shaking, and completely incapable of doing anything but letting him have his way with her. Have his way, he did, teasing a nipple with his teeth, tormenting between her thighs with his fingers, until she would have slid to a heap on the floor if he hadn't caught her up in his arms. Setting her on the bed, he held her gaze while he tossed her robe over his shoulders.

For the briefest moment, self-consciousness again began to clear the sexual haze he'd spun around her, but then he began to undress, and my, oh my, he was magnificent. Rough, sinewy arms, broad chest, powerful thighs...and between them, he was hard and heavy. For her.

Tossing his pants aside, he caught her looking, and must have mistaken her wide-eyed look of wonder for misgivings or horror because he let out a rough laugh. "Hey, it's nothing you haven't seen before."

"It's...been a long time."

"Yeah." He put a knee on the bed, leaned over her. "But it's just me."

Just him. The only man to ever make her feel as if she would die if he didn't kiss her, touch her. "Ben..."

"No regrets," he murmured, and bent close enough to glide his lips over hers. "No recriminations, no dwelling, no thinking." He ran his hands down her arms, linked their fingers on either side of her head as he settled himself between her thighs, which opened for him of their own accord. There was no mistaking his erection nudging at her already wet center, no way she wanted to. Pulling her fingers free, she wrapped her arms around his neck and breathed his name.

"Yeah, that's it, you're remembering now." His hips arched, just a little, enough to make her head swim, and a helpless hum of pleasure escaped her when he dipped his head to run hot, wet, openmouthed kisses down her neck. His hands were everywhere, then finally…right where she wanted them the most.

"Now," she gasped, trying to pull him inside her.

"Not yet." He sank two fingers inside her, groaned when she cried out. She couldn't help it, couldn't keep still. "Shh," he murmured when she cried out again, then covered her mouth with his, eating up her wordless demands, his fingers stroking her insides, her body already halfway to heaven.

"Inside me," she begged.

His touch deepened, and she caught her breath, feeling suspended… Caught it again when he removed his hand. But then he put on a condom, braced himself and entered her.

Their twin moans floated on the air. Rachel couldn't put together coherent words to save her life, but she wanted, she needed… "Ben…please."

"I know, babe." He flexed his hips, just once. "I know."

"Oh, my…"

"More?"

"Yes."

"You feel it, don't you, Rach?"

Another slow thrust made response impossible.

"Do you?"

She thrust her hips against his. "Yes!"

With another low, slow thrust, he added a knowing, purposeful glide of his thumb, right where they were joined.

She jerked.

"There, Rach?"

She opened her mouth to answer but he made another pass of that thumb, the one that had become the center of her universe, and she exploded on impact. She flew high and hard, remembering now what it felt like to be so filled, so heated, so high, and she might have said so if she wasn't struck blind, deaf and dumb by the fireworks going off in her head, in her body. And until the ripples within her eased, she didn't realize Ben was breathing every bit as harshly as she, his muscles quaking as he held himself on his elbows so that he didn't crush her with his weight.

Still buried deep within her, he lifted his head. Smiled slowly. "Hey," he said softly.

"Hey."

He ran his thumb over her sensitive lower lip. "So."

In spite of her uncertainty, she had to smile. "So."

"Did you feel the need to fake anything?"

She blinked. "What?"

"The orgasm. Real or Memorex?"

A laugh shuddered out of her.

"You think that's funny." He slid his hands to her hips and rolled to his back, pulling her over the top of him. "I'm going to take that as a good thing."

"You could."

"*Real* good?"

"Yes, *real* good," she said softly, suddenly feeling shy about it, which was ridiculous given that she lay sprawled, naked, over the top of him.

He cupped her face. "You're so beautiful, Rachel.

You *are*," he insisted when she made a doubtful little sound. "Why haven't you shared this with anyone in all this time?"

"I thought we weren't going to talk about other people."

"We weren't going to talk about other *women*," he corrected. "But this is about you."

"Ben—"

He rolled them over again, and she found herself very carefully pinned beneath him. "I see your cuts and bruises healing," he murmured. "I see your body healing, but there's still so much hurt inside you. Where does it come from, Rach? Why won't you share it? If not with anyone else, at least why not with me?"

She struggled to free herself, but he held her effortlessly. "Talk to me."

"Why?" She swallowed hard but the sudden lump in her throat didn't budge. "You're leaving."

He went utterly still, then let her wriggle out from beneath him while he flopped to his back and stared at the ceiling. "Always comes back to that, doesn't it?" Then, without another word, he rolled out of the bed and went into her bathroom.

Rachel pulled the covers up to her chin and tried to concentrate on the good. There was her body for one, still humming with sexual pleasure. And the warmth of his body, which still lingered in her bed.

Damn it, she'd known going in this was temporary, and she refused to agonize or anticipate.

It was done.

But a moment later he came out, walking toward her in all his nude glory. Not cocky, not strutting, just utterly comfortable with himself. At the side of the bed, he stopped. "You want me to go?"

Yes, her mind demanded. Go.

But it was her body in control at the moment, not her brain, and because of that, she scooted over and lifted the edge of the covers.

He climbed in, turned on his side and held out his arms.

With a sigh, she scooted right into them, entwining their legs. Pressing her face into his neck, which smelled so inherently Ben, she let out another little sigh.

"Okay?" He stroked a hand down her back.

"For now."

"For now is all that matters," he breathed, and hugged her close.

And if that statement wasn't a sum of all their differences, she didn't know what was, but she didn't care.

She would live in the moment, and enjoy it.

And worry about future moments in…well, a future moment.

## CHAPTER SEVENTEEN

BEN AWOKE to the sun in his eyes and his arms empty. No big surprise, he'd always awoken alone. Different bed, of course, different continent and time zone, but always with the same vague feeling that he was missing something.

Now he knew exactly what that something was. Or who.

Rachel.

Last night had been nothing short of earth-shattering. The way she'd given herself, the way he'd responded. He hoped to hell she didn't hate him for it, because he was afraid he'd just fallen in love with her all over again.

He might as well have jumped off a three-hundred-foot cliff because it wouldn't change anything. He still wasn't meant for this kind of life. He still didn't want the same address and same view from the same porch every morning. In light of that, it was past time to get the hell out of this bed with the fluffy white pillows and thick comforter. He rolled from his belly to his back, then nearly had heart failure. His daughter was sitting at his hip, grinning at him.

Scrubbing his hands over his face, he sat up and had enough wits about him to be grateful for the sheet at his waist since he was still quite naked. ''Uh…hi.''

She just kept grinning.

He checked the sheet to make sure it was still covering

the essentials, not wanting to be the one to educate this girl in the ways of male morning anatomy. "What's so funny?"

"You're in Mom's bed."

True. And he had no idea how to explain this. He wasn't in the habit of sleeping with a woman all night long, not when by morning he'd always been overcome by claustrophobia. Actually, that claustrophobia was overcoming him now. "About that—"

"She's downstairs drinking her coffee and pretending you're not in here. In case you were wondering."

"How did you know I'd be here?"

"Well, I came up to borrow a sweatshirt. And found you instead." She hopped off the bed and twirled. "Think I'll go mention to Mom I found you here. And that you're awake."

"No!" He forced a smile to soften his tone. "Um…maybe you'd just let her keep on pretending? You know, that I'm not here?"

She cocked her head thoughtfully. "If that would help your cause."

Oh, now he was a cause. "Em—"

Bouncing closer, she tossed her arms around him and gave him a bear hug. The feel of her, thin and sweet, so goddamned sweet his throat tightened, had him wanting to hold her forever.

"I was beginning to think it wasn't going to work," she whispered against his throat. "Getting you to come here."

Ah, hell. He put his hands on her arms and pulled back enough to look into her face. "Emily, I know you think you planned this little reunion, but I've got to tell you—"

"It was wrong," she admitted. "And manipulative. I

know. But I did the right thing, Dad. I can see that I did. Mom is down there glowing. She never glows, even when I make her put on makeup!''

Ben let out a slow breath. ''Maybe she's glowing because it's sort of chilly.''

*''Dad.''*

''Or she's catching a cold. You know, that's probably it, all that physical therapy she does. And those meds she's on lowered her resistance, and—''

''It's *you,* Dad. She's glowing 'cause of you and you know it.''

He stared at his beautiful, precious daughter and had no idea what to say or do. For most of her life she'd been out of his reach, and the rest of it would probably be more of the same. But for right now, for this little slice of time, he had her. He could be more than a casual dad, and suddenly he wanted to strengthen their relationship, make it worth something that they could both hold on to in the years to come.

Only he had no idea how to do that.

Then Rachel walked into the bedroom, indeed looking quite rosy. At the sight of Emily sitting on her bed, the bed with Ben still in it, she stumbled.

''Look who I found, Mom.'' Emily tucked her tongue into her cheek and baited her mother with shocking ease for her age. ''Right here in your bed. Can you believe it?''

Ben closed his eyes and wondered what she'd be like when she was eighteen. *Hell on wheels,* he thought weakly. And also, unfortunately, a chip off the old block. Either old block.

''Uh…'' Rachel sounded a little breathless, so Ben opened his eyes again and found her looking a little panicked.

And majorly adorable. "Would you believe I sleep-walk?" Ben asked Emily.

She giggled. "Nope."

Rachel rolled her eyes. "Emily, we…I…" She broke off with a disparaging sound, obviously at a complete loss. "It's true. He sleepwalks."

Enjoying herself, Emily leaned back in the bed next to Ben. She crossed her bunny-slippered feet and slipped an arm around his shoulders, surveying her squirming mother. "Okay. So he sleepwalks. And even though you sleep with one eye open, he somehow managed to get in under the covers without your knowledge, is that it?"

"Well…" Rachel glared at Ben. *Help me,* her eyes demanded.

When Ben left this time he wanted it to be on good terms, and he didn't plan on thirteen years going by before he made his way back into this very bed. In light of that, he smiled. "How 'bout this, Em…it's none of your business why I'm in here. We're the adults, you're the kid, and from now on, you'll knock before you barge in."

Em's mouth opened, then shut.

"Starting five minutes ago," he added.

"You mean…"

"Exactly. Start this episode over."

"You want me to, like, actually go back out?"

"Like, actually, yes."

Emily stared at her mom, who was looking as though she liked that idea very much. "You heard your father," Rachel said primly.

Emily let out a rude noise, but got up. Halfway to the door she turned back. "You know, this having two parents in the same house is bogus."

"Knock," was all he said.

She slammed the door behind her, and Rachel lifted a brow at him. She looked good first thing in the morning, he noted, with her short, short, out-of-control hair and her cheeks quite pink…wearing that robe he'd so eagerly peeled off her last night.

Emily's knock came, and he regretted he hadn't sent her farther away…like into town.

"Aren't you going to tell her to come in?" Rachel asked.

"I still haven't worked out a good reason for being in your bed."

"Maybe you should have left it by now," she pointed out.

"Yeah." As if he didn't know that. With regret, he tossed the covers off and stood. Where had he left his clothes…? Ah, he saw them now, littered across the floor.

Another knock. "Dad? *Mom?*"

Rachel was staring at his very naked body, her mouth open a little as if she couldn't quite get enough air. "Hold on, Em!"

Picking up his jeans from the floor, Ben slid into them. His shirt was across the room, draped over the top of her dresser where it had landed in his hasty strip.

Another knock, more loudly now. *"Dad?"*

"Em, we need another minute here." He didn't take his eyes off what he'd found beneath the shirt. An opened artist's pad displaying a beautiful colored pencil rendering of nighttime South Village. The lights, the people, the shops and theater…it was all there, and in such vivid clarity and detail it could have been a photograph. Mesmerized, he turned the page, and the next picture caught him by the heart and squeezed.

It was of Emily, Patches and himself, all sitting on

the small patch of grass in front of the house, laughing, touching…so absolutely, stunningly real he could almost see Emily breathing, could almost hear the puppy barking. "My God, Rachel."

"Those are personal."

"They're incredible."

She shut the pad on his fingers.

"I thought you weren't able to work. That you were struggling."

"Do those look like *Gracie* columns to you?"

"So it's not *Gracie,* they're still amazing."

"You can't make a living off renderings, Ben."

"You can do whatever you want to do, you damn well know that."

"It's not that easy."

"Of course it is."

"Look, ever since the accident, I need my job to be…important. And it's not," she finished lamely.

"Yes, it is. People wait all week for your witty take on whatever is going on in the country."

Rachel laughed. "Right."

"They do."

"Ben…I look at you and your work, and then turn back to my easel and…" Her face fell. "It just feels insignificant. Silly."

What was she saying? That she wanted to do what he did? That she suddenly wanted to travel with him? No, that was his fantasy and his alone. "Listen to me." He took her shoulders, made her look at him. "My work…it's not for normal people, okay? You know that. I travel all the time, I have no home, nothing to call my own except my equipment. I go to countries people have never heard of and see stuff no one could put together in their worst nightmares, and—"

"Exactly!" She shoved free. "You want to fix the world, Ben, and you're not afraid to do it."

"You do, too, just in a different way, that's all." He softened his voice, stroked a hand over her hair. "Don't doubt yourself because of me, babe. I don't think I could stand that. You are who you are, a damn strong, beautiful, intelligent woman, with the sense to keep her feet firmly planted. Me…I'm missing that gene entirely. What I do…that's all I know."

She lifted her gaze to his, and must have seen some of his thoughts, because resignation came into her eyes. "Last night…was that goodbye?"

Emily knocked again. "*Hey!* Can I come in or what?"

Ben couldn't take his eyes off Rachel, the woman he'd seen in the face of every woman he'd been with in all these years. The woman who'd given him Emily. The one woman who, if he were crazy enough to consider settling down, would be the one to make him want to do it.

Too bad he was missing that gene, too. "Yeah. That was goodbye."

She stared at him, still a little dewy-eyed, and he felt his heart crack. "It has to be," he whispered back.

She nodded, and went into the bathroom.

A FEW HOURS LATER, Agent Brewer called Ben. "We've got news."

Ben sat down, gripped the phone. "Tell me you have Asada in your hot little custody."

"Not our custody. The South American authorities claim to have him."

"Claim?"

"They say he was found dead in his hometown village."

"Are they sure?"

"They think so."

"And what do you think?"

"I'd like it better if we'd been able to ID the body before they cremated him."

*Shit.* Ben rubbed his eyes. "No one from the States IDed him first?"

"No, but he was reportedly identified by a handful of people who have known and hated him for years."

"So…it's over."

"It's over."

Ben hung up the phone, then waited for the relief to overwhelm him.

But oddly enough, the relief never came.

From: Emily Wellers
To: Alicia Jones
Subject: Sucky days…

Alicia, my dad is leaving on Tuesday for Africa. I know I told you he was going to stay, that's what I had hoped for, but it's okay. I think he and my mom got close on this trip, and I'm going to make sure there's more trips in the near future.

Emily stopped typing and sat back. What else could she say? She felt bad because Alicia had gotten lonely in the past few weeks when she'd been so busy. But the truth was, suddenly Emily didn't feel like doing e-mail every single day.

Before my dad goes, we're taking a short camping trip over the weekend. Summer is almost here and Dad says we're celebrating the upcoming season.

He even talked Mom into coming. Can you believe it? The homebody out on an overnight camping trip. Shockers. She must really like him to agree, don't you think?

Emily grinned. She thought about how her mother had looked just that morning while staring at her father in her bed, as if not quite sure exactly how he'd gotten there. Oh yeah, things were heating up.

Anyway, I know you wanted us to meet tomorrow but it'll have to be next week, okay? I still haven't asked my mom, she thinks there's only psychos on the net. I'll start easing her into it today.
Emily

THEY WERE ON their way to Joshua Tree National Forest. Rachel had never been and she had visions of—not to mention serious misgivings about—spiders, rocks beneath her sleeping bag and more spiders.

She also had visions of Asada coming back from the dead, but Ben assured her even if Asada hadn't died, he'd never find them in the desert. The authorities knew they were going and seemed to think it was a good idea for them to get away. But still, she couldn't shake the feeling that this Asada thing wasn't over. She shivered and glanced at Emily, who was smiling in anticipation from ear to ear, with her head bobbing to some noisy group coming out of her headphones.

Rachel glanced at Ben, who took his gaze off the road briefly and shot her that smile that never failed to turn her heart on its side.

"How are you feeling?" he asked.

She thought about that in a way she never used to, but the truth was, she felt…moderately okay. There were still aches and pains, and she still tired far too easily, but overall, things were so vastly improved, she had to smile back. "Fine, actually."

He grinned. "This is going to be great."

Well, at least two of them were excited, so that had to be something. How she'd ended up in the car was beyond her. One moment Ben and Emily had been planning this last thing together, just the two of them, and the next, they'd included her as if…as if they were a family.

But they weren't, not really.

And what would happen tonight? Alone in the dark? When their hormones kicked into gear again? Yes, they had Emily as a chaperon, so nothing much could happen, but Ben was nothing if not inventive. Would he want to sleep with her again? Instincts said yes, no matter that they'd already said goodbye. She knew resisting him would be her biggest challenge, especially when just thinking about it made her body feel soft and needy. And hopeful.

Rachel watched the scenery change and found herself putting aside her anxiety. Instead, she itched for a pad and pencils to capture the vast open space, the rock formations…everything. Spring had been extremely wet this year, and the primroses, sunflowers and other showy varieties bloomed madly across the desert floor. So different and yet so beautiful. The Joshua trees, for which the area had gotten its name, sprouted out of the dessert floor, some up to twenty-five-feet tall. From a distance, they looked like spiny, reaching ghosts.

"It's like being on another planet," she said in wonder as they pulled into a campground.

The place appeared deserted except for one other party, who'd gone much farther down the road and around a rock outcropping, leaving them with the illusion of being completely alone.

"It's early in the season yet." Ben pulled out the equipment they'd rented—a tent, stove, lantern. He wore jeans sinfully faded and threadbare, with holes in both knees, and one threatening the back of his left thigh. He had a red flannel shirt opened over his T-shirt that looked as soft and ancient as his jeans, and boots that had been around awhile. He was outdoors personified. "Spring can still get pretty brutal weatherwise out here." He tipped his head back to study the sky.

She tore her gaze off his body at that and looked upward. Was that a thundercloud? "And so we came here because…why?"

Emily grinned and danced around. She wore jeans, too, and though they were relatively new, she'd cut holes in the knees to look like her father's. Rachel's heart tugged just looking at her.

"This is going to be so much fun! Can we roast the marshmallows now, or should we go for a hike, Dad? Or how about taking some pictures? Can we?"

*Because of that, Rachel. You're here, already freezing your tush off, to make her happy. To see her smile.*

"How about we set up the tent?" Ben pulled lightly on Emily's ponytail, smiling into her happy face, making Rachel swallow hard at the bittersweet feelings just looking at the two of them together provoked.

The late-afternoon sun reflected off the desert floor. She would have said the desert was brown, brown and more brown, but here in the flesh, she was stunned by how wrong she'd have been. The Joshua trees reaching out for the sky were a vivid green, with dark-brown trunks. The jagged rock formations were a myriad of colors, red and purple and yellow…she couldn't stop looking around her, feeling the urgent need to get it all down on paper.

They put together camp. Rather *Ben* put together camp, with assistance from his eager daughter, while Rachel, feeling stiff and achy due to the surprising chill in the late-afternoon air, was forced to sit in a chair and watch.

The wind kicked up, blowing the flannel away from Ben's body, tossing his hair around his face and shoulders as he put together the tent without directions.

Rachel needed directions just to run her coffeemaker.

Ben laughed at something Emily said, laughed again as the poles Emily was working on fell to the ground, dumping the tent as well. Frustration bubbled over that she couldn't get up and help, be involved, but watching had its own merits. Her daughter—their daughter, she reminded herself—was in heaven.

Had her father have ever laughed with her like that? Smiled at her with such love shining from his eyes? Swallowing hard, she had to admit, Ben had turned out to be an amazing father, and Emily deserved every second she could get with him.

The tent did eventually go up. The tag on it claimed to sleep four people but Rachel eyed the tiny thing and wondered exactly what size those four people were supposed to be, as it hardly looked big enough for *one* sleeping bag. The three of them would be packed in there like sardines…

At least they'd have Emily with them, because being so close to Ben in nothing more than a sleeping bag sounded…damn tempting. In spite of her chill she started to warm up a little, from the inside out, just thinking about it.

"Mom, we're going to go on a hike up that peak over there." Emily was still bouncing around as she pointed to a rock formation a ways off, one that looked high and formidable. "Want to try to come?"

"Uh…" Now that she'd stopped thinking about Ben in a sleeping bag, and was looking at that mountain they wanted to scramble up, her warmth dissipated. Every single one of her injuries, healed or otherwise, had made itself known in the chill. "I don't think so."

Emily's smile faded. "You okay?"

Other than feeling ancient? Other than the fact that just a few months ago she could have outenergized her own daughter? "I'm fine, hon. Just a little sore today."

"I thought you were all better."

Her own fault, as pride had made her hide any lingering problems from the accident. "Mostly."

Ben started a fire, then came out of nowhere with her artist pad and pencils, which he set in her lap. "To help you pass the time."

She stared down at her things and was shocked to find them blurring with her own tears.

"Just do it for fun," he said softly, mistaking her emotion for distress. "Don't think of it as work, just think of it as—"

She put her hands over his and squeezed, swallowing the lump in her throat. "It's perfect, thank you."

He smiled into her eyes, then leaned forward to give her a kiss that brought back some of the warmth. "Look for us, we'll wave to you from the top."

"Ben—" She grabbed his hand when he would have pulled away.

He touched her face. "You're safe here, Rachel."

"I know." She felt safe. She always felt safe around him, she realized. "Be careful with our daughter, she's a bouncing bubble of energy waiting for disaster."

He glanced over his shoulder at the girl in question, who was already on the edge of their campsite, shifting impatiently back and forth with a camera around her neck. No laptop in sight. Ben turned back to her, his eyes lit with such heat it took her breath. "That's the first time you've ever said 'our' daughter." His voice was low and a little thick. "It's always been your daughter or my daughter, never…ours." He stroked a finger over the hand that held her pencils. "I've never really thanked you for her—"

"Ben—"

"So thank you," he said, and kissed her again, just once, just softly, and by the time she opened her eyes Ben and Emily were nearly out of sight already. But for the longest time she could still feel him. Taste him.

To keep her mind off that, she opened her pad. Surprising how she could jump right in to sketching out here in the wilderness, when she was still a little cold, not so comfortable in the chair, and worried about her precocious daughter stepping off a mountain and falling to her death, but jump she did. Maybe it was the absence of telephone calls, doorbells, clocks to watch…but whatever the reason, without the day-to-day distractions, she worked as she hadn't in months.

Thirty minutes later, she stared down in surprise. She'd drawn Gracie at the helm of a rowboat with her pencil high in the air pointing the way, towing her daughter and Patches, forging on against all odds. Out of nowhere, she'd pulled out a full *Gracie* column. No agony, no anxiety, nothing but the pure joy of the work. She leaned back and looked at the startlingly blue sky.

A few white clouds. No sound except a light wind whistling through the canyon and a few scattered birds. And a distant cry of...*Mom?* Someone was yelling *Mom!*

Emily!

Forgetting her aches and pains she leaped out of her chair, dropping her pad and pencils onto the ground as she scanned the horizon, heart in her throat. She knew it, Emily had gotten herself hurt or—

There. On top of the nearest rock outcropping, just where Ben had promised they'd stop and wave to her, stood her daughter and the man who'd changed her life forever with just one smile so long ago. Even from that distance she could sense he was giving her another of those smiles now, and she waved wildly, grinning in spite of herself, relief and something else crowding the heart that had stopped in fear only a second before.

They both waved back, Ben putting an arm on the exuberant Emily before she danced herself right off the cliff.

"Love you, Mom!" came Emily's voice, and then they were gone from view.

"Love you, too," Rachel whispered to no one, not even sure which of them she was talking to.

NIGHT FELL with shocking swiftness. No simple dusk for this place. One moment the sun slowly sank in golds and yellows and reds behind the rocks, and then the next, utter and still blackness.

Rachel crossed her arms in front of her, watching as Ben resurrected the fire she'd managed to kill. On his knees, he poked at the embers with a stick and the flames leaped to life for him. He glanced at her and she rolled her eyes.

At that, he laughed. The sound made her stomach tingle.

They'd met their neighboring campers—Joe, Matt, Liz and Shel, a group of four twenty-somethings claiming to be camping their way across the States before settling down to "real" life. The two couples had seemed a little wary of them until Ben had introduced himself, and within five minutes had made everyone feel quite at home.

Later, when Emily expressed worry at their new friends' lack of a home, lack of things and family, Ben told her that he suspected they were happy with the life they'd chosen, and could always change it if they wanted. Not everyone had to have a home or things. Or even family.

Rachel had watched him explain this to Emily and had to swallow hard. He was like that, happy without a home, things. Family.

She might have brooded over that, but Emily pulled out a deck of cards and challenged them to a gin rummy tournament. They played next to the fire, surrounded by wide-open vast space and a blanket of stars, with only their own laughter for company.

It was perfect. Rachel looked at Ben. Oh, yes, so perfect. She knew she should be sad, regretful, even resentful, that this would be it, their only foray into the whole family dynamic, the three of them, but suddenly she felt something else as well. Grateful.

Ben looked up, caught her looking at him. His hair had been long when he came, but it was longer now, and fell across his forehead. He shoved his fingers through it, shoving it out of his way. He looked tall, lean...beautiful. When he looked at her, she had to close her eyes.

He was leaving. Tuesday. Couldn't wait to leave.

"Let's hit the sack," he said abruptly, putting the cards aside, as if his thoughts had turned as troubled as hers.

"Dad—"

"Storm's blowing in." He pointed to the dark cloud mass coming in from the north, slowly blotting out the stars. "Let's get warm and cozy inside before it hits."

Five minutes later Rachel was kneeling in the center of the miniscule tent, staring at the three overlapping sleeping bags.

"I want the door," Emily said, having a good time whipping the beam from her flashlight over everything.

"I got the door, sweetness," Ben said.

Rachel waited for the inevitable argument, as Emily never accepted anything less than her own way, but at Ben's no-nonsense tone, she simply grabbed her sleeping bag. "Well, then I get the far wall beneath the window."

"Fine," Ben said.

Fine? That wasn't fine. Emily by the wall would put her in the middle, where Ben's hard, warm strength would be against her all night long. She couldn't handle it, she—

"Get in, Mom." Emily pointed to the bag that overlapped Ben's by a good third. "Tonight, *I* tuck *you* in."

Kneeling on his bag, Ben pulled off his flannel shirt, leaving just the T-shirt, and slid into his sleeping bag. He looked at Rachel, his brow raised in a silent, amused dare.

Rachel lay down, pulled the bag up to her chin. She shifted her body around, expecting rocks beneath her. "Hey, this is…soft."

"Dad put a mat down for you." Emily grinned.

"Didn't want you complaining." She kissed Rachel's cheek, then turned over, facing away from her and Ben with obvious delight. "I could sleep in the car, you know."

"No," Ben said in that dad tone, and once again Rachel was shocked when her daughter turned off the flashlight and stayed silent. Her breathing evened out, faked or otherwise.

In the dark Rachel could feel Ben looking at her, could feel the warmth of his body. Hard to miss it when they were practically pinned side to side.

"You doing okay?" he whispered.

Depended on his definition of *okay*. "I'm...good."

"Warm enough?"

Hard not to be with his body acting as her personal furnace. "I'm good," she repeated, and listened to his soft, sexy laugh.

"Then why are you holding your breath?"

Yes. Yes, she was. She let it out slowly. Outside, the storm moved in, the wind howled, the tent walls flapped noisily. Inside was like their own personal cocoon. A sinewy arm snaked out, gripped her waist and tugged her against a hard chest. "You're awfully quiet," he murmured, his mouth to her ear. "You sure you're okay?"

"I'm..." His fingers were playing lightly over her ribs, stealing her thoughts.

"Good?" he tested softly. "You're good?"

Lord, she was trying to be. "Go to sleep, Ben."

Another soft laugh escaped him, and he snuggled his face close to hers. "I will if you will, babe."

Babe. "Ben—"

"Dream of me."

Not surprisingly, she did.

From: Emily Wellers
To: Alicia Jones
Subject: We're back!

Camping was so cool! A storm came in the middle of the night and knocked our tent down, LOL. And then when we crawled out from beneath it, it started to snow. Snow! In May, can you believe it? And then while my dad helped my mom and I into the car, the tent blew away, just went rolling across the desert like a toy. You should have seen my mom's face, it was pretty funny. Dad laughed like crazy when he saw her.

Then, before we left, my dad gave all our leftovers to these two couples we met. I think they were homeless. I thought that was so cool of him. Mom did, too, though she didn't say so. She just looked at him with a sort of mushy look.

And oh! The best part of the weekend! I got an e-mail from Van, that cute guy from my history class I told you about? He said he wants to keep in touch over the summer! *scream!*

Anyway, I got your letter. I'd love to meet you this week. If Mom will let me get a bus into Los Angeles, it's on. I'll let you know which day.

Emily.

From: Alicia Jones
To: Emily Wellers
Subject: Best friends forever

Dear Emily,
Your camping trip sounded like fun, maybe next

time your parents would let you bring a friend.
Like me!

Cool about Van, but don't forget me, okay?

Beg your mom to let you take the bus to LA. Can't
wait to see you.

Your best friend,
Alicia.

## CHAPTER EIGHTEEN

MELANIE HIT the freeway, enjoying the sun and wind in her face courtesy of eighty miles an hour in the Miata, a car she could no longer afford since she'd lost her job this morning.

Talk about lousy Monday mornings. Worries started to creep in past the numbness, so she sped up.

A girl had to do what a girl had to do. And what she had to do was ignore the fact that she had no job, no rich husband and her thirty-fourth birthday looming around the corner.

How had she gotten so damn old? Craning her neck, she stared at her face in the rearview mirror. Great hair, artfully wild. Makeup emphasizing her still fab mouth and eyes. Clothes designed to make a grown man stand up and beg. She looked downright amazing, if she said so herself.

And she would have stayed home and proven that, if she'd had anywhere to go or someone to do it with, but the sorry truth was, most of her friends had long ago settled down, and the few that hadn't were going bar-hopping, ''slumming'' as they called it, and quite frankly, she'd felt exhausted at the thought.

''Oh, God,'' she muttered, gripping the wheel. ''I *am* old!'' Maybe she should turn around and do the barhopping thing, just to show she could still flaunt it. Maybe...ah, hell, she was already here.

Getting off the freeway at the first South Village exit, she ran into midmorning traffic. Then she had to circle Rachel's block twice before she got a parking spot, so by the time she got out of her car, she was good and ready to rumble.

Halfway up the walk, someone called her name, and not just any someone, but a tall, dark and handsome someone with a voice that had haunted her dreams ever since New Year's Eve. *Garrett*.

She could still hear his last words to her whenever she closed her eyes. *A one-night stand isn't going to be enough for me, Melanie. Not with you. If you ever want more, you know where I live.*

She bared her teeth at him in the closest thing to a smile she had at the moment. "I don't want more, in case you're asking."

He'd been raking his small front yard, wearing soft jeans and a T-shirt—both of which emphasized his long, muscled form—looking nothing like what she'd have pictured a stodgy dentist looking like on his day off.

But then again, there wasn't a stodgy inch on Garrett, not a one. Setting the rake in front of him, he leaned on it and studied her. "I wasn't asking."

"Why not?" she let out before she could stop herself. Damn it, that question had come out sounding far too needy. Terrific. Well, chalk it up to a spectacularly bad day.

And why was she attracted to a man who'd called her a bad sister anyway? But attracted she was, and knew by the quiet heat in his eyes that she wasn't the only one feeling it.

"I wasn't asking," he said, "because this is something you have to decide on for yourself."

Her breath caught at the calm certainty in his voice. "Decide what?"

He tossed aside the rake and moved close. His big body should have intimidated her; instead, the way he stood so near felt...protective, even lightly possessive, and her knees wobbled.

"Decide when it's time for the games to be over," he said quietly. "So there can be an us."

*"Us?"*

"Oh, yeah." His fingers swept a strand of hair out of her face, and the touch to her cheek made her shiver. "There could be such a perfect us, Melanie. If you'd let it happen."

Baffled, confused and extremely, humiliatingly close to tears, she ripped her sunglasses off and stared up at him. "Don't mess with me, Garrett. Not today, it's been a pisser."

"I'm not messing with you."

"But...you don't even know me."

"Don't tell me you believe in *lust* at first sight, but not love?"

"Love." The word choked her, she had no experience with it, none at all. "You're insane, you know that?"

With another gentle, tender touch that made those burning tears spring to her eyes, he lifted her chin. "Tell me you don't feel it, Melanie. That you haven't felt it since that night."

"That night we both agreed what we'd done was stupid."

"I never thought anything of the sort. *Never*," he added firmly when she bit her lower lip. "I only wished we'd waited until you'd been ready for what really happened between us that night."

"Which was?"

"The emotional connection. Look me in the eyes and tell me, and I'll believe you."

"I…" His eyes were deep, intense…and sincere. Oh, God, he meant it. And because he did, she couldn't muster up a bravado smile or a lie, not to save her sorry soul.

"Say it. Say the word and I'll walk away."

"I…can't," she whispered, shocked.

He rewarded her by lowering his mouth to hers in a kiss that didn't involve instant ravaging. No tongue, no teeth, no dirty words. Just firm, warm lips with so much emotion behind it, she found herself clinging.

And then *he* pulled away. "I only ask one thing," he said a little huskily. "But it's a deal-breaker if you can't give it."

Dazed, she looked up at him. Didn't he know she'd give him anything? It shocked her to the very core, but it was the truth.

"I trust you. But in return, Melanie, you have to trust me implicitly."

"What does trust have to do with anything?"

He smiled, and the sadness in it surprised her. "Everything. Take, for instance, the way you do everything in your power to make sure Ben and Rachel don't get back together, even though you know in your heart that's where they belong."

"Wait a minute. I don't—"

"Don't you? Come on, Melanie. You must know in your heart they belong together, and yet you can't quite handle the thought of Rachel being happy before you."

"No, I—"

"You've purposely sabotaged her happiness because you're not happy."

My God, that was insane. She wouldn't do that to her sister, she—

*She'd done that to her sister.*

Staggering back, she sat on the front step, ignoring the silk of her dress and how she couldn't afford to replace it. "My God. I'm a bitch."

"No." Hunkering down before her, he took her hand in his. "You're passionate and willful and a free spirit. I trust you to fix this. So, I guess the question is, do you trust me in return? To be there for you?"

In her book, *trust* was a dirtier word than *love,* and finding her pride, she yanked her hand free. "You're right, that's a deal-breaker." She stood up. Her heart cried out at the prospect of walking away, but that's what she was doing.

She'd hauled open the front door of Rachel's house when he spoke again, his voice low and hoarse with regret. "Goodbye, Melanie."

She opened her mouth, but her goodbye wouldn't come. So she simply let herself inside and shut the door.

Then leaned against it and took a deep, shaky breath. A very small part of her feared she'd just ruined the best thing that might have ever happened to her.

The bigger part of her said screw the big jerk. She stormed the stairs and found Rachel in her studio. "Am I selfish?" she demanded.

"Well, hello to you, too," Rachel said.

"Yeah, yeah, hello. Hugs and kisses." Melanie put her hands on her hips and studied her sister critically. She wore nothing over her head today, and the soft fuzz had indeed grown into hair, albeit short, short hair. But somehow the way it fell against her face suited her. So did the peach lip gloss, which happened to be the only makeup she had on. Though she was still too thin, the

cutoff jeans and tank top emphasized her small frame
and the few curves she had. Rachel was, Melanie had to
admit, still beautiful. "So am I? Selfish?"

Rachel studied her for a long moment. "You can be,"
she said honestly.

Yeah. Damn it. She'd known it. "Did you do Ben
yet?"

Rachel blinked. "I thought you wanted me to do
Adam."

Melanie stalked the rest of the way into the studio, a
little put out to realize how right Garrett had been. She'd
always thrived off Rachel needing her—*her* and no one
else. With Ben around, and Rachel glowing…she'd indeed felt threatened.

God, she hated that about herself. "Okay, look. The
truth is, the sexual tension between you and Ben is hot
enough to boil water, so maybe you should get it over
with."

Rachel put down her pencil. "What are you up to?"

It was automatic to deny, and she opened her mouth
to do just that, but then shut it and sighed. "Oh, Rach.
I've screwed up good this time."

"Oh, honey, I'm sorry." Rachel immediately came
toward her, arms out, offering a hug. "What's happened? It's Monday. Shouldn't you be at work?"

Melanie soaked up the affection she didn't deserve,
then pulled back. "Forget that for now. I have to tell
you something. And I don't really have a gentle way to
say it."

"You don't have a gentle bone in your body. Why
start now? Just spill whatever it is. You'll feel better."

She doubted that. "Well… I lost my job."

"Oh, Mel."

She lifted her hands, shook her head. "Wait. No.

That's not what I meant to say. For once, this is about you, not me.'' She dragged in a deep breath. ''Okay, here goes. I discouraged you from Ben because I didn't want you to be happy.''

Rachel blinked. ''What?''

''I mean, I wanted you to be happy, which is why I was into the whole Adam thing, but to be really, really, *really* happy you need Ben, and I discouraged that because I didn't want you to be really, really, *really* happy until I was.''

Rachel let out a little laugh. ''I thought you gave up smoking dope.''

''I did. Damn it, I haven't been smoking. And I mean it. I encouraged the wrong man, Rach, and I'm trying like hell here to fix that. Ben floats your boat, feeds your soul, is your other half, however you want to say it, and we both know it.''

Rachel stared at her for a long beat, then turned away. ''Yeah. Well, it's too late. He's leaving. Tomorrow, in fact.''

''And you're going to let him?''

''Let him?'' Rachel laughed again, though there was no mirth in the sound. ''Melanie, no one stops that man when he's got an idea in his head.''

''You could.''

''And have him regret it? No way. He was meant to go.''

''And you're just going to watch him do it. Again.''

''That's right.''

Melanie nodded. Fine. She'd done what she could. Anymore and she'd have to be a saint. There was no doubt she was not a saint.

Goodbye, Ben.

*Goodbye, Garrett.*

She grabbed her purse. Yes, it was early, but this was South Village. She could shop till she dropped around the clock, and she needed that desperately now.

Thank God for credit cards...

BEN HAD GOTTEN UP early to take his last photos of the people in South Village. Midmorning, he stepped back inside the foyer of Rachel's house and smelled burned eggs, which meant Emily was cooking again. She had the morning off school for teacher conferences. A smile tugged at his lips that she'd cooked rather than sleep in, before he remembered this would be his last day enjoying his daughter's attempts at cooking.

His flight was tomorrow. Smile gone, he moved into the kitchen in time to hear Rachel say, "I don't like the idea of you going into Los Angeles for someone you met off the Internet."

"Mom! It's not a porn convention, it's *Alicia.*"

"You have no idea if this Alicia is who she says she is."

"But she is! She's twelve, like me, and goes to a middle school that sucks, like me. She's my best friend and we want to meet."

"Who's idea was it? Yours or hers?"

"Both."

"And how long have you two been talking?"

"You know this already. A couple of months."

"It sounds unsafe, honey."

Emily tossed down the wooden spoon on the stove. "You're so mean!"

"Stop," Ben said, grabbing her when she would have whirled out the room. "Hold on. I don't want to hear you talking to your mom in that tone."

"But she talks to *me* like I'm a baby."

Rachel stood up. "You *are* my baby."

"Mom!"

"Okay, hold on." Ben spun Emily around so she and Rachel faced each other. "Look at your mom. Listen to her."

"But Dad—"

*"Listen."* He glanced at Rachel. "Obviously you're worried about the whole unknown factor with Alicia."

"Of course! She's too young to take the bus by herself into the heart of L.A. and meet someone I don't know."

"I agree." Ben gently squeezed the glaring Emily. "So why don't I go with you, Em? Wouldn't that work?"

"I've been informed parents aren't allowed," Rachel told him.

"Bad choice, sweetness." Ben tsked at Emily over that. "If you change your mind about that today, let me know and I'll—"

*"Us,"* Rachel corrected. "We'll both go."

*"Us.* If you change your mind and want *us* to take you, then you've got a deal."

"But you're leaving," Emily reminded him, reminded them all, and her voice cracked a little on the last syllable, cracking his heart as well.

"Yeah." *Leaving.* His middle name. "But I could take you into L.A. with your mom tomorrow and then leave right after."

Emily brooded over that for a moment. "Could we go to, like, a restaurant or something, and you guys let us have our own table?"

Ben slid his gaze to Rachel. "Rach?"

"Fine. But I still don't like it—" She broke off when Emily leaped forward and bear-hugged the life right out of her.

"You're the best, Mom!"

Rachel shook her head and laughed. "Could you do me a favor and try to remember that?"

With a grin, Emily danced out of the room. A moment later they heard the front door slam as she left to catch her bus.

"I wish you hadn't agreed to that," Rachel said, sitting back down at the table.

"Why? After this Asada thing, meeting an online friend seems pretty tame, especially with us right there."

"At a different table."

"I'm not going to let anything happen to her, Rach."

"You're not going to always be there."

He stared at her bowed head as she calmly paid bills, and marveled that she never broke stride in writing her checks while she managed to dig in hard at his heart. "I thought we were okay."

"We are."

"So what's the matter?"

"Do you really need me to spell it out?"

"I'm a guy," he said so despondently she actually let out a laugh. "I need everything spelled out."

"Well, we could start with Asada."

Just the name on her lips swamped him with guilt. "Who's dead as a doornail."

"Not in my dreams, he's not."

Another nail in his heart. "Rach—"

"No. I'm sorry." Tipping her head back, she stared at the ceiling. "It's Emily, too. I just realized how much she's growing up. I mean look at her, she no longer even needs me, and I've…I've just come to understand my show of strength with her is really just a farce."

"You're an incredible mom."

"Thanks. It's just…"

"Just what, Rach?"

"You're out of here tomorrow." She smiled sadly. "And I just might admit to missing you this time."

He reached for her hand, took the pen out of it and linked their fingers. "I'm going to miss you, too. So *damn* much. Do you remember the other night? In your bed? Where we came together like we'd never been apart?"

"I remember."

"You were into my touch, and God knows, I was into yours." He pulled her up against him. "Neither of us can have what we really want," he whispered, skimming his lips over her ear. "But wouldn't it be nice if we could have one more night?"

"Ben—"

He opened his mouth and sucked the edge of her earlobe into his mouth. Her fingers tightened on his, her breath left her lungs in a whoosh. As he took his mouth on a tour down her throat, her eyes drifted closed. "Ben, what are you doing?"

"Getting you there," he said. "To that one spot we can both share, where we can both be happy."

"Mindless sex?"

"If that's all we can have, what's wrong with that?"

"Spoken like a true red-blooded male," she said on a breathless laugh, but he had her, he could feel her softening beneath his hands, which were roaming her body now, could hear it in her breathing against his shoulder. She tilted her face a little, and when he gently touched his mouth to hers, she opened for him, nipping at his lower lip, then soothing it with a lazy swipe of her tongue.

As an act of acquiescence, it was an irresistible offer, an artless seduction.

"Mel's here. She went shopping though."

"Shopping is good."

"This won't change anything." She sucked on a patch of skin at his throat, making his knees weak. "Nothing at all."

"No," he agreed, catching his breath when her hands ran down his chest. "Rach…" His eyes crossed when she boldly caressed his thighs…between them. He struggled to remember they were right in the kitchen. "Upstairs—"

Her fingers did the talking, outlining the erection he sported, which was threatening the seams on his jeans. His body arched slowly into her exploring hand. Stifling a groan, he caught her fingers, then lifted her in his arms.

With a laughing gasp, she held on. "Bedroom?"

"Bedroom."

"And I thought you were so adventurous."

"I'll give you adventurous in your bed."

When they got there, he tumbled her to the mattress and followed her down, carefully pinning her arms over her head, holding her captive while he slowly and surely stripped her bare. Insinuating himself between her thighs, he looked into her beautiful eyes. Her beautiful, *wet* eyes. His heart cracked and broke. "Ah, no. Rach—"

"Love me, Ben. Just shut up and love me."

Hadn't he always?

"This has to last us," she whispered. "After this…I can't do it again, I can't—" Her breath hitched. "I can't keep watching you go—"

"Shh." He bent his head for a kiss, filling his hand with her breast, indulging himself in her softness, the feel of her, the sounds that came from her throat, the taste of her skin… She was hot, ready and more than willing when he slid down farther, running his mouth over every inch.

The way she arched and squirmed and cried out nearly undid him, so he held her writhing, damp body still. If she so much as touched him, she'd take him right over the edge. He might have let her, too, if he hadn't wanted more, so much more.

"Ben...please, now."

"Now," he agreed, and put his lips on her, *there.*

She bucked right into his mouth. Perfect. Holding on, he took her slowly, using his tongue, his teeth, teasing her with soft, little licks, and when she was mewling at him, he pushed her harder, switching to long, languid strokes that choked another cry out of her.

Her head thrashed on the pillow, her fingers fisted in his hair, pulling, holding him...as if he intended to go anywhere. "Come for me," he whispered. "Come in my mouth." He slipped a finger into her soft folds, coaxing the sweet spot on her body into a hard little bud.

"Don't stop," she begged him, shamelessly arching into his hand. "Please...don't stop."

"Not on my life," he promised, and watched her fall apart for him.

When she'd stopped shuddering, he surged to his knees and managed, barely, to get on a condom.

Then, while she was still sighing with pleasure, he sank inside her. At the hot, wet feel of her surrounding him, hunger and desire mingled, skittering down his spine, pooling between his legs. Curling his toes. Moving his mouth to hers, holding her to him, he thrust all the way home, and she went wild beneath him.

Watching her, hearing her, with the taste of her still on his lips, he thrust again, catching her every whimper, her every breath, with his mouth. Her shudders rippled down her body to his. Another thrust and his body started to tighten and contract, too, pulsing with the need for release. Again. Then again, losing himself in her soft, wet heat, following her over, shattering into nirvana as he poured himself into her.

Dazed, spent, he stared down into her face, knowing the truth.

There was no doubt now.

He'd gone and fallen all the way in love with her.

Again.

## CHAPTER NINETEEN

RACHEL LAY SIDEWAYS on the bed, her head hanging off, and a heavy weight on her chest that turned out to be Ben.

With a groan, Ben lifted his head. "Did you ID whatever hit us?"

"Don't worry, it's on its way to Africa." It came out of her mouth before she could think, and of course, she regretted it immediately. "Ben…"

"No. It's okay." He rolled to his side, putting a hand flat on her belly to hold her to the bed. His fingers danced over her skin, and even now, when she should be sated and limp as a noodle, he drew shivers with his touch. "I can't change, Rachel."

"Because you're too stubborn? Or too old?"

While he pondered that, she pushed his hand away and sat up. Forcing her boneless legs to function, she got off the bed in search of her clothes.

Which, apparently, they'd lost far before the bedroom, as there wasn't a single item to be found.

"Here." He came up behind her with her robe, then turned her to face him, his eyes filled with so much pain she could hardly look at him. *Try my pain on for size,* she wanted to cry, but she fisted her hands rather than beat them over his chest. He was a grown man, and she wouldn't beg. She wouldn't even ask. "I can take Em to L.A. tomorrow. You can catch an earlier flight out. Tonight, if you'd like.''

"I have one last night," he said in a low voice. "Don't take it from me."

*You could have an infinite number of nights if you'd but ask.* Pride made her push instead. "I wouldn't take a thing from you, Ben Asher."

"But you'd see me go early?"

She stared up at him, the lie backing up in her throat, but it was far too late to save her heart. She'd long ago lost it—to the only man she'd ever given it to. The very man standing in front of her, stricken, lost. Alone.

*Of his own making,* she reminded herself. "Yes, I'd see you go early."

"No," he said in such a low voice she almost missed it. "But I'll stay out of your way."

"Fine."

"Goodbye, Rachel."

She didn't answer, and Ben had no idea if that was because she didn't know how or she didn't care.

Once, he'd wondered if anything could hurt as much as losing her all those years ago, and now, as he walked out of her room, he had his answer.

This hurt as much. This hurt worse. His insides shattered along with his heart and soul, and as he entered his bedroom and grabbed his duffel bag out from under the bed to pack it, everything within him rebelled.

This trip had been *temporary,* he reminded himself. He'd wanted temporary, he lived for temporary.

But that had been before. Before he'd gotten to know Emily as a father should. Before he'd lived the actual little details of everyday life and found them not nearly as tedious as he'd imagined them.

Before, the urge to move around had consumed him,

but somehow that urge had vanished, and in its stead came a different yearning all together. A yearning for a place to call his own. A home.

*Too bad you've blown it, Ace.* He started tossing his things into his duffel bag, knowing that by tomorrow night he'd be fifteen thousand miles away from the bed Rachel had kicked him out of.

Out of her bed and out of her heart. He deserved it, he supposed, both for being who he was and for bringing her the danger in the first place. Resigned to his fate, he zipped his bag closed.

RACHEL STAYED in her robe trying to console herself with an extralarge bag of assorted baby chocolate bars. Halfway through her own private pity party, she called Melanie on her cell. "Aren't you done shopping yet?"

"My credit card is still working. Why?"

"I've eaten a pound of chocolate and it's not helping."

"What's the matter?"

She opened her mouth to say…*Gracie. Emily. Everything.* "Ben," she said, and burst into tears.

"Oh, honey, I'll be there in five minutes."

*YOUR FAULT,* Melanie told herself as she drove around Rachel's block searching for a parking spot. *You messed with her head, and now you're responsible for hurting the only person who ever truly cared about you.*

And all this time she'd thought she hated Garrett for making her feel so rotten to the core, when it was herself she hated. All her life she'd skated through without caring about anyone or anything too much. Somehow that had slowly started to change.

It was hard work, caring. And so far, she didn't see any rewards for it.

Finally, she found a parking spot and ran into the house. It was quiet. "Rachel?" Moving through the rooms, she started to panic until she caught sight of her sister in the backyard. Stepping through the glass doors of the living room, she waved.

Her sister, sitting on the grass with the puppy in her lap, stuffed what appeared to be a chip loaded with cheese into her mouth and didn't wave back. "You didn't have to stop shopping just because I'm drowning in stupidity," she said.

Mel plopped down next to her and tried not to picture what the grass would do to her silk dress. "You've never been stupid. You've been crying?"

"Sugar overload. I've moved on to straight fat calories." She gestured to an almost empty plate of nachos sitting next to her.

"All because of a man?"

"Don't be ridiculous. A man has nothing to do with this."

"Liar."

Rachel's head jerked up at that, but after a beat, her shoulders sagged in defeat. "He's going tomorrow. Right after dinner in Los Angles with Emily and her new friend. Just hopping on a plane and leaving. *Again.*"

"Did you tell him to go? *Again?*"

Something close to guilt flashed across Rachel's face and Melanie shook her head. "You did."

"What does it matter?"

"Because he loves you. Jeez, you're as big an idiot as I am. *He loves you,*" she repeated to her now pale sister, thinking Garrett should see her now, the jerk. She was willingly being...*good.* "He's always loved you, but because of how he grew up, you know damn well he'd never stay where he thinks he's not wanted."

"What?" Suddenly Rachel looked like a good wind could knock her over. "What did you just say?"

"Oh, God, this do-good thing is going to kill me," she muttered to the sky.

"Ben doesn't love me."

"Have you seen the man look at you? *Please.* He's got stars in his eyes, okay? He came across the entire world for you, dropping everything, and once here, even with his job waiting and his entire soul yearning to be wild and free, he stayed. God, Rachel, he stayed. For you. You know what that cost a man like him? Do you have any idea?"

Rachel just stared at her. "How did you know about how he grew up?"

"Everyone knew."

"I didn't," she whispered. "I didn't know details until recently, when he finally told me."

"Yeah, well, don't take this wrong, sis, but you're not real big on opening up or getting other people to do the same."

"I should have tried harder."

"Why? You were either in bed with him or in denial over how you felt. Black and white, that's always been you, Rach." She watched agony cross her sister's face and sighed. "Look, help me do the right thing here. I encouraged you off him before and I was wrong. Flat, dead wrong. And..." Ah, damn it all to hell. "Rach...there's more. All those years when I took Emily to him? I never once saw him with another woman."

"But you said—"

"I know, I said he'd become a slut. I lied. And—"

She bit her lip, all that guilt she never let herself feel swamping her now. "And he always asked about you. Always."

"He..." Rachel looked stunned. And hurt. Slowly she shook her head. "I don't get it. Why would you lie to me?"

*Truth,* Melanie. "I told you, I wanted to be happy first. And...um...while I'm being honest, I should also tell you I sort of had one wild night with your neighbor." She lifted a hand when Rachel went even more pale. "I promise you, it was a horrible lapse in judgment."

*"Garrett?"*

"Remember last New Year's Eve? You went to bed early, and I...didn't. I went looking for trouble in a bar on Sixth, and he was there... God, I don't know how it happened exactly. But we never again, not once."

"I...see."

Her sister had put that quiet voice on, and her eyes had cleared of all emotion. Damn, she was good at it, too.

"So you wanted me with Adam because that would make me only a little happy, and you could be happier than me and feel better about yourself." She nodded. "In some twisted way I actually understand that. And not telling me about Garrett, well...that's your business, I suppose. But Mel, what I don't understand is lying about Ben."

"Yeah, join the club." She scrubbed her hands over her face. "Look, Rach, I'm sorry. I never meant to hurt you."

"But you did. When you told me those things about Ben, I believed you, and it changed how I thought about him for years. *Years,* Mel. What you did was incredibly selfish.''

''Yes.'' Okay, this was not going as smooth as she'd hoped. ''But in all fairness, that's really nothing new, right?'' She tried a smile.

Rachel didn't return it.

''I'm trying to make it right,'' Mel whispered. ''I'm trying to fix things.''

''You can't always do that.''

''Rach—''

''Okay, stop.'' She put her fingers to her temples. ''You know what? I just need to think. I need to be alone.''

Her chest feeling restricted, Mel nodded. ''All right, I'll just go inside—''

''No. I think you should go home.'' Then she turned away.

Rachel couldn't help it, she was reeling. Mel had tried to sabotage her happiness. That was really nothing new or shocking. But that her sister of all people had come up with an astute, accurate and horrifying reason for Ben walking away from her. *Twice.*

And Rachel had missed it. How she had was beyond her.

*Of course* Ben was extremely sensitive to not staying where he wasn't wanted—he'd grown up that way.

*Of course* he'd walk away without looking back if someone said to go. No one had ever cared if he'd stayed or gone, not ever.

She'd been trying so desperately to protect herself from hurt, and in doing so she'd hurt the one person who truly, unconditionally loved her. That ugly truth would haunt her forever.

And yet she had no idea, no idea at all, how to fix it.

MELANIE RACED through Rachel's house like the devil himself was on her heels, emotions flogging her with every step—remorse, anger, humiliation, regret... Without Rachel's forgiveness, her entire world had splintered.

*Go home.*

Well, damn it, she didn't have a home, she had a leased condo she could no longer afford, with someone else's furniture in it, and someone else's tastes on the walls. Unlike Rachel, who'd taken from their childhood a need to settle and had followed through with that need, Melanie had done nothing for herself. She hadn't really cared to.

By the time she slammed out the front door, her throat was closed, her heart shriveled, and she could hardly see for the tears pooling in her eyes, the tears she refused to let fall.

She took a step toward her car, or at least that's the message her brain signaled to her body, but suddenly she found herself running, running like hell across the neighboring lawn and up to the front door there, knocking with three bold knocks.

After a moment, Garrett answered. He wore trousers and an open shirt exposing a wedge of hard chest spattered with dark hair, a chest she knew to be warm and perfectly capable of holding her weight while she burrowed in.

"Melanie," he said with surprise.

She took one look into his face, with his dark, passionate eyes and wide, firm mouth that always, *always,* spoke the truth, no matter what, and did the most horrifying thing.

She burst into tears and covered her face.

A steady hand settled on her elbow, just a simple, comforting touch. It made her fall apart even more, and her breath hitched in her chest as she continued to sob, utterly unable to stop.

"Are you coming in?" His other hand came up to steady her as well. "Yes or no, sweetheart. You come in and we deal with this, all of it, or you run off again. You make the call."

"I can't...."

"Yes or no," he repeated quietly.

"Yes!"

He drew her in. She heard the door shut, but resisted when he tried to pull her close because though her feet had brought her here, she still didn't feel like she deserved his sympathy.

"Come here," he said, and ran his hands up and down her spine, not grabbing her butt, not trying to cop a feel, just...holding her.

She couldn't remember a time when a man had offered her such simple comfort, wanting nothing in return. Or if she'd ever wanted one to. But she wanted that now, so much. Gripping his shirt in her fists, she buried her face in the crook of his neck, inhaling his scent, wetting his skin, feeling soothed by the steady beat of his heart beneath her ear. She had no idea how long they stood there, with buckets of her tears falling at their feet, the sounds of her crying muffled by his shoulder and the occasional wordless murmur he made as he held her.

Eventually she ran out of steam, which left her drained and weary. His hand swept back up her spine, gently stroking the back of her neck, before sinking his fingers into her hair to tug her face up. "Better?"

She sniffed, and for once didn't care that her mascara was probably all over her face or that she needed to blow her nose. "Yes," she said, marveling that it was true.

He led her through his living room to his kitchen,

where he sat her at a bar stool and poured a glass of water for her parched throat. When she'd taken a long sip, he sat next to her. Reaching for her hand, he brought it up to his mouth. "Talk to me."

She stared at him, feeling goose bumps rise on her arms from nothing more than the feel of his mouth on her palm. Lust, yes, but good God, this was more than any simple lust she'd ever felt. "Garrett..." She let out a surprised little laugh. "I can't think with your mouth on me."

"That's new," he said, and set her hand back on the counter.

"Yeah...*no*," she corrected, and nervously licked her lips. She was anxious, she realized. With a man. She was never anxious with a man. "It's not new. I've felt this way around you for a long time, I just couldn't admit it to myself, much less you."

His eyes lit with such emotion she could hardly breathe. "Can you tell me why you're here? Why you came to me?"

"Because you're the only one I wanted to come to." Every time she spoke, revealing another little truth she'd kept to herself, it was like lifting a brick off her heart. "You were right before."

"Really? About what?"

"That I was hurting Rachel. That I did it because I wanted a little tiny bit of what I saw in her eyes. Some of that happiness." She put a hand on her heart as it hitched. "I didn't know I had to get it from within me."

"Have you found that happiness?"

"I'm not sure," she answered honestly, and another brick came off her chest. "I went to Rachel, tried to tell her how sorry I was...it didn't go well. I was running away, you know. Running home, but then I realized, I don't have one. And then I ended up here.'' She looked into his eyes. One more brick fell away. ''I wanted to be with you all along. I was just terrified of that wanting. Oh, Garrett.'' She reached for his hand and squeezed, hoping to God she wasn't too late.

He cupped her cheek. ''Are you talking love?''

She held her breath, then let it out slowly, no longer willing to cajole, coax or lie. Not ever again. ''I don't really know the meaning of the word. I was thinking...'' She stared at his fingers.

''Yes?''

What was it about him that gave her such strength, such hope? She looked into his eyes. ''Maybe you could help me out with that.''

His smile was slow and full and filled her with such hope it hurt to breathe. ''How's this for a start? I love you, Melanie Wellers. I love you with everything I've got. That means that I think of you night and day, and being with you makes me feel alive. I want you happy. Do you think that could work for you, love in that context?''

''Oh, yes,'' she gasped, starting to cry again. ''And in that context, Garrett, I can honestly say...I love you back.''

''Be sure,'' he said a little huskily now, getting off the stool to stand between her legs. He slid his hands into her hair. ''Because I play for keeps.''

''For keeps is good,'' she whispered, and reached up for a kiss to seal the deal.

## CHAPTER TWENTY

ON TUESDAY, Ben drove them into Los Angeles. Rachel rode shotgun, staring silently out the window. Emily, in the back seat, sat surprisingly quiet as well, a set of headphones on her ears that might have been a brick wall between them for all she even looked at her parents.

The silence stretched, then stretched some more, until the tension in the car became the fourth passenger. Ben knew why Rachel was quiet; there was a whole host of reasons for that. She resented him for leaving, she didn't want to be here, she didn't want her daughter to be here.

But Emily, her silence seemed out of character for the preteen who lately had only two gears—fast-asleep and hyperspeed.

"You cool enough?" he asked Rachel, reaching for the air-conditioning.

She didn't look at him. "Fine."

He glanced in the rearview mirror to make sure Emily's head was still bopping to the music only she could hear. "Look, Rach, I wish things could be different."

"Really? What things?"

"Us, damn it. I know there are things about me that…"

"That what, Ben?"

"That scare you."

Now her eyes frosted over to match her voice. "You don't scare me."

"Bullshit." He checked the rearview mirror again. "Come on, Rach, truth. We don't enough time left for anything else."

"Okay." She took off her sunglasses. "Truth. Because God knows how important the truth is when you're getting on a plane in a couple of hours."

"It *is* important." He glanced at her, needing her to agree.

"Yeah, okay." She closed her eyes. "You're right. It is. And yes, you scare me."

The victory was hollow. "This is who I am," he said quietly. "It's always been who I am. You're the most important person in my life, you and Emily, and I'd do anything for you. Anything. Except hold back. I've tried and I can't, not even for you."

Her eyes filled. "I know." She no longer looked cold and frosty, just…sad. "I know. Ben, let's just do this, okay? And get it over with."

Get it over with. The goodbye, she meant. But first they had Emily's friend Alicia to meet, and suddenly, inexplicably, Ben felt uneasy about that. It made no sense, of course. They'd gone camping, they'd let Emily ride a school bus, they'd lowered their guard all over the place, slowly, gradually.

And Asada was dead.

He glanced at Emily again, his baby, his precious daughter whom he'd spent far too little time with. "God, I have no idea what I was thinking, urging her out of her shell, letting her do this. It's crazy."

Rachel sighed. "It'll be good for her to stretch her boundaries, good for both of us. I've kept us so contained, Ben, and all because of my own fears and insecurities."

He reached for her hand. "It's not your fault, it's the

way you grew up moving around like a vagabond. You want to stay still now and have a real home. That's understandable.''

''Well, you didn't grow up any easier than I did, and you're—''

''What? Consumed by the opposite need?'' he asked wryly. ''I guess we're both screwed up.''

''There's got to be a happy medium, for Emily.'' She squeezed his fingers. ''I want to give her that. No more hiding behind my insecurities and fear. If nothing else, you taught me that.''

Unbearably touched, he didn't know what to say. And as Emily pulled off her headphones, it didn't matter.

''We there yet?'' she asked, scowling when both her parents laughed. ''What?''

''The age-old question,'' Rachel said, and pulled her hand from Ben's.

The loss had his smile fading. It was really almost over. Within a couple of hours, he'd have what he'd wanted so badly. His freedom.

Only he couldn't remember why he'd even wanted it so badly or what he was running to.

EMILY HAD ARRANGED to meet Alicia at five o'clock. It was ten minutes until the hour and Ben circled the block yet again, unable to find a parking spot.

''Let me out,'' Emily said from the back seat. ''I'll go get us a table.''

''No way,'' Ben said.

''I have to go to the bathroom, Dad!''

''I'll go with her,'' Rachel said to Ben.

''Mom!''

''Either you hold it or you go with your mom.'' Ben shocked himself with how much like a father he sounded. He nearly laughed at the thought, except that he *liked* sounding like a father, and this was his last chance to do it for a while.

After one more circle of the block, Emily was bouncing off the walls in the back seat. "I have to go!"

"Fine." Stressed out, and with no reason for it, Ben pulled over. He grabbed Rachel's hand as she left the car. "Don't let her out of your sight."

He had no idea what the sudden panic was about, but his instincts had saved his life more than once.

"Ben—"

"Just promise me."

And only when Rachel nodded did he let go of her hand. "I'll be right there," he promised, silently vowing to park illegally, ditch the car, whatever it took.

It was still an agonizing five minutes before he ran back to the restaurant, out of breath from adrenaline and anxiety by the time he got there.

Naturally, the place was packed. For a interminably long moment he couldn't find either Rachel or Emily, and his heart stopped, though he had no idea what he thought could happen in such a busy place.

"Ben." From behind, Rachel put her hand on her arm. "We're waiting for a table, the hostess said it'd only be a moment because we had reservations."

"Emily," he said hoarsely. "Where's—"

"Bathroom."

"Which way?"

She frowned. "Behind the bar, but— Ben?" she called after him as he took off, weaving through the people to get behind the bar.

A waiter with a full tray growled at him when he nearly plowed him over in his haste. Then a three-hundred-pound woman inadvertently blocked his way, and they did a sort of dance trying to get around each other in the narrow hallway. Finally he dived under her arm to get around her.

Rachel did the same. "There," she said, pointing to the women's bathroom. "There's only one stall in there, so she locked the door and I came back to find you."

Innocent. Easy. So why were his instincts screaming? He tried the door handle, still locked. "Emily?"

To her credit, Rachel didn't doubt the panic she could no doubt see in his eyes. She knocked on the door. "Emily!" She looked at Ben with her own sudden panic. "Why isn't she answering?"

Because there was no Alicia. Ben knew that with a sudden, painful clarity. Alicia was Asada, who wasn't dead at all. Ben should have never believed that without a body. And he'd just hand-delivered his daughter to the man. Using his shoulder, he plowed into the door. The wood jamb started to splinter, and he did it again.

"Hey!" The bartender got a look at what they were doing and started to round the bar. "Get back from there—" he shouted just as the door gave, propelling Ben inside the bathroom.

Emily was on the floor, bound and gagged, with a two-ton goon kneeling at her side shoving a needle into her arm. A second goon had removed the window and was reaching down for Emily's lifeless body.

Ben lunged for him, and they both went down like a load of concrete to the tile floor. He got one punch in before he was rolled to his back and socked in the head. Stars danced across his vision, cutting off for a new pain when he took another in the gut. Using his knee as effectively as he could from flat on the floor, Ben leveled it into the guy's crotch, then nearly suffocated when all two hundred pounds of solid muscle landed on him,

knocking the air from his lungs. Trying to shove free of
the dead weight, he died a thousand deaths at the sound
of Rachel's sudden scream.

The other goon had dropped Emily and turned toward
Rachel, knife out, an unholy gleam in his eye.

Rachel lifted something and sprayed. Mace, Ben
thought with a surge of pride as the man screamed and
dropped like a sack of potatoes.

Rachel looked up at Ben, her eyes dilated. *"Ben!"*

He whipped around just in time to watch goon number
one, still holding his family jewels with one hand, pull
a gun from his pocket with the other. "I'm going to
shoot yours right off," he growled, and believing him,
Ben took a flying leap at him.

Not quite quick enough though, because a shot rang
out. And as things switched to an old silent film, Ben
had time to lash himself with guilt.

*His fault they were here,* he thought as he crashed to
the floor, a burning ripping through his upper thigh as
the bone shattered under the speeding bullet. *His fault
Emily had come to any harm.*

At least he landed on top of the guy, because the way
the goon's head bounced off that concrete, making the
sound of a pumpkin squishing, couldn't be good. And
while getting shot had sent searing agony roaring
through every part of Ben, he had to admit to being glad
it was his leg and not the promised family jewels.

The other guy was sitting on the floor, screaming
about his eyes.

Rachel weaved, then sat down hard, but unharmed.

Emily lay on the ground, facing away from Ben, far
too still. He crawled toward her, dragging his bad leg.
It took too long, and for a moment he couldn't remember
why the unbelievable agony was accompanying his

every breath, until Rachel appeared at his side, touching his thigh, which made more fiery waves of agony go through him. Scooping Emily against his chest, he sank back against the wall and closed his eyes. Sirens sounded in the distance.

Sirens were good. He had Rachel on the floor beside him, teeth chattering, eyes glassy as she clearly went into shock, and Emily in his arms, unconscious and possibly overdosed from God knows what. Oh, and he needed to throw up.

God, he'd screwed up good this time. He might have even said so to Rachel, but damn, he hurt. Beyond the screaming agony in his leg, he could hear her crying, feel her tears soaking through his T-shirt.

Oh, yeah, he'd definitely screwed up. "Rachel," he said with regret, or tried to, but his vision faded to black.

ASADA GOT THE NEWS on his ham radio. He stared out into the dark night. That's all he had left now, darkness. No less than he deserved for failing. He was truly all alone, as the last of his two loyal minions had been hauled off to a Southern California jail cell for attempted kidnapping.

Odd, how it felt, to fail. He'd never experienced it before Ben Asher. Desolation, certainly. Sadness. It shouldn't have come to this, but it had, and now there was only one thing left to do.

With a calm he hadn't felt in a good, long time, he pulled out his last five-gallon drum of gasoline. Weakened by his exile and circumstance, he had some trouble dragging the thing around the perimeter of the dark, dank cellar he'd been living in, but as the gasoline splashed on the ground, the container became lighter and lighter.

So did his heart.

When he'd completed his large circle, he tossed the container aside and pulled out a lighter. Stepping inside the circle, he bent and lit the gasoline.

And stood tall as he prepared to die.

THREE IN THE MORNING in a hospital, any hospital, was the most unpleasant place in the entire world. For Rachel, who'd spent far too many late nights in a hospital recently, the sensations were the worst. The smell of antiseptic and pain. The sight of white, white and more white. The sounds of hushed murmurs and cries.

The taste of fear and hopelessness.

Thank God the last didn't apply to her tonight. She sat in a chair by Emily's bed, holding her daughter's lax hand. Emily was going to be fine, the tranquilizer that had been shot into her unwilling body had worn off by now. She slept easily and of her own will. Except for her various bumps and bruises from where she'd fought her captors—Rachel's heart hitched at the thought of what her baby had gone through before they'd broken into the bathroom—she would be fine. She was even being released in the morning.

Ben, however, hadn't gotten so lucky. He'd come out of surgery with a steel plate in his thigh to hold the shattered bone together, and had required a transfusion of blood to keep him alive.

He would not be released in the morning. Or any time soon.

She lifted her gaze off Emily's still, pale face and looked at the chair on the other side of the bed, a wheelchair.

The nurses had told him no. The doctors had told him no. Ben had simply gritted his teeth, gotten out of bed and demanded crutches. Worried about his well-being, they'd given in, but after he'd nearly killed himself, they'd taken away the crutches and replaced them with the wheelchair.

The man was a stubborn, idiotic fool.

He was also the most amazing, passionate, heroic, quick-thinking fool she'd ever met. He wore a hospital gown and an IV and nothing else. Slouched in the chair, head twisted at what had to be an uncomfortable angle, his good long leg stretched out next to his wrapped one, he looked...what was it he'd said to her his first day? He looked *alive*. Even with the tousled hair, the five o'clock shadow along his jaw, the dark circles of pain and exhaustion beneath his eyes...eyes that suddenly were opened and on Emily.

"She's okay," she whispered.

"Yeah." Fierce and protective, he relaxed only when he saw she still slept. "No thanks to me."

"Ben—"

A slight shake of his head stopped her. His jaw was tight with the pain, but she knew better than to move to his side and offer sympathy. An hour ago she'd tried, and an hour before that as well. Both times he'd refused her touch.

In his head, had he already gone? No, she knew him better than that. In his head he'd put all the blame for what had happened firmly on his own shoulders.

She watched as his eyes grew heavy on his daughter, as slowly the exhaustion and lingering anesthesia from surgery claimed him again. The depth of grief and guilt he felt stunned her. The depth of emotion *she* felt in return stunned her as well. My God, she'd really fallen for him again. Or maybe the word was *still*.

There was no lingering doubt now. After all these years, she still loved him.

Having to go to him, she rounded the bed, kneeled at his side, all the love she'd just realized she had for him swamping her, needing to spill out.

As if he could read her mind, he lifted his hand and put a finger over her mouth. A grimace crossed his face. "Don't. Don't say it."

She gripped his fingers in hers. "Why not?"

His face twisted in a mask of torment. "Did you somehow miss the part where I nearly got Emily killed today?"

Tears filled her eyes for what seemed the thousandth time that night. "No. That wasn't you, that was Asada. Ben...don't take this on yourself."

"I have to." He stared at her, his own eyes suspiciously wet. "It was my fault, Rach...all of it. Every single moment of your pain from the moment you were hit by that car, to when I had to darken your doorstep again, to now..." He looked at the very still Emily. "Watching our daughter lie in that hospital bed."

She cupped his face and waited until his eyes shifted off Emily to hers. His pupils were dilated, his skin hot and dry to the touch. The words she wanted, needed, to tell him backed up in her throat at the heat of him. "My God. You're burning up." Surging up, she went behind his wheelchair.

"What are you doing?"

"What I should have done a long time ago," she said, mirroring his long-ago words to her. "I'm taking you to bed."

# CHAPTER TWENTY-ONE

FOUR PINS, a steel plate and one more surgery later, Ben was released from the hospital. He blinked into the bright sunlight, nearly tripping over the crutches he'd been so determined not to need but would for a long time.

At least he was alive, more than he could say for his nemesis, who'd actually chosen death by his own hand. And this time Asada's body had been positively identified by a United States FBI agent.

There'd be no more reign of terror.

After all this time of being on edge, Ben still couldn't believe it was truly over. His mind was having a hard time wrapping itself around that fact.

"Here." Rachel opened the passenger door of her car and smiled at him. "Bending to get in is the hard part, I'll just hold on to you—"

At the feel of her hands sliding around his waist he sucked in a breath and looked at her. He'd been surprised when she'd shown up as he was signing the release papers, though in retrospect, he shouldn't have been. She'd come every day, bringing Emily... Those memories made him swallow hard. His baby, his precious baby with the bruise still over her jaw where she'd been hit.

On her first visit, Emily had taken one look at his leg and burst into tears. He'd been terrified that she'd suffered some long-lasting emotional trauma, that she'd never be the same lighthearted kid, but she'd lifted her tear-streaked face and had said, "You can't camp with your leg like that."

He'd laughed. His first.

Rachel had confirmed that their daughter had indeed bounced back. A miracle. *Their* miracle, she'd said softly.

But Ben's miracle had her arms around him and was trying to get him into her car. A place he couldn't go because he knew where she'd drive him.

Home. *Her* home. His heart skipped a beat just thinking about it. He needed to get on a plane, *now,* before he did something stupid, like admit he didn't want to go at all.

"Come on, Ben. Get in."

"Why?

"Why?" She seemed stunned by the question. "Because I'm driving."

"I mean, why are you doing this?"

They stood in the parking lot of the hospital. The street was busy and noisy around them. And the sky, the goddamned sky, was so bright he could hardly stand it. Rachel stood at his side, the breeze brushing over her short, short blond hair, putting color into her cheeks. She looked bright too, so bright he could no more look at her than he could the sky.

"Why am I doing this?" she repeated. "Because I'm taking you home to recover."

"Your home."

"Well, yes," she said, the first hint of temper in her voice. "As you don't happen to have one."

"Rachel. *No.*"

She stared at him, a hand on her hip. It took her a

moment to speak, and when she did, her voice was husky with emotion. "You're not in condition to traipse off to the four corners, not quite yet."

She thought he was in a hurry to leave her. And though his leg was screaming, as well as the rest of his body because just the walk out had sapped his strength, he leaned on his crutches so that he could reach out and grab her hand. "I hurt, Rach."

"Oh! My God, you should have said so!" She patted down her pockets, then came up with his pain prescription. "I have—"

"No," he said tightly. "I mean I hurt here." He put her hand over his heart. "I hurt for Emily, for what might have been. I hurt for what I let happen, because there's no way the two of you can ever forgive—"

"Ben—"

"Hell, *I* can't forgive me." He drew in a shaky breath. "Look, the best thing we all can do is get on with our lives."

"Just like that? Just forget that you came here, how we all connected despite ourselves? We should forget everything, just like that?"

He stared into her wet eyes and closed his. "Yeah. Just like that."

"Fine." Now her voice was tight. "But get in the car. Not even you, superhero, can get on a plane tonight. You'll need rest first, at least one night's worth. I'm offering you that." When he just looked at her, she shook her head. "Don't worry, I'm not going to tie you down, physically or otherwise. Just come, use a damn bed, then go. Go the hell away."

*Again.* She didn't say it, but she didn't have to. He'd pissed her off good now, which hadn't been his intention. He'd wanted to go away immediately to avoid just that. To avoid all the emotional stuff they'd drudge up by having to say goodbye yet again.

"Are you getting in?" she asked, arms crossed. "Or are you going to be stupid and catch a cab to the airport?"

They both looked at the short line of cabs along the sidewalk.

"I'd bet my last dollar you have your passport and all you need right there in your backpack," she said softly. "Am I right?"

"Aren't you always?" he tried to quip, even added a half smile, but she just lifted a brow. "Yeah," he admitted on a long breath. "I've got everything I need."

She looked away. "Well then."

He touched her, ran his fingers along her hair, the edge of her ear, watching her shiver, wanting that last touch, that last memory. It would have to hold him awhile; he didn't think he could come back any time soon and be able to stand it. That he was thinking of coming back at all made him realize just how weak he must really be. "I'll...uh..."

"Send for Emily?"

"Yeah." He cleared his throat. "Rach—"

"Just go," she whispered, and covered her face for one beat before dropping her hands and walking around toward her car door. "Just stop dragging it out and go the hell away."

Beating him to the punch, she got in, revved the engine, and drove off.

Leaving him weaving like a drunk on the unaccustomed crutches wondering how it had come to this, with them destroying each other all over again.

BEN GOT ON the first plane out of Los Angeles, heading toward Africa, determined to lose himself in other people's miseries and to forget.

But as he rubbed his aching leg, all he could see were the lights of South Village, California, and the disappointment and hurt on Emily's face.

And the real love in Rachel's eyes, whether she'd admitted it or not.

THANKS TO THE STORY of Asada hitting the papers and the ensuing resurge in *Gracie's* popularity, none of it really hit Rachel for about three weeks.

But after it'd all died down, there was no getting around it. Ben was gone, really and truly gone. It seemed as if she'd just gotten used to having him around again, and now that he'd left, she felt...different.

Odd how she'd been able to work with a broken heart, but she had. Maybe it was *because* of her broken heart. In any case, she gathered her latest drawing off her easel, of Gracie kayaking through the rough waters of life, with the handicap of one hand tied behind her back and a short oar. The handicaps of everyday living.

At the sound of the truck outside her window, her concentration broke. The trash men were late again. They were also in a hurry, given that the guy dumped half the contents of her trash on the sidewalk. "Hey!" She leaned out the window to make sure he heard her. "You need to clean that up!"

Startled, he looked up. Flushing with guilt, he bent to retrieve the fallen trash.

"Mom!" Emily came running into the room. "What's the matter?"

"Absolutely nothing." She dusted off her hands. She

watched with satisfaction as the man picked up the last of the scraps he'd dropped.

"But...you were yelling."

"Yes, and you know what?" She turned around to face Emily. "It felt wonderful— Oh, my God." Her daughter's hair was...gone. "What on earth have you done?"

Emily grinned and tugged at the extremely short tufts still on her head. "Do you like it?"

"You...cut it all off?"

"Yep." She squared her shoulders, lifted her chin. "I've always wanted it this short but you kept saying no."

"I would have said no again!" She had to consciously lower her voice at her daughter's stricken expression. "I understand it's your hair, and you're stretching your wings and becoming a teenager and all that, but—"

"M-ooo-mmm," Emily said, drawing the word out into five syllables.

"You should have asked!" She was yelling again and didn't care.

"I wanted to be like you!" Emily yelled back.

Rachel stared at her. "You...really?"

"Really." Emily's eyes filled. "But you hate it. And you're yelling. Why are you yelling, Mom? You never yell."

"Oh, baby, I don't hate it, I promise." Rachel gathered her in for a hug and had to laugh at them both as she swiped at a tear on Emily's face. "I guess I still want you to be my little girl, needing me for everything."

"I do need you, I'll always need you."

Rachel buried her face in her baby's short, *short* hair. "I'm glad to hear that. I've...felt a little shaky lately."

"Without Daddy?"

Even now, the thought of Ben was like a knife to the chest. "Yeah."

"Is *that* why you're yelling?"

"I'm yelling because…well, because it feels good." Rachel drew back and smiled. "I'm not going to hold back everything anymore, Em. I'm not going to pretend my feelings and emotions don't exist."

"Uh-oh." A wary expression crossed her face. "Does that mean you're going to want to yell at me a lot?"

Rachel laughed. "I'll try to control myself on the decibel level, okay?"

"Jeez, Rach…" Melanie came into the studio. "I don't think the people in China heard you, why don't you scream at the guy a little louder. Hey, cutie," she said to Emily, and ruffled the new short cut. "Cool 'do."

Emily shot Rachel a "see?" look.

Rachel rolled her eyes.

Melanie hesitated. "So…am I interrupting?"

The old Melanie would never have asked such a question, she wouldn't have cared. This new Melanie not only looked as if she'd been recently kissed by Garrett for a good long time, but she had a glow to her, one that wasn't purely sexual, but…joy.

Rachel knew she had Garrett to thank for that. They'd been living together, and Mel had gotten a job—in Garrett's dental office. "You're not interrupting at all. We're going to have a snack."

"Always up for that," Mel said, and grabbed a chair. She paused for a moment then said, "You know, Rachel, we never really talked about…"

"About me telling you to go home that day?" Rachel sighed. "I was wrong to do that to you, Mel. I'm sorry."

"I'm the sorry one. But I can tell you, I've changed."

"I know." Rachel's newfound determination to speak

her mind made her say, "I just want to be able to trust you, and I want you to be happy."

"You can. And I am." Melanie came closer, and surprised Rachel by reaching out for the hug first. "I love you, Rachel."

Stunned, Rachel felt her throat clog at the unexpected admission. "I love you, too. And just so you know, I'm going to tell you a lot." She squeezed her tight. "Because ask Em...I'm not holding back anything anymore."

"Yeah, watch out," Emily said.

Melanie smiled at Rachel. "Feels good to feel, huh?"

"Oh, yeah."

Melanie reached out and snagged Emily close, too. "How about a soda, kiddo?"

"You just want me to scat so you can talk without me listening again."

"Yeah, but a soda would be good, too. And get that snack while you're at it. Make it fattening, okay?"

"Okay, but it's only going to take me two minutes to get down to the kitchen and back, so talk quick."

Mel did. "So. With this new *feeling* kick you're on...does it mean you're going to tell Ben you didn't want him to go?"

"Well...that part is complicated." Rachel had a new list of emotions, and topping it was her unwavering love for Ben. She'd hurt him, and all in the name of her pathetic fears. She had no idea why she hadn't seen it sooner.

She glanced down at the drawings in her hand, giving them one last look before putting them into the courier envelope. Her favorite was *Gracie* on her soap box about fake do-gooders. She'd even spoofed Asada in another column, really getting into the swing of it, in her own way warning people off giving blindly to charities they knew nothing about. The drawings, the sharp, caustic one-liners were good. More than good, they were relevant and damn important. Enough to make her want to keep doing it.

*Gracie* was back.

Ironic, really, when she thought about it. Her life had come full circle.

And yet there could be no denying, things had changed. She'd learned to feel, to love, to really love…

Too bad it had come too late.

"Rach?"

"I don't know, Mel." Or was it too late? "I'm thinking about it. All of it."

Emily came back into the room with a tray of goodies.

"Do you have your dad's cell phone number handy?" Rachel asked her.

"What's the matter?" Emily looked worried. "Why do you need him?"

Melanie stared at Rachel, then slowly smiled as she put an arm around her niece. "She's done thinking."

"Huh?"

"She's going after him."

Rachel smiled. Yep. She was going after him. With her stomach in her throat, she dialed his cell. Heart pounding, palms sweaty, she wondered what she'd say.

Turns out it didn't matter, because she got the message "the cell user you are trying to reach is not available."

The story of Ben's life.

"You miss him," Emily said with a smile. "I knew it. You just miss him."

"I miss him," Rachel agreed softly, and cupped Emily's face. "And you know what? I just realized I haven't left South Village in far too long. What do you say to a vacation?''

"I have three days left of school before summer break.''

"It'll take three days to pack.''

"For where?''

"Where else? Africa.''

Emily's grin spread.

IT ACTUALLY TOOK two weeks to prepare for the trip. Ben wasn't so easy to track down. All Rachel had known of his plans ahead of time was the name of the place he'd hoped to stay at while covering his story, and once they got the details on the rugged, isolated terrain they were heading into, she had to swallow hard.

This was no cozy little planned-out vacation. This was an adventure of the highest magnitude. This was going against the grain. She'd be leaving behind her three Ss— security, stability and safety in a big way. She felt as if she were perched on the edge of the steepest cliff.

And yet she wanted to jump. Couldn't wait to jump.

And then finally they had their bags packed, their tickets in hand, their passports ready. Melanie had gone to get her car. She was taking them to the airport, to the trip that would hopefully change their lives forever.

Assuming Rachel could convince Ben to give them another shot, that is. A real shot. Their *first* real shot. She looked at Emily, waiting so patiently and trusting for her to get her life together, and love swamped her. "Emmie, I love you.''

"Oh, no! You're changing your mind!''

"No, I'm not.'' Rachel laughed at the horror on Emily's face. "I just wanted to say I love you, that's all.''

"Oh. Okay.'' Obviously not believing her, Emily

tugged on her hand. "Come on, let's wait outside for Aunt Mel, I think I hear her coming now."

Outside was good, it would get her one foot closer to Ben. With a deep breath, she hauled the door open and nearly plowed right into…Ben?

Her heart stopped.

He looked right into her eyes and gave her one of his slow smiles, the kind that never failed to tip her heart on its side, but this time his seemed shaky. Uncertain.

"Ben?" Uncertain herself, she twisted around to look at Emily.

Emily shook her head. It wasn't any crazy new stunt of hers to bring him here this time, which meant… She whipped back to face him. He stood there looking bleak and hollow, leaning on the jamb in a way that spoke of bone deep exhaustion. Misery radiated off him, matching the misery she'd pretended not to feel since he'd been gone.

Since she'd sent him away.

"Yeah. Just me," he said in a grainy voice, and with a heavy limp, stepped inside. He hugged and kissed Emily, then turned to Rachel.

Her heart, which had stopped only seconds before, began a heavy, dull pounding. "I can't believe you're here."

He took in their packed bags, and lifted his gaze to hers. "You were just leaving."

"Yes," she said with a half-hysterical laugh. "We were coming to—"

"No. I'm sorry, Rachel, but I have to go first. I've been thinking of this for fifteen thousand miles." Taking her shoulders, he drew her closer, grimacing a little when she stumbled and he was forced to support her weight for a moment.

"Ben!" She tried to look down at his leg, but he'd cupped her face. "You've got to sit down."

"I've got to tell you something first."

"But you're shaking!"

"That's not because of my leg." He lowered his forehead to hers. "I wanted to roam the earth. I wanted that with every thing I was."

She felt her heart crack at the desolation in his voice, in his eyes, and stroked a strand of hair out of his eyes. "I know. It's who you are, it's always been who you are. Ben, I shouldn't have—"

"No, listen. When I got there this time, it no longer worked for me."

She stared at him, forced herself to breathe. "Go on."

"I want a home, Rach. I want it with you and Emily. For keeps."

Her mouth fell open. A little laugh escaped. "You're going to really wish you'd let me talk first."

But he wasn't done trying to convince her. "You can tell me to go away all you want, but you'll have to convince me that's what you really want this time. No more hiding, no more pretending what we have doesn't exist. I love you, damn it, and I always have."

"Ben—"

"So go ahead," he dared. "Tell me you're not interested. Make me believe it."

"*Ben*—"

His mouth came down over hers, and proceeded to melt all her brain cells with the hot, greedy, needy connection. When he lifted his head, she clung to him, a little stunned that he could have sidetracked her with one simple kiss when she had so much to say. "Can I talk now?"

He looked wary. "I'm not sure. You going to tell me to go?"

"No." She looked at Emily, who lifted her hands and covered her eyes.

"I'm not looking, Mom. Just don't make me leave, I want to hear this! Tell him. Tell him quick or I will."

"Tell me what?" asked the poor, confused man who'd done the unthinkable and come back for her. He'd come back.

Rachel put a hand on his chest, which he reached up to hold there over the steady beat of his big, beautiful heart.

"Ben…" She let out a low laugh. "We were coming to you. We were going to hike through all of Africa, if that's what it took to locate you."

"You…what?"

"I love you back," she whispered, her eyes filling. "I never should have sent you away. I want another chance to prove we could make this work, even if we have to plan out a time schedule on how to meet up between your jobs. We belong together, Ben, even if we have to be apart for long periods of time. It doesn't matter. I love you," she said again, stronger now. "And I always have."

Ben stared at her for one beat before hauling her even closer, burying his face at the crook of her neck, his arms banding tight around her body. They were *both* shaking, she realized as she hugged him back.

"I want to be here," he whispered. "*Here*. With you."

"Not Africa?"

"Not Africa."

"Not South America?"

"Not South America."

"Not—"

"With you, Rachel," he said, and reached out for Emily, pulling her into the fray. "With Emmie. The three of us."

Rachel pulled back, bit her lower lip. "I was wondering how you would feel about four."

Ben stared at her, then dropped his stunned gaze down to her still-flat belly. "Four?"

"No, not yet…I was just wondering…"

"Are you kidding?" His voice was hoarse. "I would love to have another baby with you."

Emily closed her eyes as her parents squeezed her tight between them, her heart overflowing. She'd done it, she'd really done it. She'd gotten them back together, and now they were going to be a family. And maybe even add to that family! Hmm…did she want a sister to boss around, or a brother? Yeah, definitely a brother.

Oh, yeah, she was good. She'd made this happen.

She wondered what she could do next.

\* \* \* \* \*

*If you enjoyed*
*THE STREET WHERE SHE LIVES*
*look for the next book by Jill Shalvis,*
*a Harlequin Flipside title,*
*NATURAL BLOND INSTINCTS.*

*Coming in December 2003*
*to your favorite local retailer.*
*Don't miss it!*

*Immerse yourself in holiday romance with*

# BETTY NEELS

*Christmas Wishes*

Two Christmas stories from the
#1 Harlequin Romance® author.

The joy and magic of this beloved author
will make this volume a classic
to be added to your collection.

Available in retail stores in October 2003.

"Betty Neels pleases her faithful readership with
inviting characters and a gracious love story."
—*Romantic Times*

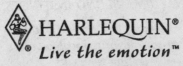

HARLEQUIN®
*Live the emotion*™

**Visit us at www.eHarlequin.com**

PHCW

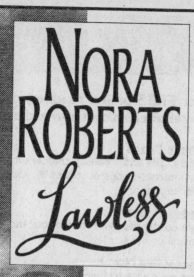

# NORA ROBERTS

*Lawless*

A rare historical romance novel
from #1 *New York Times*
bestselling author
**Nora Roberts**

Half-Apache and all man,
Jake Redman is more than
a match for the wild Arizona
Territory...but can he handle
Eastern lady Sarah Conway
as easily?

*Available in October 2003,
wherever books are sold!*

HARLEQUIN®
*Live the emotion*™

Visit us at www.eHarlequin.com

PHLAW

# eHARLEQUIN.com

**For FREE online reading,** visit
www.eHarlequin.com now and enjoy:

### Online Reads
Read **Daily** and **Weekly** chapters from
our Internet-exclusive stories by your
favorite authors.

### Red-Hot Reads
Turn up the heat with one of our more
sensual online stories!

### Interactive Novels
Cast your vote to help decide how these
stories unfold...then stay tuned!

### Quick Reads
For shorter romantic reads, try our
collection of Poems, Toasts, & More!

### Online Read Library
Miss one of our online reads?
Come here to catch up!

### Reading Groups
Discuss, share and rave with other
community members!

## For great reading online,
## visit www.eHarlequin.com today!

INTONL

If you enjoyed what you just read,
then we've got an offer you can't resist!

## Take 2
## bestselling novels FREE!
## Plus get a FREE surprise gift!

**Clip this page and mail it to The Best of the Best™**

**IN U.S.A.**
3010 Walden Ave.
P.O. Box 1867
Buffalo, N.Y. 14240-1867

**IN CANADA**
P.O. Box 609
Fort Erie, Ontario
L2A 5X3

**YES!** Please send me 2 free Best of the Best™ novels and my free surprise gift. After receiving them, if I don't wish to receive anymore, I can return the shipping statement marked cancel. If I don't cancel, I will receive 4 brand-new novels every month, before they're available in stores! In the U.S.A., bill me at the bargain price of $4.74 plus 25¢ shipping and handling per book and applicable sales tax, if any*. In Canada, bill me at the bargain price of $5.24 plus 25¢ shipping and handling per book and applicable taxes**. That's the complete price and a savings of over 20% off the cover prices—what a great deal! I understand that accepting the 2 free books and gift places me under no obligation ever to buy any books. I can always return a shipment and cancel at any time. Even if I never buy another The Best of the Best™ book, the 2 free books and gift are mine to keep forever.

185 MDN DNWF
385 MDN DNWG

| Name | (PLEASE PRINT) | |
|------|------|------|
| Address | Apt.# | |
| City | State/Prov. | Zip/Postal Code |

\* Terms and prices subject to change without notice. Sales tax applicable in N.Y.
\*\* Canadian residents will be charged applicable provincial taxes and GST.
All orders subject to approval. Offer limited to one per household and not valid to current The Best of the Best™ subscribers.
® are registered trademarks of Harlequin Enterprises Limited.

BOB02-R                    ©1998 Harlequin Enterprises Limited

## *Forrester Square*
### LEGACIES. LIES. LOVE.

*The Kinards, the Richardses and the Webbers were Seattle's Kennedys, living in elegant Forrester Square—until one fateful night tore these families apart.*

*Now, twenty years later, memories and secrets are about to be revealed...unless one person has their way!*

Coming in October 2003...

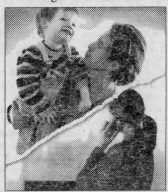

# THE LAST THING SHE NEEDED
### by Top Harlequin Temptation® author
# Kate Hoffmann

When Dani O'Malley's childhood friend died, she suddenly found herself guardian to three scared, unruly kids—and terribly overwhelmed! If it weren't for Brad Cullen, she'd be lost. The sexy cowboy had a way with the kids...and with her!

*Forrester Square...Legacies. Lies. Love.*

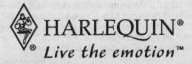

## HARLEQUIN®
### *Live the emotion*™

**Visit us at www.forrestersquare.com**

PHFS3

A **brand-new**
*Maitland Maternity*
story!

# MAITLAND MATERNITY

# Adopt
## –a–Dad
by
# Marion Lennox

The second in a quartet of *Maitland Maternity*
novels connected by a mother's legacy of love.

When Michael Lord's
secretary, Jenny Morrow,
found herself widowed and
pregnant, the confirmed
bachelor was determined
to help. Michael had an idea
to make things easier for Jenny
and her baby immediately—
a temporary husband!

*Coming to a retail outlet
near you in October 2003.*

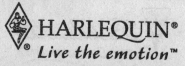

**HARLEQUIN**®
*Live the emotion*™

**Visit us at www.eHarlequin.com**

CPAAD

Brody Fortune is about to get the surprise of his life...
in this brand-new *Fortunes of Texas* romance

# THE EXPECTANT SECRETARY

by

# LEANNA Wilson

When Brody Fortune saw
Jillian Tanner pregnant with
another man's child, he was
shocked. She was the
woman he'd never
forgotten...but time and
circumstances had torn
them apart. Now many
years later, were they
ready for a second chance
at love?

**Available in November at
your favorite retail outlet.**

### THE FORTUNES OF TEXAS™

*Membership in this family has its privileges...and its price.
But what a fortune can't buy, a true-bred Texas love is sure to bring!*

*Silhouette*®
*Where love comes alive*™

Visit Silhouette at www.eHarlequin.com                    CPTES